ROGUE

"Don't let anybody tell you you can't do anything."

- Tim Peake

ROGUE

DANNY LENIHAN

ISBN: 978-1-8384764-0-3
eISBN: 978-1-8384764-1-0

For Tim, for being the geek I needed,
to over-explain the stuff I made up.

And for Alison, for being the first to say, "I'll read it."

CONTENTS

PROLOGUE

I NEVER KNEW LIFE when it was deemed safe. Or at least free of potential cataclysms. Neither did my grandparents, or their grandparents.

My life was ordinary in the early years. My parents, now long dead, were poor, and we lived in the city limits in one of the steel canyons, way up in the "nosebleeds" as they used to say. It stuck, and now everyone calls it The Bleeds. The air was fresher up there, away from the landfill on which they built these metal monstrosities. Most days were ordinary, unless the mag-lifts packed up. On those days we'd have to stay in the commune, over in City Park—an ironically titled slab of concrete just north of Kingston. It used to take us an hour to get there, walking, but still a half-day quicker than climbing six hundred and fourteen floors, and we were less likely to stumble over a body. As kids, the journey to the commune was an adventure, especially if we had enough credit for the tram. For adults, it was wearisome and soul-destroying.

I had very little to complain about. We'd been safe out on the streets, playing, blissfully unaware of the impending annihilation.

Of course, they'd taught us about it in school. I didn't really pay much attention.

Two hundred and thirty years ago, some scientists charted a new planet roughly the size of Earth's Moon. There were trillions of these wandering or *rogue* planets, untethered to any system, drifting through the vast emptiness of space. Some ancient cosmic event had sent this one hurtling towards Earth. They watched it for a decade before they told anyone. Then another twenty years before anyone actually did anything. Thirty years just watching, as it got closer. It was almost another century before they notified the public, though how they'd kept it a secret for a hundred years was beyond me. Kid gets hit by a cyber-car these days and within eight minutes it's on the news. But this was a planet, hurtling through space at an unfathomable speed, on a trajectory that potentially brought it on a collision course with Earth, in two hundred and thirty-odd years.

Nobody was sure if it would actually hit. There were simply too many variables to consider. Projections showed it might hit Saturn first, or several other cosmic anomalies, including asteroids and meteor belts.

The only thing anyone agreed on was that, should the *Rogue* (as it had been dubbed early on) avoid all obstacles en route to Earth, it would amount to our annihilation. A meteorite hit one hundred million years ago and wiped out the dinosaurs, and that was only eighty-one kilometres in diameter. This was a planet, thirty-five hundred kilometres in diameter, travelling at incredible speed, through the endless void of space, the product of a star colliding with a black hole. Speculation was that it would destroy Earth just by getting close enough, with billions being sucked off the planet in its awesome wake. If it collided, it would destroy Earth in the blink of an eye.

So they created two plans, with two hundred and two years to execute them. Simply put, Plan A dealt with the planet—how to destroy it, or divert it or, frankly, how to even get near it, and Plan B—evacuate Earth.

It boggled the mind how they expected to do either. These were ancient times, when people still used hand-held devices to communicate. When fossil fuels were simultaneously powering and killing the planet. Countries had borders back then, with papers required to move between them. Eventually they concluded that reaching the planet was impossible, and so all eggs went into the one basket.

In the early days, I think the prevailing mood was hopelessness. We had neither the technology nor the ingenuity to tackle either problem. Strangely, the hopelessness galvanised the planet, creating unity between nations and cultures. History showed that in the face of overwhelming odds, humanity would be selfish, and an every-man-for-himself attitude would prevail, but this was a threat of a different magnitude. The world got a lot smaller the day the threat was announced.

Despite this, there were still millions of nutjobs preaching about redemption and revelations. It was easier back then to go against the establishment. The threat wasn't imminent, and nobody would live long enough to see the End Times. People were glib and dismissive. Why should they worry about a threat that may or may not materialise in two-hundred-and-something years? Then we got within fifty years and divisions formed. People couldn't see past their own future ending, and economies collapsed as workers shunned their employers for family. Time was running out, and where people worked to live, they now lived to live.

Now, global unemployment sits at a little over seventy per cent. Those who remain employed are contractors for the space station and emergency services, or essential services such as food manufacturing, sanitation and utilities. Some schools are still open, but nobody knows what we are educating our kids for. The travel industry collapsed long ago. You can catch a mag-tram or a cyber-car, but there are no flights; at least not on a commercial level. My grandparents once told me that the skies were full of aeroplanes and hollocopters, and the seas hosted thousands of ships and hydrofoils. I'd never seen the ocean. Our island isn't large, but everyone stays close to home these days.

We're now four years away from our extinction, and the mood has changed.

PART I

CHAPTER ONE

TEN YEARS AGO they announced a lottery for a place on the Bertram Ramsay. It was a huge space station that had taken one hundred years to build, partly on Earth, but mostly constructed in space. It was so-named after the Admiral Sir Bertram Home Ramsay, the senior officer who oversaw the evacuation of Dunkirk during World War II in the early twentieth century.

The Bertram Ramsay was a complex network of titanium and glass spheres with interlocking tunnels and walkways, much like a snowflake. Each sphere would house one million people; there were nine for accommodation, plus four for command and control, defence, warehousing and transportation, and agriculture. There were also a bunch of smaller domes attached to each sphere, with fresh-water recycling plants and reclaimers, oxygen, crops, propulsion and engineering. The structure was impressive, capable of moving in and out of Earth's orbit, and scheduled to head into deeper space six months before the event that would change everything. It was visible to the naked eye as it passed over, even in daylight.

They chose me in the lottery. They'd already pre-selected two million people from a pool of occupations deemed crucial to our success and continued life: scientists, farmers, emergency services, doctors, nurses and teachers. There was no sentimental predisposition towards carrying relics and antiquities. Our survival was the only agenda.

I became a random choice in another seven million people. I had neither discernible skills nor talent according to my mandatory aptitude tests, so my designation was 'occupant'. It wasn't inspiring, but certainly better than being left on Earth. The evacuation started eight years ago, mostly for personnel needed to set up hospitals, defence, catering and agriculture. The things we'd need up and running long before the first occupants joined.

Six months ago there was a knock on my apartment door. I opened it to find two ICP officers standing outside holding an envelope which, it transpired, was my evacuation order.

"Mr Jaxon Leith, we have randomly selected you to join the evacuation on the Bertram Ramsay. You are not obligated to do so, but you must tell us should you decide not to join."

"Got it." I could feel my heart pounding at the news. Nobody in The Bleeds expected a ticket. How the hell had I got the nod?

"You have six months to get your affairs in order. You will be collected at the date and time shown in the letter. Lateness is not an option, so don't lose that." He nodded towards the envelope.

I was handed a tiny holdall which looked like it would just about hold a sandwich.

"No clothes or personal care items. This is just for those small sentimental items you wish to take with you. Everything else will be provided to you once you're in Compression. Okay?"

"OK. What do I wear for the transport?"

"It doesn't matter. Compression is a sterile facility, so they will incinerate your clothes upon arrival." They made it sound like a nudist colony, and I had to stifle a laugh. These were serious-looking people.

It was an odd conversation, and not one I was likely to forget. I didn't have any personal possessions, so when they arrived this morning and I handed over my empty bag, they looked at me with pity, and perhaps a little resentment. I imagined they were wondering how I'd got lucky, when I had nothing to show for my life. Their thoughts weren't my problem, so I just climbed into the transport and tried to relax.

Today I moved to a specialist facility called Compression. I was going to spend the next three months in an internment camp, being assessed, trained and conditioned for a life in space, and eventually allocated a job for the duration of the voyage.

I had to say goodbye to The Bleeds, a place I'd lived my entire life. I'd never even travelled beyond the city limits before, so this was a novel experience for me.

The bus was bumping along slowly, leaving the transportation base in Abingdon, Oxfordshire. I didn't know our destination, so I was nervous. It didn't help to be sat on a fifty-seat coach, with just eleven people on board, including two ICP officers who I assumed were there to escort us. They had full fatigues, body armour and combat weapons which just made me more apprehensive. How rough was this journey going to be?

They'd formed the Intercontinental Police way back when the borders had come down and the earth became a single state. I knew little about them beyond my occasional run-ins with them in The Bleeds, but I'd say they were more of a military unit than a police force.

The other eight passengers were occupants, like me, picked randomly by a computer to embark upon a historic voyage, and ensure the continuity of our species. All were late-twenty-to-mid-thirty-something by the looks of it, and they all looked just as anxious. Six were women, and two men. I wondered if that was random too, or perhaps by design. The thought made me shudder, as if these women were hand-picked as broodmares for the men to stud them. If there was a single moment that could have changed my mind, and spurred me to walk away, it was right there, right then. I was grateful for the departure, truly, but I hadn't signed up to be part of some social experiment. I felt unclean. I shook these thoughts from my head.

They'd collected each of us from our apartment buildings by separate cars. We each carried that small holdall; our allowance was just two kilos, for us to bring tokens from home.

I watched the streets for forty minutes, the first twenty of which were in the shadows of The Bleeds, before crossing the city boundaries and being caught in the glare of light. The car took me to the bus station on the outskirts of a converted air force base, where I had my documentation checked, before walking through two sets of body scanners.

I counted sixteen buses, all with armed ICP outside, and a cordon of ICP officers around the depot. As we pulled in there were crowds shouting and screaming at us, waving boards with proclamations of anger, of judgement, of God's will and revelations. I'd been told to expect this and to just keep my head down and not look at any of the protesters. This was impossible, though. They surrounded us on all sides, pushing and hitting the cyber-car, shouting and screaming at its occupants.

All except one guy.

He stood there, hoodie pulled over his head, just staring at me, completely still and showing no emotion at all. Once I caught his eye, I couldn't look away. I felt a pang of discomfort—maybe fear; I wasn't sure. Then, just as I thought my eyes would dry out from staring back, we passed through the gates into the depot. I didn't look back.

The depot itself was ordinary. A bare structure was at the rear which presumably had the ticket office and amenities, and several diagonal bays with coaches parked in them. Each was at least a bay apart, and temporary fencing created a path, funnelling passengers to their allocated transports. I opened the car door and a female ICP officer asked me to step out, and then escorted me to a holding pen of sorts, where about twenty others were being ushered through the security cordon. I handed over my papers and received a lanyard with a barcode and the moniker JAXON LEITH above it.

I walked to the next pen, as directed, and then further down the left pathway to Bay 16 at the far end of the depot. A sea of lost and emotional faces passed either side of me, shuffling along to their buses. I felt depressed looking at them, and a little sad. I'd left nobody and nothing behind, so to me this was an escape, not an incarceration.

I stepped onto the bus and had my lanyard scanned and inspected, and was told to take Seat 23, just about halfway down by the emergency exit.

A high-pitched whine and a powerful throb coursed through me as the fusion engine kicked into life. The soft hiss that followed marked the beginning of our last journey on Earth, confirmed by the mechanical clunk of the hydraulic doors sealing.

There were so few occupants on board that it finally dawned on me just how many people were being left behind. Twenty-six billion souls would stay on Earth and face their collective fate, and

I wondered how they must be feeling. Six months ago I was in the same position, but I didn't dwell on the future when my present was so bleak. I didn't waste time praying or living in false hope that this was all a huge mistake.

We were nearing the endgame now, and I couldn't comprehend the emotions those people would go through every day, as each sunset concluded another strike off the countdown clock.

The bus rolled forward, and as we exited the compound I looked out at the crowd. There he was, amongst a sea of angry faces, hooded, silent, still and looking straight at me. Something about him unnerved me, and his face haunted my thoughts for months to come.

Brigadier General Phillip Hawlsey looked up from his desk at the sound of a knock on the door.

"Come."

The rusty creak of the hinges echoed down the hallway. A uniformed ICP officer entered and stopped smartly in front of the ancient desk.

"Andrew, please take a seat." Then, seeing the look on his face, Hawlsey enquired, "What's on your mind, Colonel?"

Colonel Andrew Grealish removed his hat and ruffled his dark crew cut. The stress of the current situation was taking a toll on his usual youthful vigour, and his boyish face had aged in recent weeks. The meticulously-kept stubble looked unusually haphazard, as if his only intention had been to shave in a manner that vaguely resembled the norm. He looked up at the brigadier through blue-grey eyes and shifted uncomfortably in his seat. Stalling the conversation wasn't likely to make it any easier.

He glanced up at the brigadier. "It's the AoG, Sir. Communications with our operative inside their network is becoming more difficult and dangerous. The latest intel she sent stipulates that they're planning a major operation on the Bertram."

"We've had this sort of intel before, Andrew. You know what our security is like. Why is this latest warning any different?"

"She thinks there are at least two Acolytes in the system already, Sir. She's not sure if they're already on the Bertram, or in Compression, but her sources inside the network have confirmed infiltration."

"Christ." The brigadier shook his head and sighed. He always knew that the day would come when the Acolytes of Gaia would constitute a legitimate threat to the evacuation.

"How did they get so powerful, Andrew? Two hundred years ago they were barely a cult."

"Ah, well, they weren't the first, Sir. The Mayans were obsessed with eschatology, and there are dozens of religions that are predicated on the world ending in some manner. But their beliefs were simply that: *beliefs*. These zealots know that our way of life is ending. They're preying on people with fear, and their ability to sow discord and enmity far and wide, with modern technology, is the heart of the issue." He sighed and scratched his head. "The problem for us is that they just don't conform to the usual cult profile. They gather followers from all faiths, religions, cultures and countries."

"It feels like they're ramping up their efforts, Andrew. We've been through this before and look what happened then. We can't afford this sort of disruption when we're so close."

Grealish frowned. The brigadier was bringing up ancient history, and it simply wasn't relevant to the current threat. "Sir, that bomb was sixty years ago. And it was never formally associated with the AoG. We are without doubt better equipped to handle the latest threats, as and when they materialise."

"That bomb killed two pilots, one of which was my father, and four ground crew, and halted transportation of supplies and critical personnel to and from the Bertram Ramsay for seven months. Seven months, Andrew. We leave in six. If something happens, it's over for us. There's no happy ending."

"Sir, we're doing what we can, but I need more assets. Their resources are limitless. They have a pool of twenty-six billion people who aren't flying to safety, desperate for any opportunity to save themselves, ready to do whatever it takes to escape this impending cataclysm, or else bitter and angry enough to sabotage it for everyone. I need more people inside, investigating quietly and negating any potential threat before they get to the Bertram."

The brigadier leaned back in his chair and sighed. What they had achieved was nothing short of sensational. The Bertram Ramsay was a feat of engineering that scholars and engineers, a century ago, had scoffed at. They said it simply couldn't be done. Space flight was still in its infancy, having barely progressed from manned rockets pummelling through the atmosphere with brute force and blind luck, to controlled ascents, and meaningful reconnaissance of the planet.

The plan had progressed, regardless of the scorn and cynicism. They built the initial command structure on Earth, disassembled and shuttled it to the ISS4 where NASA's best engineers began assembling it in space. It took them thirty years to complete the first structure, with all amenities and accommodation, and specialist construction equipment that had been unavailable to the ISS crew because of the constraints of its size.

Once the Command Sphere was operational, everything moved at much greater speed. With a crew of eight thousand engineers and scientists, and a further thousand civilian crew members including doctors, nurses, chefs, maintenance workers and communications specialists, the build began in earnest, and the second sphere took only three years to complete.

As they completed each sphere, they shuttled more crew to the Bertram to aid its construction, and by the time the space station was fifty years old, all thirteen of the sphere structures were built and connected. It was Earth's greatest ever feat of engineering. Even as an incomplete structure, it was impressive to behold.

"Sir?" There was a bite of impatience in the colonel's voice. The old man was daydreaming.

The brigadier looked up and furrowed his brow. "Andrew, I'll pass this up the chain and get a response. In the meantime, let's double down on security of all Compression centres, and sweep every site from front to back. You can have your extra assets, whatever it takes. Put together a plan for implementation and get your team leaders into the conference room at 16:00 to thrash it out. We'll worry about the other sites when ours is squared away."

CHAPTER TWO

*T*HE MAN WATCHED *as one by one they were carted into the depot. These people, these lost souls, were fleeing the very land that gave them life. They could not be permitted to desecrate the fundamental laws of nature. Each time man sends a rocket into space, it is depleting the fabric of our lifeblood, chipping away the sacred minerals that feed our Mother Earth.*

In the two hundred years since the founders created this temple and this doctrine, the threat has increased exponentially. The Acolytes will prevail in their mission to save the Earth Mother, because their faith is limitless and their determination boundless.

He went to his communicator, a small incongruous chipset inserted into the back of his forearm, once the bus pulled out of the depot, pleased with what he had seen.

"She is in. The documents worked. We will need more, but for now you can relax. Call me when they arrive, so that we may be certain of our success."

"Yes, Sir. I do not think they suspect, but we should exercise caution. There is an increase in activity in their security around Echo, so we must not be complacent. If she makes it inside, then she will be alone."

"She knows what has to be done. Her sacrifice is pure. She will succeed."

She kept looking over her shoulders at me from a few rows in front. Inquisitive eyes, which averted the moment I looked up. I watched her for a while, and twice caught her looking back at me, only to see her face flush and her long red hair flick back around to cover it. She wasn't beautiful in the traditional sense, but there was something about her that attracted me instantly.

I looked out of the window for a spell. A man at the front had asked the ICP officers where we were going, but they ignored him and remained alert. We were on a country road, farms and villages flashing past as we trundled onwards. I didn't recognise any of the place names we passed—Kingston Bagpuize first, then Brighthampton and Ducklington—before joining a major road. Judging by the sun, we were heading west.

It was over an hour before the landscape changed significantly, and we passed a sign for Cheltenham. We travelled on for a few more minutes, turning left at a roundabout, and that's when I saw it for the first time. A huge circular building on the right side, surrounded by military vehicles, ICP command posts and a sea of protesters.

If the crowd at the bus depot had been agitated, it was nothing compared to the seething mass of despair and vitriol that engulfed us on our approach. Gone were the placards and signs, and the peaceful declarations of God's will. Bricks and bottles were smashing against the bus. Petrol bombs were exploding in front of the ICP blockades, and fire crews and medics were rushing around to put out the blazes and treat the wounded. The angry mob was swelling, and the ICP was charging back. I couldn't make out the individual voices—there were just too many; but the message was clear: Why do you get to live?

I felt a sudden sense of profound loss. I can't explain why I felt this so powerfully at this moment, but seeing the hate and the anger in the faces of thousands—no, tens of thousands—left a mark on my soul. We were answering the call: abandon ship. And there just weren't enough seats on the lifeboat.

I looked around at the people on the bus. All I saw was fear.

Surrounded by armed ICP, the driver edged the bus through the blockade, and once free of the missiles and screamed threats, rolled to the entry compound and opened the doors. A few went to stand up but were told quickly to sit and stay. Six ICP officers climbed on board, whilst several others ran mirrors and dogs around the exterior of the vehicle. They asked me to present my lanyard, which I did, and had it scanned for a third time. The ICP officers exited, leaving the two original escorts, before the gate opened and the bus hummed forward, slowly and deliberately, coming to a halt in front of another building with an exterior sign: Compression Echo.

We disembarked methodically from the front to the back, so I was the fifth person out behind the redhead. I sensed an eagerness to get out from this metal shell, mixed with trepidation of our future pathway.

They ushered us into a small anteroom just inside the first building. Muffled voices and the metallic clank of pots and pans permeated the far wall, giving the impression of a well-occupied facility.

There were a dozen or so cheap chairs around the edges, screwed to the floor. My first thought was that you'd have to be a pretty desperate thief to want a chair so badly that the facility had to screw it down. I must have smiled, as at that moment the door at the far end opened and a woman in ICP fatigues broke the silence.

"Something amusing?"

I did that comical thing and looked around just in case she wasn't talking to me. I don't know why. She was looking directly at me. Her name patch said simply 'Cooper'. She had a face that most models would die for and dark hair pulled back fiercely into a bun at the back: what we used to call a 'Croydon facelift'. I must have smiled again because she cocked her head to one side and stared at me, without anger, but with enough force that I knew to take her seriously.

"No, not particularly," I eventually replied under her penetrating gaze. She held her piercing hazel eyes on mine for another few seconds, just long enough to make it uncomfortable, and then looked up and around the room.

"Welcome to Echo. Follow me, please."

We walked single-file through the second door, into a room with bio-detectors, screens and several ICP Command officers. There were three benches against the far wall, with a small box every metre or so. I counted nine in all. These must be our welcome packages.

"Boxes are marked with your names. Please collect yours and make your way to one of the screens opposite."

Nobody moved, each of us staring around at each other to see who would go first. A tall man, heavily built, was closest. He muttered something under his breath and then swept along the benches until he'd located his box and picked it up. I shrugged and headed over, finding mine on the second bench, and then walked back to the screens, picking number four and stepping behind it. I had expected there to be a chair or something, figuring they were asking us to change, but behind my screen was an open door and an ICP officer, who scanned my lanyard once more and then nodded through the doorway.

The passage beyond was just four or five metres long and opened onto a circular room with two recesses about the size of a shower.

"Box down, kit off, and into cubicle one please, Sir," came a surprisingly gentle voice from the ICP officer. He was pretty square in a kind of alpha-male way, jutting jaw, crew cut, broad shoulders, and arms muscular enough that he couldn't put his hands flat to his sides.

I could hear voices, presumably in the other chambers, all being told to do the same thing.

"Don't be shy, Sir. It'll be over in a couple of minutes." He nodded at the first cubicle and then turned himself at an angle that let me know he wasn't looking, yet wasn't looking away.

I stripped off and started to fold my clothes up on the bench.

"Don't bother, Sir. Just post them through the hatch on your left."

There was a small black metal door in the wall, with a handle. I opened it, deposited my clothes, and closed it again. Once into the cubicle the opening slid shut, and there was an electronic voice, not in a robotic way but more like a bad intercom.

"Please face the red circle on the wall and stand with your feet on the red pads. Then please close your eyes. This might catch your breath a little, but keep your eyes closed for your own safety."

I barely had a moment to wonder what was going to happen when what felt like freezing oil cascaded unceremoniously over me. It was so cold I gasped, and a few drops splashed into my mouth. I almost gagged. It was like a combination of antiseptic and alcohol.

"That's it. Stand still for just a moment longer."

Then several jets, presumably water, and considerably warmer, hit me from all sides. My face, ears, torso, legs, arms were all pounded simultaneously with quite some force, causing me to flinch.

"Please keep your eyes closed until the process has finished," came the metallic voice.

I was being pummelled for what felt like an eternity, but was probably only a minute or two, before the jets stopped. Almost instantly a whirring noise fired up and a warm fan kicked in, billowing the water droplets from my body.

A minute later the fans stopped, and the voice told me I could open my eyes. Ahead of me, where the red circle had been, was an archway to the second cubicle. They instructed me to walk through, where I found my box on a bench inside. I opened it and pulled out the contents. A blue flight suit with 'Leith' on a Velcro patch above the left breast, some white shorts, white socks and a pair of faux-leather boots that weighed almost nothing. My lanyard was gone, but in the box's bottom was a metal-link wristband. It looked like a watch strap with the watch missing and had a thin polymer surface which made it much more tactile than it looked. I rolled it around my wrist and it magnetically sealed as the trailing end contacted the beginning.

As the two ends connected, a series of lights flashed around it, and a short, high tone emitted.

The cubicle wall rotated again, and an opening appeared on my left. I checked my box to make sure I had missed nothing and walked through a corridor to a heavy door with a red light above it. The light changed to green, and the door hissed and slid open. I was in a four by two metre room with identical doors at both ends. The door I'd just stepped through closed behind me and a moment later the room started to squeeze me, as the pressure inside increased. I could feel my ears pop, and it took a few yawning movements to clear them. The second door hissed and opened.

"Please move to the seating area in the centre," came a voice from a staging area on the right. I was the second one through. One of the six women whom I had paid no attention to was already seated in the middle. She had white-blonde hair, and I wondered why I hadn't noticed her before. I mean, there's blonde, and there's platinum, but she almost glowed. I walked over and sat beside her, and was about to introduce myself when several hisses behind me indicated the others coming through. Over the course of about a minute, the airlock opened several times, and each occupant entered the room, some furiously wiggling their fingers in their ears, and others making yawning motions as I had, until all of us were sitting, facing a small platform. A man stepped out in white fatigues. His breast patch said 'Harris' and he looked like he could handle himself. Muscular, dark, of average height and clearly in peak physical condition, with a close, military crew cut and eyes so black they looked like onyx.

"My name is Sergeant Tyrone Harris. I am an astronaut, and a marine. The two are not mutually exclusive.

"I will take you through your induction processes over the next few weeks before we move on to assessments and work placements. Your crew is Echo 41, and this is encoded into your wristbands, along with your identification. You may not remove your wristband unless instructed to do so, or in case of a medical emergency.

"You have just been through decontamination. As your ultimate destination is a space station, we have to be very careful not to introduce bacteria or foreign DNA of any sort into the clean areas. You will go through this process again, if we deem it necessary, to enable us to maintain a sterile facility. Some of you may experience a minor discomfort. We pressurise the facility to keep out bacteria and viruses. Once you are through Stage 3, you will depressurise before departure. Any of you with ears still popping should not worry. It will clear in the next hour, but if you feel any further discomfort, notify me immediately for your own safety. Keeping this facility clean is crucial to our success. For those that know your history, the Spanish flu killed millions in the early 20th century. COVID-19 killed millions more in 2020 and 2021. Imagine if a virus gets on board a space station, with enclosed living spaces and recirculated air. It would be nothing less than catastrophic, and so we ask each of you to observe the protocols we have implemented.

"We have strict rules in this facility, which you will adhere to, or find yourself no longer eligible to move on to the Bertram Ramsay. You were not randomly selected, as you were previously told. Each of you has been assessed independently of this facility, and the results have rewarded you with a place in this Compression centre. In order to move on to the Bertram Ramsay, you are required to undergo several further assessments, both physical and mental. These assessments are designed to challenge you, but not harm you. Please keep that in mind.

"Rule number one: Treat each other with respect. You are not competing with each other. Learn to operate as part of a team. If you cannot do so, with just nine people, then it seems unlikely you will manage to work in an enclosed sphere, with a million other occupants, forty million miles from Earth.

"Rule number two: You will do as you are ordered to do, when you are ordered to do it, by any officer wearing a white BRMC uniform, like the one I am dutifully modelling for you now."

There were a couple of chuckles at this remark, and the tension eased considerably. I looked around at my fellow crew mates and could see palpable relief on a few faces.

"Rule number three: You are each going to be issued with a waist pack, like mine. It may look like a padded belt, but it is in fact your lifeline should we sustain a loss of oxygen. Inside it is an inflatable helmet with a hose that runs to the pack. If you hear seven blasts of the alarm siren, you are to depress the blue button on the right side, like so..."

He pressed a button that I couldn't see from my vantage point, with his right hand, without looking down. There was an audible click, and a clear bag attached to a hose rolled out and dangled below his knee. I looked around at my fellow occupants. Each of them had looks of deep concentration, desperately trying to follow the demonstration. Some of them were subconsciously mimicking his movements. I watched as hands reached down to click invisible buttons on invisible belt kits and smiled.

I refocussed my attention on Harris, just as he was pulling the clear bag over his head. The bag suddenly inflated, making it look like he was wearing a goldfish bowl. The internal pressure pushed out the creases and brought into focus a small silver disc just below his chin.

"This device will prolong your life if we suffer depressurisation in space at any point and will save your life if there is a chemical or biological accident or attack. Your pack acts as a rebreather, recirculating the air you are breathing for a full forty minutes before the excess carbon dioxide causes nitrogen to build in your bloodstream, at which point you will suffer and die." He smiled mischievously.

This produced a stunned silence from us all. The reality of space travel had not really impacted until this point, but more alarmingly he had casually thrown out the word 'attack'.

He depressed the blue button again; the bag deflated, and sucked back into its small pack size, before neatly folding back into the belt pack with the thin hose.

He looked up at us, smiling. "It will be uncomfortable the first time you try your rebreather, as the bag creates a seal against your neck. You are not to panic—this is a perfectly breathable environment that protects you from the extreme elements in space. Of course, if you find yourself sucked into space with just one of these, your body will freeze in under three seconds, and breathing will become a luxury you no longer require.

"Space is dangerous. It is formidable and unforgiving. It will not comply, and it will not relent. These rules are in place to keep you alive, not to scare you. If adhered to and respected, you will live long and happy lives and become part of a unique community of citizens that will save humanity from extinction. It is our job to ensure the continuity of our species. No, our *obligation.* We are tasked with the single most important mission in the history of the human race, and we take this responsibility seriously.

"Which brings me to our final rule: You and you alone are responsible for the upkeep and maintenance of your equipment. You are to treat it with care, and test everything regularly. It may save your life one day. That also goes for your suits—we will eventually replace these with fatigues that have thermal controls and bio-monitors. We will initiate our first test of all equipment and teach you how to maintain it tomorrow. It's been a long day for all of you, so for now I shall take you through the accommodation and show you where you will eat and sleep. Catering is twenty-four hours to enable flexible working, depending on your assignments, but I would encourage all of you to adopt a routine and stick to it where possible. I will take any questions from you tomorrow, but for now let's get you settled. Please collect your waist belts from the hatch on the left and form a line by the door."

Colonel Grealish left the brigadier and headed down the hall to Amy Cooper's office. He knocked twice and entered, finding Lieutenant Cooper on her comms with her back to the desk and staring out of the window. She swung round as he entered and held up a finger to indicate the call was finishing.

Grealish caught his breath and tried not to stare. She was an extraordinarily beautiful woman, even wearing full combat fatigues, belts, holsters and all that comes with it. She had mid-length dark hair, pulled up into a tight bun to accommodate her cap, but an easy, relaxed aura about her. Cooper clicked off her comms, looked up at Grealish and smiled.

"I've just been over to Echo to start the process on Crew 41. One or two characters in that bunch. Harris has just called to say they're in digs for the evening. What can I do for you, Andrew?"

Grealish sat down, rotated the chair to the desk and leaned forward with his forearms flat on the desk and fingers clasped together. He must have seemed a little agitated because Cooper leaned back in her chair, put her hands on her legs, cocked her head to the side as she always did when she was thinking.

"Sir? Is everything okay?"

"I've told you before Amy, it's Andrew when we're one-to-one. Save the 'Sirs' for the brigadier."

"Sorry, Andrew. You just looked, officially official. I'm just trying to strike the right tone. What's the issue?"

"Crew 41 is the problem, and what I'm about to tell you from an officially official point is absolutely classified, and a mile above your clearance, so bear with me. I need someone on the inside, undercover, and going through the process like any other pleb, and I think you're it."

"Something wrong with Crew 41? And it's classified? That doesn't sound good."

"Actually, it may not be Echo 41. It may be Charlie 38, although I think it's more likely to be 41. Get Harris over here at 05:00. Let me start from scratch and bring you up to speed. We'll meet in this office. Don't advertise it, and ask Harris to be discreet. That'll give me time to bring up your clearance level, and Tyrone's. Bring your own coffee. I don't want catering wandering in."

"Yes, Sir. 05:00," said Cooper to the colonel's retreating back.

COMPRESSION ECHO

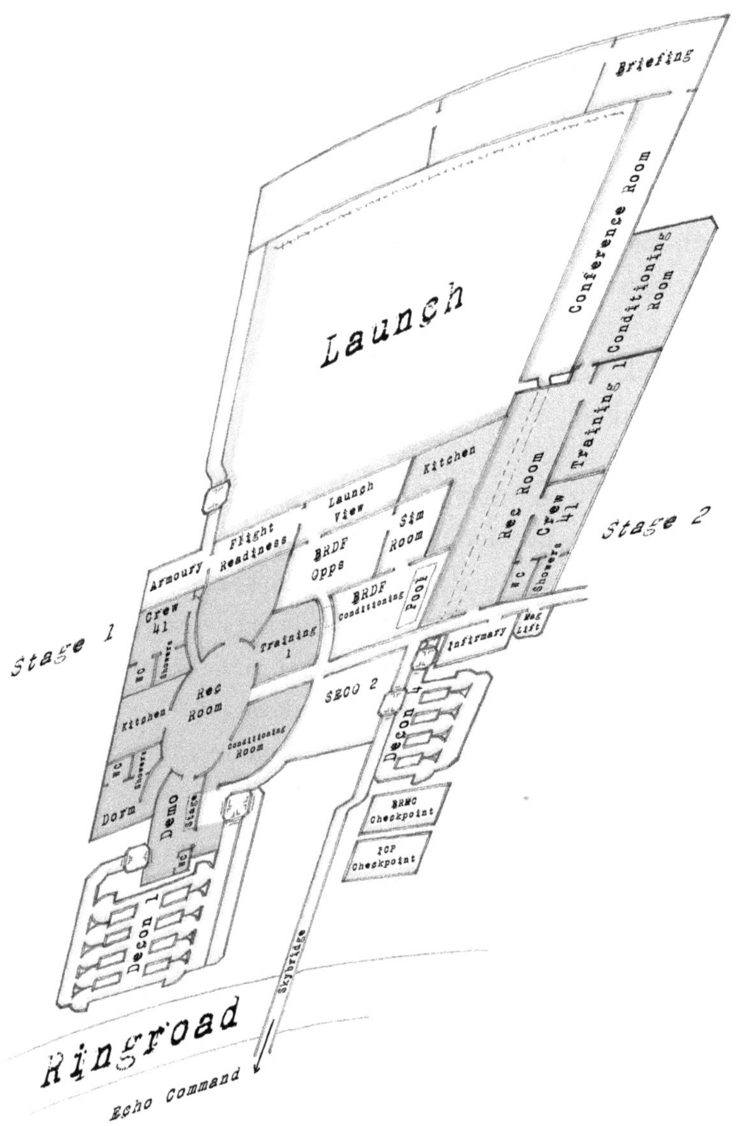

CHAPTER THREE

THEY LED US through a small tunnel to an oval hall with several other tunnels leading from it. I was about fourth from the back, so couldn't see much until we were actually inside. Harris gave us a quick summary of each 'spoke' and told us this was the 'rec room'. There were various areas with sofas, chairs, tables, coffee machines, water and juice dispensers, and an open hatch on the left with tables in front, lined with trays, cutlery and napkins. At one end of the rec room were half a dozen small tables with four seats at each one, presumably for mealtimes.

There were one or two people milling about. A guy in his early forties was sitting on one of the sofas with a coffee, immersed in a hollotab, and a woman was sitting at one of the far tables with her back to me. There was artwork around the walls. Photos and drawings of the Bertram Ramsay, plus some photos of Earth and the Moon. It seemed cosy enough. It was lit well, but not so bright that it seemed like a hospital, and not so dark that you couldn't see people across the room. There were some spotlights over the dining tables, but only the occupied one was illuminated.

Harris indicated we should continue on and took us to the far end of the oval room in the third tunnel which was wide enough for three or four of us to stand shoulder to shoulder. From there we walked maybe twenty metres to what I could only describe as a barrack or dormitory at the end. There were twelve beds neatly spaced around the room, each against a wall, and each with its own cubbyhole in the wall. Two of the beds were bunks, which left eight singles. I wondered who'd end up using a bunk. I suspected it might be me.

On the far wall there were two archways leading through to communal areas—showers and toilets. Clearly these were mixed facilities. I could see a few eyebrows being raised by the women. That's when I realised the redhead was not with us. I looked around to see if she'd fallen behind, but she wasn't anywhere to be seen. Plus, we were all accounted for. Nine on the bus, and nine in the room. Six women, three men. It seemed nobody else had noticed, but now all I could think about was which one of the women had replaced her. I hadn't looked hard enough at any of them when I got on the bus to be sure. I'd only noticed the redhead because she was looking at me.

People were already claiming beds and lifting the small washbags to inspect. Our bags were all on a shelf at one end of the room, so one by one people claimed their own, and set their knick-knacks and photos by their chosen beds. I left my bag where it was. There wasn't anything in it, so there was no point collecting it.

My thoughts turned back to the redhead. I was trying to think back to when I last saw her. Obviously on the bus because she stepped off right in front of me. I tried to place her in the anteroom, but the only thing I remember there was the big guy and the woman called Cooper. For a moment I visualised each step methodically until I arrived at the room through the airlock where

I was alone, except for Blondie. I hadn't paid her much attention since, but I looked around now, and sure enough, she was in the third bed by the first bunk. The bunk was still empty, so I walked over and claimed it. I rummaged through my washbag, not really looking at anything, occasionally looking up at the blonde and wondering why I hadn't noticed her on the bus. Or in the anteroom. Or the corridor.

Harris had finished his pep talk. I'd barely paid attention since entering the dorm, so I was hoping he hadn't imparted with any crucial information while I was daydreaming about the mysterious redhead.

The lights suddenly dimmed, and a soft tone sounded from a speaker in the ceiling. I wondered what time it was. I went to check my watch, before remembering I didn't have one, but the action of bringing up my wrist caused my bracelet to glow. I looked down, and across one link was a blue display showing 22:00. Useful.

I sorted out my bunk as best as I could. The sheets and covers were stacked neatly in the middle, so I pulled them out and set to work. There was a small spotlight mounted on the wall at one end for reading, I assumed, so that's where I placed the pillows, although with nothing to read it seemed pointless. Some others were getting into bed, a couple of the women clearly trying to undress under the covers. I doubted that modesty would last with the communal showers and toilets. I wasn't hugely enamoured with taking a dump in a room full of women, but shrugged; it's the same for everyone. Eventually you just have to get it out of the way.

The two other guys were conversing over by the seventh and eighth beds, occasionally looking around at the women. No need to eavesdrop that convo.

I removed my flight suit and folded it into my locker, along with my socks and white tee shirt, and climbed under the covers. It had been a long day. I had barely a moment longer to ponder on the mysterious disappearance of the redhead before I fell asleep.

At 05:00 the colonel trudged wearily down the endless corridor, stopping at Lieutenant Cooper's office. He knocked once and stepped inside. Harris was sitting in the far chair and he rushed to his feet as the colonel arrived, but Grealish waved him down before he was fully stood. Cooper sat behind her desk looking remarkably alert given that she couldn't have had more than five or six hours' sleep.

Grealish took the other seat and sat back heavily, bringing both his hands up to his head and ruffling his hair to wake himself up. He looked up, sighed once, steeled himself and sat upright. One thing that was burned into him over and over at the Academy was "If you need to command a situation, look like you're in command of the situation, and not the other way round". Sound advice, he reflected.

"Harris, Cooper… I've upgraded your clearance to Delta 4. That's eyes-only stuff. You won't have access to the system, but nobody will challenge you for having Delta 4 information, understood?" They both nodded and exchanged looks before focussing on Grealish.

"Tyrone, I know you're BRMC and not ICP, but whilst in this facility you're under my command. I appreciate you are obliged to report this meeting back to your superiors, but I must ask you not to. We have a serious situation, and trust is a problem. You're here because Amy trusts you, and I trust Amy, and because you are potentially in harm's way." Tyrone's eyes widened in concern. "Not directly, so don't be alarmed. You'll understand more in a minute."

Harris nodded and waited for the colonel to continue.

"Andrew, what's going on? Why all the cloak and dagger?" As usual, Cooper's voice and presence had a disarming effect on the colonel, and he relaxed a little.

Grealish surveyed them both. "Six years ago, we sent a female operative on a mission to infiltrate the AoG. It took her almost four years to penetrate deeply enough to have access to meaningful intelligence. Only three other people outside of this room know that she exists." He paused, allowing the gravity of his words to sink in. "It has become so dangerous for her that she now has to make dead drops at one of sixteen different locations in order to avoid detection. The ICP is tasked with checking each location, twice daily, and have done so for the last seven months since electronic communication became an impossibility."

"Sixteen?! Jesus!" Cooper's eyes were wide. Dead drops were difficult to manage covertly when there was only one location.

"Quite. The officers collecting don't know what they are collecting or who they are collecting from, or for, but the fact that we've had to check sixteen dead drops twice daily for seven months should give you some idea of the level of resource dedicated to this intel.

"Each dead drop holds two items: a watch and a ring, both digital storage devices with encryption. The ones left behind are blank and untraceable, so anyone accidentally stumbling upon them won't know what they are and can't compromise us or our operative in any way. When our operative has active intel, she goes to a drop, swaps her ring for ours, or the watch, and walks away. It's clean, and the safest way for her to communicate with us."

Grealish stood up and walked to the corner and back. He paced for a few moments, and then turned to face Cooper and Tyrone, leaning down on the desk with his fists.

"This morning, we recovered a drop. By the time they decrypted the intel, and passed along the chain to us, there was nothing we could do in the way of prevention."

The colonel pulled a ring out of his pocket and a small hollopad. He placed the hollopad on the desk, pressed down on it once, and waited for five seconds as the green lights around the edge blinked and turned solid. He placed the ring on the centre, and a screen projected up from the hollopad. A hooded figure appeared on-screen, too dark to discern features or gender, and spoke in a soft voice, clearly manipulated to protect their identity.

"They've infiltrated. I don't know who or where. What I know is that their timetable says '4 pm, 5.15 pm, 6.45 pm final.' I got a look at it during a meeting. They keep mentioning 'The Valiant', but without any context. Then I heard, 'Congratulations on the second'. I take this to mean that they already have one inside, and that this timetable is for their second infiltrator."

The screen flickered and vanished.

"That's it?" said Harris, looking between Cooper and Grealish.

"That's it," replied Grealish.

"With respect, Sir, that's nothing," replied Cooper.

"Actually, it isn't," said Grealish, pocketing the hollopad and the ring, and lowering himself back into his seat.

"Yesterday we had two collections scheduled for 4 pm pick up, and then transferred onto a bus at 5.15 pm, arriving at this facility at 6.45 pm. One is Charlie 38, and the other is Echo 41.

In one of those crews lies an AoG agent. Charlie 38 was actually scheduled to arrive at 6.50 pm but arrived at 6.45 pm. We know they couldn't know that the bus would be early, so it seems most likely to be Echo 41 at this moment. I'm putting a few things in motion in Charlie 38, just so we don't get blindsided by our own assumptions, but the three of us are going to concentrate our efforts on Echo 41, okay?"

"When you say 'concentrate our efforts' what did you have in mind, Sir?" asked Harris. "I only ask because Echo is a big facility, and of the three of us in this room, only one of us has air-side clearance."

"I agree with you, Tyrone. It's an impossible task for one person, but, as fortune would have it, we had an agent of our own on the second transport. They pulled her out before we received this intel, right as they all entered DECON 1. Annoyingly, she was on a Grasshopper back to ICP Whitehall and halfway back before I'd heard the message. I put a call in while the new crew were still going through decontamination and managed to get someone scrubbed out and in civvies before they were through the airlock."

"So that's why Hennessey was in the group? You took a chance there, not communicating that to me. She gave me the nod as I walked in, but I could so easily have blown her cover. We need to get better comms going if we're to pull this off, Sir." Harris looked irritated.

"There was no time, Tyrone. If Sara hadn't been in SECO 2 when I put the call through, we'd have missed the window. The brass in London have sent the other officer back for debrief in a couple of hours, so I'll need you both back here at 07.00."

"How much is she likely to tell us Andrew? How long was she on the bus? Ninety minutes?"

"Less. And you're probably right. She's unlikely to have gleaned anything meaningful on a guarded fusion-bus with only eight other passengers, but we have to ask, check and double-check. If we really have cleared an AoG spy into Stage 1, we're going to need to flush them out before they get too far into the process and compromise our security. Any intelligence leak would be a disaster for the evacuation."

"Okay, granted, it's a problem," admitted Harris, "but that entire facility is locked down. No information can flow in or out without coming through us. They don't even have access to external networks or communications. Echo's occupants are locked up in a pressurised bubble, twenty-four hours a day for the next three months. They can't have brought anything in with them—we incinerate everything in DECON 1. What are the actual risks we face here?" Harris's tone wasn't challenging. It was factual and open.

Amy Cooper let out an audible sigh—more of a blow—and covered her eyes. "Oh, shit."

Grealish looked up. "I see you've understood the problem, Amy."

"What problem? What am I missing here?" replied Harris.

Cooper looked directly at him. "What are the chances of us selecting an occupant for the Bertram Ramsay, without doing a thorough background check, and tearing apart the lives of each one, for any hint of a connection to international terrorism, Tyrone?"

"Zero. You guys always do your homework first. What's your point?"

"That's right, Tyrone," Cooper interjected, "so if it's impossible for us to accidentally select someone with ties to the AoG, then the only alternative is that someone in the ICP deliberately selected a candidate with ties to the AoG. They manage the lanyard printing and distribution on site. They're dispatched directly to the depot, under armed escort, in a secure pouch. There's at least thirty people involved in the complete process from bang to bullets."

"Oh, shit."

"Quite."

There was an audible silence for a minute as each of them internally weighed up the ramifications of this revelation. Grealish broke the silence.

"This is why all the cloak and dagger, Amy. You two and I are the only ones who know about this. I told the brigadier yesterday that we've got intelligence of an infiltrator, but I kept it vague. Silly old fart is still reminiscing about stuff that happened sixty years ago. We have absolutely no clue who they already have on the inside, but it's a fair assumption that whoever it is was referenced in the message earlier."

Grealish held up one hand and started counting off his fingers. "We know they have two inside. We know one arrived yesterday, and we know that someone already inside helped them do it. Two operatives. One with every access to outside networks and communications. Trained in counter-intel, as we all are, and armed to the teeth by the very people they're infiltrating."

"Well, the good news is, Echo is sterile. No weapons in or out. Every time I go in or come out, I have to go through DECON 4. You don't burn my fatigues—they stay in a lockbox land-side, but my Proxy stays locked in the armoury and is coded to my bio-band, anyway. The only routes in are through the delivery chambers, which are buried in cameras, thermal imaging, X-ray screens, bio-sensors, chemical alert beacons, and twenty-odd heavily armed ICP guards on one side, and an equivalent number of BRMC on the other. The bad news is, this problem is mine. I cannot clear the both of you to be inside Echo beyond the anteroom. I suggest that's the first thing we deal with. Simply put, I don't have the clout, or the bollocks, to resolve that, so that's one for you, Sir. Respectfully, of course," Harris said.

"Well, that's a starting point at least, Tyrone. It's good that the compound is as secure as you say from the inside."

"Actually, Sir, not so good. In order for them to be effective and to communicate with this new operative that we think arrived yesterday, there'd have to be someone else on the inside that has access to both land and air-sides. ICP control land, BRMC control air, but BRMC have access to both, as local assets and staff come in daily. There are some long-termers in the BRMC barracks, but that's a totally separate unit, and none of them work in Echo."

"Hang on a minute. Are you suggesting there's three inside? That's a gigantic leap from the intel we heard for the first time five minutes ago," replied Cooper. She looked agitated.

Harris shrugged. "Logically there has to be. Unless the two units are completely disconnected. We could assume that the ICP infil is there to facilitate further infiltrations, and that this is their only role, and that the agent on the inside is alone, with an agenda that doesn't include communicating outside of the facility. We could assume that, but if we do, then we have to assume they don't come into play until they're already on the Bertram. What would be the point of sabotaging this facility? There are fifty other sites around the world. All they'd do is bottle-neck the intake for a short period. Maybe cause some damage. But they'd have to do it with what's available to them, which isn't much. Once they get on the shuttle, they could potentially down the flight, but that achieves nothing either. No, it makes more sense to do meaningful damage once they're on the Bertram. In the meantime, I think we have to check to see if there's any possibility of communication between an internal asset and an external one. I think we have to assume there's three, because if it's only two, the obvious and right thing to do right now is remove everyone currently in the program, and rotate staff, BRMC and ICP off the facility."

"We can't do that. It would be a sticking plaster. We must also assume this isn't the only facility compromised. It's hardly a soft target. Look out the window—it's built on the fucking grounds of GCHQ. No, you're going to have to find them en route to the Bertram. Amy, I'll get you levelled up so you can cross to the air-side. Tyrone, you'll have to bring Amy up to speed on the internal stuff, and we'll have to develop some cover story—cross-force training or something. I'll stay on the periphery here. You both have enough legitimate contact with me that our meeting won't raise eyebrows, but if I started wandering in and out of Echo, people will notice. Back here at 07:00. God help us if we don't find them."

CHAPTER FOUR

I WOKE EARLY. NOT by design, just couldn't switch my brain off. The redhead disappearing was bothering me, particularly since I was in a facility surrounded by security. How someone stepped off the bus and just vanished was beyond me. Our numbers were still the same which suggests that one of us was already inside. *Blondie.* For a moment I wondered if there wasn't another body on the bus that I didn't see, but that was improbable given how few of us were on it. Besides, there were nine welcome packages, nine washbags and nine mini-holdalls.

It was making my brain ache thinking about it. I got myself up and moseyed through to the toilets in my shorts. No point being shy with everyone still asleep. The toilets were all in separate cubicles, although the doors were miniature, so you could see over the top of them when you sat down. There were six cubicles and a line of mirrors along the back wall with four sinks underneath. The walls were magnolia or cream and were spotless. There wasn't so much as a crack in the paintwork or a cobweb anywhere. Duel skylights illuminated the room, dousing it in a soft orange glow from the dawn sunrise. I rinsed my hands off and wandered back out and round to the shower block. The showers were also separate cubicles, with an open side so that you couldn't see into them as you entered the room. That's something, I thought. The showers were decorated identically to the toilets, but with white, ceramic brick-like tiles on all the shower walls. On the far wall was a unit packed with folded towels, in two sizes that looked to be large and small. Next to the unit was a cube stack, with freshly laundered underwear, tee shirts and socks in each section, split into genders and sizes—small, medium, large and extra-large. I was almost indignant on behalf of people that were bigger or smaller than these sizes, and then I remembered we weren't random selections, and our size probably formed part of the assessment. It hadn't previously occurred to me, but thinking about it, space travel is probably physically demanding, so they'll have selected candidates who could handle the rigours of our training and life on the Bertram.

I grabbed a large towel and slung it over the wall of the third cubicle. I'd already taken my shorts off and lobbed them into the laundry bin, so I stepped into the cubicle and turned the shower on. On the wall were three bottles of shampoo, shower gel and body lotion. The body lotion seemed unnecessary, but no point dwelling on something I'll never appreciate. The shower was hot and the water pressure was great, so I let the water drench me for a good ten minutes before switching off. I wrapped the towel round my waist and walked over to the cube stack, grabbed some fresh underwear and strolled back out to my bunk. There were a few stirring noises from the other beds, so I quickly towelled off and dressed before I drew too much attention to myself. I headed out to the rec room to check it out. As I turned to leave, Blondie smiled at me from the next bed. I wondered how long she'd been looking.

The rec room was exactly as it was the night before, although with a lot more natural light from four frosted skylights in the ceiling that I couldn't have seen in the evening gloom. It was empty, and clean, and dappled in that same orange glow from the morning sun, with a newsdock stationed by the table in the middle, and a stack of hollotabs, kinetically charging from the surface. I poured myself a black coffee from the machine and grabbed a hollotab from the pile before sitting back on one of the large sofas in the middle section. It was 5.30am, and I was about to read the news when Harris walked in.

He looked up as he crossed the room and nodded to me before grabbing himself a coffee and joining me in the armchair opposite.

"How was your first night?" he asked. The concern on his face suggested that he had some experience of the internal conflict we were each facing.

I shrugged. "I slept okay. Lights out the moment I got my head down." Then I remembered the redhead. "Hey, can I ask you a question, Sir?"

"Call me Tyrone, or Harris, or just about anything but Sir. What should I call you?"

"Jax or Jaxon is fine. Don't think I've used my surname for about a decade."

"Okay, Jax. We can change that name on your flight suit if you like. What is it you wanted to ask me?"

"It's a strange one, and it's the reason I was awake so early. There was a woman with red hair on the bus yesterday, and nine of us in total. Six women, three guys, including me. She looked at me a couple of times, and I got off the bus behind her. But she's not here."

Harris shifted in his seat, his furrowed brow belying the calm exterior.

"It's like she just vanished. I don't remember seeing her after the bus, in any of the rooms, and yet there's still six women and three men. This woman had vivid red hair. Unless it was dyed, and the decontamination process washed it out?"

Harris leaned forward, elbows on his knees. "No, that can't happen. The oily stuff is actually a protein that magnetises bacteria, dirt and other impurities to itself. We dunk you in it, and everything on you that shouldn't be there sticks to the oil. Then we use the jets to wash it off. It's completely impervious to water, so it falls off in clumps into a drainage sieve, where the water runs off it and into the sewers. The sieve is propelled through a tube into the furnace and they incinerate the oil. Hugely flammable, smokeless and burns at 850 Kelvin in about ten seconds, so anything stuck to it is destroyed. That's how we keep the place clean from sickness and disease."

She definitely hadn't entered Compression then. "So where could she have gone?"

Harris side-stepped the question and asked one in return. "Did any of the six women seem out of place to you when you re-formed as a group after you'd been through DECON?"

"I'm not sure I'd say 'out of place'. When I came out in my flight suit, through the airlock, there was already one woman sat in the middle. She had white-blonde hair, and it wasn't until later that I thought it was odd that I hadn't noticed her before. She's not exactly inconspicuous."

Harris smiled, and it was disarming. "Well, there are six women in your crew, and only three men. It's an unusual gender bias, certainly not one we see very often, so you'd be forgiven for being confused."

"I'm not confused. The redhead was on the bus. She isn't here now." I was relieved to hear that our specific gender-imbalance was unusual. The walls had been closing in on me every time I thought about that. The building was suddenly less claustrophobic.

"Would you say you're quite observant, Jax?"

That raised a shrug from me. "I haven't really given it any thought. I'm more of a thinker than a talker, so maybe I notice more. Maybe I don't."

"How many skylights in the far end of this room behind you?"

"Four. Why?"

"Well, they're behind you, and this is your first time in this room in daylight. Your hair is still wet, and your coffee hot and full, so you haven't been in here long. Yet you know how many skylights there are. And you don't think you're observant? It's a useful skill to have. I think we're going to see good things from you in the next three months."

He raised his cup to me, inclined his head a little and drained the rest of the coffee, before getting to his feet and walking back out through the tunnel.

An hour later, Harris entered the ICP Command centre and took the stairs to the second floor, turning left through the double doors and down the never-ending corridor to Amy Cooper's office. He knocked, entered, expecting to see Grealish and Cooper, only to find an extra body in the room. Vivid red hair, pretty face, made so much more interesting by her ICP dress uniform. She wasn't in

Cooper's league, he mused, but all the same... he let the thought linger perhaps a moment too long.

"Harris, this is Sergeant Laura Watkins. Sergeant, this is Sergeant Harris, BRMC."

They shook hands and Harris couldn't help a wry smile.

"What's so amusing, Tyrone?" Cooper was giving him one of her fierce looks. Harris looked at each of them and then back to Watkins as he took his seat.

"He made you, you know?" He gesticulated towards Sergeant Watkins.

"Who?"

"Jaxon Leith. I've just been in Echo to gear up before coming over, and he was sitting alone in the rec room. I asked how his first night went and he brushed it aside and asked me what happened to Watkins here."

"What?"

"Yep, cool as you like. He's also spotted the plant. Sara doesn't know yet, but he's got her nailed as an imposter."

"Christ, that's all we need." This came from Grealish in the corner. He turned to face Watkins.

"You're supposed to be inconspicuous. Blend in. How bloody obvious were you?" Grealish hadn't slept well, and his manner was irritable.

Watkins looked up, a fierce expression on her face. "Sir, I was supposed to observe the new Occos. I can't do that with eyes forward and a stiff neck. When my orders came in, I protested the infil should happen from depot to dorm, and not a switch, because that's what we always do. It's an insert for a week and then ejection, and then I get rotated through again two weeks later. Changing protocol was always a risk. I got my head bitten off and told to crack on. So that's what I did." She looked huffy and dangerous, and clearly quite capable of holding her own in a room full of higher ranks.

"Okay, let's take this down a notch." Cooper raised a placatory hand vaguely into the room, to prevent the tension from escalating. "Before we get to the 'What the fuck do we do now?' section, tell us about the depot and our new Occos."

Watkins sat back in her chair, surveying the room. "Very little to tell. The usual protest outside the fence, and a couple of faces we recognised but don't have any intel on. There was an entire team of plain clothes ops walking through the crowds and observing from across the street. Your chap, Jaxon, locked eyes with one of them on the way in and on the way out," she shrugged, "but impossible to know if it was morbid curiosity or recognition."

"Jesus Christ! Why weren't we told when you exfil'd? I'd say that's a fairly important observation, wouldn't you?" Grealish was pacing now, not at all as composed as he usually was. He must have realised because he stopped, closed his eyes, took a breath, and then turned back to the room.

"Okay, what else did you observe?"

Watkins was bristling. "To answer your first question, Colonel, I didn't tell you when I exfiltrated because I didn't know until I'd landed back at command. It wasn't my observation. I only found out during the debrief. I was in the holding pen before any of them arrived, as per the SOP, and I was concentrating on the civilian personnel and anyone with access to the buses at that point. My job was to observe everything. Not just the new Occos. As things stand, there isn't much to tell. Everyone seemed to be getting on with things as they normally would. No suspicious movements, eyes lingering too long in the wrong place, that sort of thing." She briefly raised her eyebrows at Harris. "No one where they shouldn't be. It was actually very efficient. Two of the guys arrived first, and they were through the pens and onto the bus inside three minutes. I followed them on board. Then came the five women, and last on was your boy, Jaxon. And I admit, I took a special interest in him. He was looking at everything. At everyone. Not invasively; I got the impression he was just very observant, and given the current circumstances I'd say I arrived at the correct conclusion, wouldn't you?"

"Mind your tone, Sergeant." Cooper looked sternly across.

Watkins immediately flared up. "My tone? This was a botched operation from the moment it was hatched. I made my objections, did my job to the letter, and then got barked at by the CO, and dragged back here for a second debrief, so you'll forgive me if I'm not glowing and happy about it." She glared at Cooper.

"Alright, alright." Grealish's turn to calm proceedings.

Watkins took a breath and turned to the colonel. "Sorry, Sir."

Grealish waved off the apology. "What about the rest of them? Anything unusual?"

"Nothing at all. Didn't speak to each other, did little of anything. Usually we get two or three that want to introduce themselves and get to know their fellow Occos, but this group just sat down, stared out of the windows and stayed silent the entire journey. It was almost bizarre, but it didn't feel forced or unnatural." She shrugged.

"What about when you left the bus? What was your exfiltration strategy?"

"Not much to tell. Orders were to step off, tie my shoelace while they filed past me as they all got ushered straight into Echo, and then step back onto the bus. The bus drove me for about twelve seconds, I crossed the yard out of sight of Echo and jumped on a Grasshopper. Back in Whitehall inside twenty minutes. Job done, Sir."

Cooper took a sideways glance at Watkins and then addressed Harris. "Is Jaxon going to be a problem, Tyrone?"

Harris's turn to shrug. "He could be a valuable player. Very observant, and at the very first opportunity he told a staffer about something that didn't seem right. Not like he was grassing someone up." He blinked. "He seemed genuinely put out by the whole situation. It's not uncommon. His brain is telling him something is wrong, and also that he doesn't have enough information to make that determination. What is uncommon is that, rather than sweat on it, he just spilled to me. Shows integrity, confidence, assertiveness and great observation skills."

"Okay, so what's the play?" Cooper looked at Grealish. Grealish took in the room and settled his eyes on Watkins. He was about to speak when Harris interrupted.

"Sir, if I may?"

"Go on, Tyrone."

"Why don't we reinsert Watkins? Her cover isn't blown. We could introduce Senior Instructor Captain Sara Hennessey out of the group when they first assemble, reintroduce Laura here, publicly apologise to her for pulling her out and isolating her overnight, and then give some speech about teaching them to observe everything, and a pat on the back to Mr Leith for making a good call? Sara's out, Laura's in. Plausible." He opened his hands out as if to say: 'works for me'.

Grealish looked at him, considering his options.

Cooper weighed in. "Sir, it would save Tyrone having to build a legend for me. Plus, they saw me when they first arrived, so I'd have to go in as a staffer, and not an Occo. Tyrone's idea kills two birds with one stone."

"I don't have flight status," replied Watkins.

Grealish looked at her and back at Cooper. "How many reserve placements do we have?"

"At least another thirty, Sir. We could bump Laura up pretty easily."

"Why does she need flight status?" fired back Harris.

Cooper rolled her eyes. "Because if you enter Compression, you can't suddenly bug out before launch."

"We've flunked several Occos and kept them back because they simply couldn't cut it in training, or because they've displayed a poor attitude. There's a protocol for it."

"Yes, but only up to Stage 2. Once they get to Stage 3 they're accepted and working on all the safety stuff and classrooms on protocols. And in order to be convincing, and of any actual use, Laura can't be seen to be incompetent, or she won't earn their trust. She's there to observe and potentially develop assets. No, if we're doing this at all, we're doing it right."

"And what if I don't want to? You're talking about inserting me this morning, and I might have family I need to say goodbye to, or a husband or something. And by the way, what the actual fuck is going on here?" She looked haughtily at them all.

Cooper opened a file on her desk, turned over the first leaf and read, "Laura Jane Watkins, twenty-eight years old, raised by maternal grandparents after both parents killed by AoG while working at Evac Command in Whitehall, in a botched bomb blast meant for the Brigadier General." She turned and raised her eyebrows at Grealish. "Grandfather died six years later, grandmother nine years ago. One brother, Darryl, also deceased.

Never married, no significant other, lives alone in Pimlico, no pets, non-smoker, no significant debts. Joined ICP straight out of university, where she studied Politics and Law, graduated with Honours from Cambridge, went straight into the Academy, and into the field upon passing out." She closed the file and dropped it on her desk. "Did I miss anything, or shall we continue to pretend that you're not thrilled at the idea of a live operation that actually saves your life?" She drenched the whole question in sarcasm.

Watkins flushed red, and looked like she was about to blow, when Harris started to laugh. Deep belly laughs filled the room as the sergeant completely forgot himself. Watkins glared at him, fit to burst for about five seconds as he leaned his head back and guffawed, then she softened and broke into a grin. The tension evaporated, as quickly as it had arrived.

"Okay, let's make this happen." Grealish pointed at Harris and Cooper and said, "I'll leave it to you two to sort it out. Harris, back here at 6 am every morning to brief us." He got up and started walking to the door, before turning back and addressing the room. "May I remind you all what's at stake here. Bring Laura up to speed, and no word to anyone outside this room. Laura, I'll square this away with the brass at Whitehall. You'll need to let me know what to do about your belongings and your flat. Entry cost to the Bertram Ramsay is a forfeit of all personal possessions except two kilos of whatever. No clothes, personal care items, any of that, so make a decision, let Amy here know and we'll make it happen." He paused, hand on the door frame. "In the meantime, these two will fill you in, and then you're into DECON 1 and the initial briefing just like any other pleb. Nobody air-side knows who you are, so keep it that way. Tyrone is your handler. He'll figure out a safe way to communicate, after he's decided how to tell Sara she's blown. Questions?"

Three heads shook, and Grealish turned on his heel and left.

CHAPTER FIVE

I READ THE NEWS and drank another cup of coffee before the others appeared in the rec room. Something still preoccupied me with the redhead. Harris had completely avoided giving me an answer which made me think I'd stumbled upon something that he didn't want to discuss. First out was one of the guys. Looked to be about five foot ten, with slightly gangly arms. He had a thick mop of brown hair, wavy and all over the place, and stubble a couple of days old. Despite the last twenty-four hours, he seemed pretty chilled. He nodded to me as he strolled to the coffee machine and then joined me in the middle. His patch said 'Prouse', and as he sat down he reached over with his hand and introduced himself as Leon. I shook his hand and said 'Jax'. He smiled, sat back and grabbed a hollotab from the pile. I got the impression he'd be chattier if I had boobs.

Next out was Blondie. I figured she'd be one of the first because she was awake when I came out half an hour ago. She smiled at me as she entered the room. Not sure what face I pulled, but she didn't seem put off by it. Leon looked up from his hollotab as she passed by and then winked at me. I hated being right. I ignored him and finished my coffee.

She sat next to me on the sofa, coffee in hand, and looked up. Leon leaned over and introduced himself. His face lit up like a fucking Christmas tree. She took his hand and said her name was Sara, before turning to me and offering me her hand too. Introductions complete, she asked how the first night had been. We had a bit of small talk; the usual stuff. Beds are okay, showers are decent, what's with the small doors on the toilets? Leon sexualised the convo instantly by claiming to have accidentally picked up the ladies' underwear instead of the men's and made some crass comment about it going up his arse before he realised it. Sara rolled her eyes. I cringed. Leon's face faltered, and he went back to his hollotab.

Gradually, over the next fifteen minutes, everyone joined us. The other five women introduced themselves as Libby, Eloise, Amanda, Aoife and Jennifer, and the other guy was Mark. By the time Harris walked in, the conversation was in full flow. It was an odd mix of trepidation and emotion. One of the women, the Irish girl, Aoife, became quite tearful, and a sense of profound melancholy stole through the group. I may not have left anyone behind, but some of these guys had. I can't imagine the internal struggle of coming to terms with being saved and simultaneously condemning your loved ones to an uncertain fate.

I stayed on the peripheries of it, quite content to sit and listen to the others. I wasn't ready to wear my heart on my sleeve just yet.

Harris wandered over to the group and, to my astonishment, the redhead was two steps behind him. Her hair was a little damp, and there was a ring around her neck, presumably from the mask demonstration, so I guessed she'd not long been through the airlock. Probably had a safety briefing to herself. Harris motioned her to a seat, which she took, looking a bit shell-shocked. And now there were ten.

"Listen up, people. We'll be having breakfast shortly, and then heading through to your first session, which is through the door North-East One at the far end on the right. You'll need your bracelets on to get your food from the kitchen on your left, and again to get through the door to the session. Eat well, as the first session will be a long one. I'll see you inside in thirty minutes."

He walked away and got about ten yards before Blondie stood up and called out "Sergeant?" and trotted after him. The shutters opened over by the kitchen, so I got up and headed over to the trays. Breakfast was an assortment of fruits, breads, cereals and juices, so I grabbed some toast and a grapefruit juice and headed for the dining area.

I watched the crew take their seats and mingle, small pockets of chat every few minutes, but nobody seemed particularly interested in meaningful conversation except Leon who, it seemed, had introduced himself to pretty much everyone. Half an hour later there was a soft tone from a speaker in the ceiling, and I took that as our cue to head through the door behind me. I was the first one through, and as I entered I could see that the room was laid out in a classroom setting. I took a desk on the left side in the second row—close enough to see and contribute, but not in the limelight. This also meant I'd have the entire class in my field of vision. I always preferred to have eyes on everyone in the room. The rest filed in and sat down, all except Blondie. Redhead was here and sat on the far right in the second row. Leon was front and centre, with two women to each side of him. The other guy was sitting to my right, then there was an empty seat and a woman next to Redhead.

Harris entered from the back through the door we'd just come through and took his place at the front. There was a screen wall behind him, a staple feature of any classroom. There was a desk in the corner with a sealed box on it, and a podium to the right of Harris with what looked like a holloscreen.

"Good morning, Crew 41. I trust you had a restful first night and are energised and ready for your training and assessments?" There were a few murmurs and nods.

"Before we begin, I'd like to introduce Laura Watkins to you." Redhead blushed but smiled. "She was on your transport, but we pulled her away before she could enter the building. We do this with every new crew, to check their credentials one last time, through a series of interviews. It also acts as a useful test of your awareness and observation skills. Apologies, Laura, for making you spend your first night alone, but you were the obvious choice with your distinctive hair." If it was possible for her face to turn a deeper shade of red than her hair, it probably would have.

"Tests like this rarely yield results, but I'm happy to say that one of you made the observation. Well done, Jaxon." He pointed to me, and everyone looked round. Now I knew how Redhead felt.

Leon raised his hand. "Sergeant, I noticed she was missing too." He said it in an almost sulky voice. If I didn't already dislike him, he was doing a grand job of making sure I'd be giving him a wide berth.

"Really, Mr Prouse? To whom did you report it?"

"Well, nobody. It wasn't really my business." He crossed his arms in a defiant gesture. It was like watching a six-year-old.

"But Ms Watkins here is in your crew. If one of your crew goes missing, you wouldn't report it? Tell me, Mr Prouse, do you understand the concept of what we are embarking upon here?

There are no individuals any more. You are a crew, and crews look out for each other. If you believe a member of your crew to be missing, you take steps to resolve it. Am I making myself clear?"

Prouse grunted something like a "Yes, Sergeant" and looked highly embarrassed. I wondered if Harris's only job today was to make everyone blush.

Harris looked at the entire room. "Is that clear to all of you?"

"Yes, Sergeant," came a chorus of replies mingled with the odd "Sir".

"Many crews have come through before you." Harris paused, and looked around at the silent faces. "And we are well aware of the feelings of trepidation and fear that crews experience as they enter Compression. Most of you will have left loved ones behind. You will feel emotionally compromised and are likely to experience guilt and shame and loss." He hung his head for a moment before continuing, looking for the right words. I heard a soft sob from the front row.

"There are literally hundreds of crews in these facilities, all going through this process at the same time. We crew you up in smaller groups to make the transition easier, and the training more individually focussed. Your crew is your family now. You will need each other to progress through this program. These emotions are too hard to process individually, so you will look out for each other, and care for each other." He looked at Prouse. "You have a responsibility to each and every person in your crew to ensure their wellbeing, and your own. If you see a crew mate struggling, you will help them. Or report it to me so that I can take the appropriate steps to ease their burden. If you feel yourself struggling, there is no shame in asking for help. Every person in this facility harbours these emotions. I'd like to tell you that they pass, but they merely dim with time. Coming to terms with your new life is a huge part of Compression. It is important that you learn to trust one another."

I could feel my eyes stinging, and a pressure in my chest. I couldn't quite explain why, but the reality of my situation crashed over me at that moment, rocking my very soul from within. I kept seeing my mum, laughing and smiling at me as I played. She died years ago, and I missed her every day. I had a lump in my throat that was constricting, and it took every ounce of energy to pull myself together and focus on the room.

Having instilled a sense of togetherness, Harris rounded on Prouse again. "Mr Prouse, having already confessed to possessing extraordinary observational skills, I wonder if you noticed the second thing we changed after you arrived? Any clue?"

Prouse was visibly shrinking in his seat, obviously praying for the ground to swallow him whole.

"No? Well, as it happens, someone did make a second observation and reported it to me promptly." He looked at me and said, "Well done again, Jaxon. Two out of two." He gesticulated to the back of the room. "May I introduce you to Captain Sara Hennessey, Bertram Ramsay Marine Corps."

Blondie walked in, wearing full BRMC fatigues, belt and all the trimmings that came with being an officer. The volume in the room went up a notch, as chatter broke out between the crew.

Harris raised a hand to quieten them. "Captain Hennessey is my Commanding Officer. How you perform in this crew reflects upon me. Anything to say, Ma'am?"

"Hello, Crew 41. As Sergeant Harris has already impressed upon you, teamwork is the key to our success and survival on this mission. For the next twelve weeks you will work hard and be pushed beyond your limits. We will assess you, teach you, train you and make you better. At everything. Let's get started. Tyrone?" Blondie nodded to Harris and then took a seat at the back of the room.

"Thank you, Captain. Today we are going to talk about your future lives on the Bertram Ramsay. There are several jobs available to occupants, and everybody will have one. The station itself requires the contributions of everyone on board to operate safely, efficiently and comfortably. These jobs come in grades, and every occupant has the opportunity to qualify for even the highest positions on the space station. It is our job to assess you and funnel you into the correct career so that you provide the optimum contribution possible."

Harris continued to talk, and over the course of the next hour he covered many of the positions and how they affect operational capability. Some of it was quite interesting, but I found myself daydreaming after a solid hour of holloslides and information. It was like going to a very intense career guidance counsellor. The second hour was a bit more interesting, but no less intense. Understanding different alarms, commands, orders and protocols—where to go if I heard such-and-such, where to be if this alarm sounded this many times. When the soft tone sounded to indicate a break, I was pretty wrung out. We stood up, a few of us stretching, and proceeded towards the door.

Harris and Hennessey watched the group file out of the door and looked at each other.

"What do you think, Sara?"

"I think we've got an obvious choice for a sacrifice, and one or two decent prospects in the crew."

"Jaxon is going to be their crew leader for sure. We usually wait until the first week is up to create that position, but if you don't have any objections, I'd like to make that official this afternoon?"

"Seems premature, Tyrone. He's clearly intelligent, and observant, but he's also obviously a loner. When we went into the dorm last night, he kept himself to himself, chose the bed that nobody else would, was first to sleep and first to rise. I'd only just woken when he came out of the shower block, completely oblivious to the rest of us."

"I doubt he was oblivious, based on what I've seen so far. Just because he ignored everyone, doesn't mean he didn't notice them. He is a little isolated from the group, I'll give you that. But he's not shy. It's only the first day. He wasn't nervous when asking me about you and Sergeant Watkins. Just quite matter-of-fact."

"Maybe, but we've got bigger fish to fry at the moment. I don't want to make hasty decisions in the current circumstances."

"I think, given the right motivation, Jaxon could be an asset to this investigation. He's on the inside of the crew, and he's made no bones about reporting things that made him uncomfortable. Our infiltrator wouldn't draw attention to themselves like that, which means that his questions are genuine. He could have kept his mouth shut and just let the day play out, but that's not how he handled it at all. I promise you, his contributions to the crew are going to be invaluable. How often have you known me to gamble, Sara?"

She looked at him for a moment, processing his words, and then nodded. "Well, let's push his boundaries this afternoon. See what he's made of."

As I walked through the door into the rec room, I felt a tap on my shoulder, and turned to see Redhead looking at me. "Hi," I managed, amazingly, without stuttering. I was never very good at talking to women.

"I'm Laura. You're Jaxon." She smiled, a genuine warmth emanating from her.

"You are. I am. Jax is fine." I held out my hand, and she took it.

"Okay, Jax. I just wanted to say thank you. The sergeant told me you reported me missing to him at the first opportunity. I really appreciate you looking out for me."

Up close, she was really quite breathtaking. Aside from her proclivity to blush, she had blue-green eyes that sparkled, a few laughter lines coming from the corners, and a smile that was disarming. There was an air about her—a quality in her I could sense. Some sort of feistiness, or a desire to impress and challenge. She seemed to have a steely determination, and yet a warm nature. Her hair was down and loose today, brushing the tops of her shoulders and blowing gently in the air conditioning. The effect was quite captivating.

I shrugged. "You were difficult not to notice, to be fair. I saw you on the bus sat in front of me for over an hour. And when we came through DECON 1 and you weren't there, something didn't seem right. We were in the dorm before I figured out what was missing though."

We continued to chat for a while, grabbing a coffee each and taking a seat at one of the dining tables. Mostly discussing what we'd just learned and wondering if the next three months was going to be spent in a classroom. I couldn't imagine anything more mind-numbing.

The tone sounded, and we finished our coffee and headed back to the classroom. I took the same seat as before, and Laura sat next to me. The rest of the crew filed in, and this time Leon took the far corner. He'd clearly had enough limelight for one day.

Hennessey was AWOL when Harris entered. I didn't know whether I expected her to be there. I supposed as a CO of the Echo Site, she probably had more important things to worry about than one crew. Harris had mentioned there were hundreds of crews, and certainly the ambient sound was that of a well-occupied facility, but so far, the areas we'd been in were pretty quiet.

Harris welcomed us back while he tore open the sealed carton on the desk and removed a pile of hollotabs. He handed one out to each of us, and asked us to go through the initial setup process and pair with our bracelets. The whole exercise took about ten minutes, as each of us took face scans and handprints. The hollotabs had biosecurity imprinted to each of us. We were handed small kit bags to stow them in and were told we needed to keep these with us at all times, except in the shower.

He was just starting an explanation of the assessment phase when Hennessey walked in, whispered something to Harris, who nodded and then pointed at me and motioned for me to follow her. I packed my hollotab away in the kit bag, ignored all the staring, and followed her out of the door to the left and back through the one marked 'South 1', which had been the first tunnel we came through to the rec room. We entered the induction room where our mask demonstration had been, and Hennessey walked over to a table on one side, looking behind her to make sure I was following. She asked me to take a seat, and pulled out a hollotab of her own, placing it on the table.

"Mr Leith..."

"Jax."

"... Jax. I've pulled you out of class this morning to talk to you about your journey here and learn more about you. You've already demonstrated your ability to see certain things, and you seem to do a good job of trying not to be seen yourself. These are skills that we actually develop in our agents and operatives, in different fields."

I listened and tried not to be distracted by the blonde hair, which she occasionally flicked away from her face.

"What do you remember about the day you received your seat on the Bertram?"

"Not much. I'd been out in The Bleeds that morning, running a few errands, and when I got home, I'd barely taken my jacket off when they knocked. You know the rest—I assume they gave the same speech to everybody?"

She nodded. "Have you ever seen either of those operatives before or since?"

"No."

"You seem quite certain. Were they BRMC or ICP?"

"That's an odd question. BRMC have no terrestrial responsibilities or jurisdictions. And yes, I'm certain."

"You are absolutely right, we don't have any operational capability outside of air-side facilities like this one, or the Bertram Ramsay itself."

"What is it you really want from me, Captain? You didn't bring me here to be nostalgic about receiving a ticket to a spaceship." I didn't mean it to come out so aggressively, but I'd been singled out here, and I was wondering why.

She looked at me for a moment, like she was weighing up what to say next. I was trying to look impassive, but something big was going on here.

"Okay, Jax, I'll tell you some things that you are not to repeat outside of this room. Am I clear? If I find out you've repeated them, you will be out of this facility immediately and will forfeit your place on the Bertram."

I nodded, wondering if I wanted to know.

"Part of my job is the security of this facility, and those that enter it. As you've already been told, your 'ticket' as you call it, wasn't a happy accident. We hand-picked you for this program following your aptitude tests and you were meticulously screened prior to receiving your invite."

She showed me a file on her hollopad, which held all the information they'd learned about me during a ten-year period prior to initial contact. What I read didn't really surprise me. It was my life, after all.

"Upon being told that you had a pass to the Bertram Ramsay, who did you tell?"

"No one. I don't have anyone to tell. Plus, I'm from The Bleeds. What do you suppose would happen to me if I let that slip?"

She ignored my question. "Don't you have friends?"

"None that are meaningful. There are people I like and respect, but I don't see them often enough to think of them as much more than casual acquaintances."

"Sounds lonely."

"Not really. Maybe sometimes. I've always been okay in my own company, and I see plenty of people each day. Where are you going with this?"

"Just trying to understand you, and what motivates you. You've had a few run-ins over the years with the ICP." She pressed something on her hollotab and looked up. "An arrest and a short incarceration ten years ago? Tell me about that."

"Nothing to tell. I was in a bar. Guy walks in and starts screaming and charging at a woman inside. He looked like he was going to let fly, so I stepped in front and stopped him."

"ICP report says when they arrested you, you were bear-hugging this guy who was, by all accounts, going berserk. Who was the woman?"

"I never found out."

"Okay, who was the guy?"

"Don't know that either."

"So why get involved? Help me understand why you stepped in front of an angry man and prevented him from hurting a total stranger."

"Did you see her? She was five-foot-nothing in heels and sat at a table minding her own business. She'd have blown over in a stiff breeze. It was like watching Goliath pick on a librarian."

"And what if Goliath had a weapon?"

"He didn't."

"You didn't know that."

"Yes, I did. He came in, fists swinging and screaming his lungs off. He wanted to hurt someone. Anyone with that much rage that owns a weapon comes in with the weapon in hand. He didn't, ergo no weapon. He was wearing tracksuit bottoms and a tee shirt. The tracksuit was elasticated, so no weapon in the waistband, and the legs were cuffed, so none on his ankle either."

"What if he'd struck you?"

"He did."

"So why didn't you hit back?"

"Because he was huge, and I wouldn't have walked away. He would have been fighting for something. I had no motivation at all. By far the best tactic was to get inside his swing, so he couldn't deliver a meaningful blow, hence the bear hug."

"So, you stopped a small woman, a total stranger, being beaten up by a big man, neither of which you knew. Why?"

"I've told you. He would have killed her. I didn't really think about it. I just stopped it from happening. The whole thing was over in ten seconds. ICP came in, zapped me with a Sleeper, arrested me for good measure and stuck me in a cell for six hours."

"You're an interesting man, Jaxon. Most people would have looked away and carried on with their lives."

"I don't like seeing people get hurt. Sadly, it's a daily occurrence in The Bleeds. I tried my best to be the best version of myself. Something I learned from my mum." There she was again, invading my thoughts. The lump in my throat returned at the memory of the woman who raised me. "I failed more than I succeeded."

Hennessey leaned back and looked me over. I felt like she was assessing me and deciding whether or not I'd passed muster.

"I want to show you something."

She put her hollotab in the middle of the table and double-tapped the left corner. A screen popped open between us, totally transparent, with ten pictures on it. She asked me if I'd seen any of these people before. There were nine men and one woman. I tapped on the first and it replaced the grid with that single image and then swiped through them one by one. As I got to the seventh one, I stopped. I paused for a moment and swiped through the last three, and then back to number seven.

"This one. Except he was wearing a hoodie."

"Where did you see him?"

"In the protesters at the depot where I got on the bus. He was staring at me as we drove through the demonstrators. When we left ten minutes later, he was still there and still staring at me. Who is he?"

She looked at me for a full minute, her eyes darting back and forth between mine, and then stood up and said, "Wait here."

CHAPTER SIX

I SAT ALONE IN that room for ten minutes before I decided to get up and look around. I could hear the same noises from the day before—muffled voices, pots and pans being clattered around. The hiss and whirr of the compressors, and the soft whining of the air conditioning. The two airlock doors were closed. Both lights were red. The chairs in the middle were still here, haphazardly scattered, like a group had just got up and left. I wondered if they'd been like that since we sat in them.

On the wall behind me was a huge picture of the Bertram Ramsay. It was impossibly big. I couldn't comprehend what it would be like to be up there. Each of the spheres had almost a whole city inside. Tall skyscrapers in the centre, a small area of parkland, and buildings dotted around inside each one. The land inside was layered, so the buildings all stood on one level, with what looked like farmland and factories in the lower levels. There were metal and glass tunnels connecting between the spheres and what looked like a never-ending train running the full circle between them all.

I couldn't help but marvel at its enormity. How anyone could have dreamed this up was beyond me. It was like someone decided to build a life-sized snow globe with a city inside, thirteen times, and then joined them together. It was truly impressive.

Hennessey stepped in through the door and stopped. She pointed at the desk and said, "Grab that and come with me," and then turned on her heels and left. I picked up the hollotab and the screen disappeared. I held it under my arm next to my kit bag and followed her through the door. Inside was another airlock, which we both entered. I felt my ears pop again, and then the second door opened into a short corridor that turned right into a longer one. There were no doors either side, but I could see daylight at the far end.

We exited and crossed over the road to the circular building opposite. I was asked to present my bracelet at the security gates and given a lanyard with a badge that said 'ESCORT EVERYWHERE'. Hennessey took me through a set of double doors, and then into a bank of elevators. One was open, so we stepped in. There were no buttons on the inside at all. Hennessey said "two" and the doors closed for just a few seconds and reopened onto a corridor that curved and stretch in both directions. We turned right and walked by twenty or so offices, left and right, with people working away in all of them. Nobody passed us. We eventually stopped by an office with 'Lt. Amy Cooper' printed on the plaque to the side of the door. Hennessey knocked and opened it up.

We stepped inside and sitting behind the desk was one of the most beautiful women I'd ever seen, and I'd seen her before. She was the one that had welcomed us into Echo and sent us behind the screens.

A man to my right spoke. "Mr Leith, please take a seat. My name is Colonel Andrew Grealish, and this is Lieutenant Amy Cooper. Captain Hennessey you are already acquainted with."

He turned to Hennessey and asked if we were expecting Harris.

"He's in with Crew 41, so will have to sit this one out. I'll brief him later."

"Okay, good. Mr Leith..."

"Jax."

He paused. "Jax, I appreciate that you're probably a bit confused but all will be explained in due course." He took a seat and then turned to face me.

"You've heard of the AoG?"

"Those nutters with the placards at the bus depot? 'The end is nigh' and 'Revelations is upon us' and that malarkey?" This is not how I imagined this conversation starting.

"Sadly, they are a lot more than that. For years the ICP has worked hard with media outlets to create a reputation for the AoG, of being 'nutters', as you say, but this is an organisation that is determined to undermine the Compression process and prevent the evacuation. These are zealots and extremists, and their absolute belief in the day of judgement is a powerful motivation. After two hundred years their ranks have grown, and become more sophisticated and more dangerous. They have infiltrated any number of high-level departments in world governance, and are believed to hold various positions of power in global corporations."

He went on to explain that they'd received recent intelligence that one such operative was amongst the Crew 41 in Echo. I must have made a face, because Lieutenant Cooper piped up at this point.

"You find that hard to believe, Jax? That a member of an extremist organisation could have infiltrated one of the most secure compounds in the world?"

"It's not hard to believe they'd want to, no, but they must have had help." I looked up at Grealish. "If what I've been told so far is true, I was assessed and checked and chosen for this crew. I don't know why, but Captain Hennessey here just pulled out ten years of my history on a hollotab. Presumably the same rules apply to all invitees." There were nods. "Which means that either the ICP isn't very good at vetting people, or you've already been infiltrated and someone has manipulated the data to sabotage your investigative abilities. They couldn't just sneak onto the bus or you'd be overrun, so their paperwork checked out. Incompetent or compromised—sorry to be blunt, but it's not exactly a ringing endorsement for you."

There was a moment of silence whilst the three of them exchanged looks. Clearly, I'd hit the nail on the head. Hennessey spoke.

"Jax, you're absolutely right about almost everything except one thing: there's no incompetence. Someone in your crew shouldn't be there, and someone in our team outside has placed them there. There are people working on the external problem, but the internal one is our primary concern right now. So far, the only person we can discount from your crew is you. You've demonstrated your integrity and your ability to see beyond what is happening. So we're asking you to help us."

"Help you?" I was just a bloke from The Bleeds. I failed to see how I could be any help at all.

Grealish now. "It is difficult for us to make a full assessment inside Echo. There are very few cameras, because in order for us to retain the integrity of our security, we have forgone the pleasure of being Big Brother. There are no circuits to hack, or systems connected to the external network. Everything inside Echo is a closed loop. Training centres are carefully monitored, as are exits and airlocks, but there is scant coverage of the communal or living areas. Instructors must maintain their usual routines, so as not to raise suspicions, and whilst we have taken the precaution of inserting an operative into your crew, we feel that you can be of great value to us, being on the inside."

"Laura," I said. It had to be the redhead.

"Excuse me?" replied Lieutenant Cooper.

"Laura is your operative inside." I looked at all three of them. Grealish's face crumbled and he sat heavily in his chair.

Hennessey remained impassive and was the first to break the silence. "What brings you to that conclusion?"

I shrugged. "It's obvious really. There are only three men, of which I am one. Leon is a moron with a big mouth, and the other guy, Mark is it? He's barely lifted his head since he's been in—hardly the demeanour of a spy, although I confess, I'm no expert.

"If it were either of them, you'd have two male operatives, including me apparently, which probably isn't optimal for the dynamic, given that two-thirds of the crew is female. Why is that, by the way? Tyrone told me it's unusual."

"That's actually the only real random part of the process," Cooper explained. "Crews are usually groups of ten. Any less and it's probably because someone has died between getting their evac order and entering Compression. We can't amend orders and bring a later crew member forward to take their place, because it causes a ripple effect through all the other incoming crews. It's not unusual to have a sixty-forty split, so there's nothing untoward going on."

"Fair enough. But Crew 41 is predominantly female, so given that fact I wouldn't be your choice in those circumstances. It would be easier for me to get close to the guys than it would the girls. I wouldn't even know where to start." It was true. Women had rarely taken naturally to me, either platonically or intimately. "If I were to choose someone to be on the inside, I'd probably pick a woman. In my limited experience, women find it easier to bond with both sexes. I'm not trying to be antagonistic here. It's just logic."

Grealish looked at me and nodded. "Go on."

"Well, everyone else was inserted together, except Laura, who made a mysterious disappearance, and then she only reappeared after I mentioned it to Harris. I don't know her at all, but first impressions are that she seems intelligent, and during the bus ride here, she was looking around at everyone, including me. It might have been morbid curiosity, but I don't think it was."

"Well, aren't you a regular Sherlock bloody Holmes, Mr Leith." Cooper this time.

"Who was the man?"

"Man?" Grealish now.

"Yes, the man on the hollotab. Number seven. I picked him out of a crowd and fifteen minutes later I'm sitting here. So who is he?"

Hennessey took her hollotab from my lap. I'd forgotten that I had it to be fair. She pressed a couple of buttons, then placed it on the desk and the image of the man popped up for us all to see.

"This is John Q Nobody. We don't have a name, or any information at all. He doesn't exist on any of our databases globally."

"So how do you have a picture of him, and how have I managed to pick him out of a crowd?"

"We had operatives everywhere at the depot. We always do on collection days. Some of them are in the crowd. Others are blending into the background. We have eyes and ears in the buildings opposite, and cameras everywhere. Laura's team spotted him staring at you when you arrived, and again when you left. They'd been working under the assumption that you were known to him, and therefore possibly a threat."

They had a point. "Why can't I be the threat? I mean, you've pulled me in here and asked me to help, but how do you know I'm not your spy?"

"Are you?"

"Well, that's not an intelligent question. There is only one possible answer. If I'm not the spy, I'll say no, truthfully. If I am the spy, I'll say no. Congratulations. You've gleaned precisely no information." I was becoming frustrated.

"Look, Jax, I think we're safe in the knowledge that you're not. You have a frankly quite staggering history of protecting or helping strangers. We have your entire file here, complete with arrest records, all of which absolve you of any criminal involvement. Unless something has changed in the last six months, you're not our infiltrator. But someone in your crew is, and we need to find out who, before they do something to compromise this mission."

"Okay, I'm sorry. It's all just a lot to take in. Have you thought about showing them all the photos?"

"It's fine. We know how intense these early days are. What do you mean about the photos?" Cooper responded.

I looked at the three of them. They all seemed tired. They also seemed genuinely concerned and I wondered if this threat wasn't bigger than they were making it out to be. I decided to be a bit more acquiescent.

"I don't know much about this stuff, but surely if you pull them all out of class one by one, and show them the photos, you can watch their reactions?" I tried to remember the face I'd made when I recognised him. "That guy stood out a mile. I won't have been the only one that saw him."

Hennessey looked at Grealish. "That's not going to take much effort. I can ask everyone, in a closed environment, and the ones that didn't see him are the ones we'll concentrate our efforts on. I suspect we'll eliminate most of them immediately. There may be one or two that genuinely didn't see him, but you can bet your arse that anyone who recognises him is going to flat out deny it."

Grealish beamed. "That's actually bloody clever. A denial is almost an admission in this situation." He looked back at Hennessey. "Can we set this up today?"

"Sure. We do individual assessments all the time. We'll have to do everyone, including Jaxon and Laura, so as not to raise suspicion, but it'll work."

"Can I make a suggestion?" Cooper chimed in. She had a concerned look on her face.

"Go ahead," said Hennessey.

"If we're only going to show them his photo, we'll be tipping our hand to someone who does recognise him. Why don't we round up photos of all the people they were likely to have encountered on the journey? That way we can suggest it's a test of observation, and won't end up inventing some half-arsed cover story for it. We're spoiled for options here. The bus driver, the ICP guards on the bus, the staff inside Echo. We might as well see if they've been paying attention anyway."

Grealish shrugged. "It makes sense to create some sort of meaningful analysis out of what would otherwise be a fishing expedition."

"That works. And it's probably easier to do. I'll use the opportunity to brief Laura on Jaxon's inclusion so everyone is up to speed," replied Hennessey.

"Just out of interest, who were the other nine people in the photos?" It had only just occurred to me that they might be threats, if they were on the same document as the guy I pointed my finger at.

"That, I'm afraid, I cannot tell you, Jaxon. Not yet anyway. There's still a big operation happening outside of Echo, within the ICP and it would be inappropriate to disclose that information, sorry." Cooper seemed genuinely apologetic.

Grealish held his hand out, and I took it. "Thank you, Jaxon. I think you've been gone long enough. Captain Hennessey will take you back."

CHAPTER SEVEN

SHE WATCHED AS the man called Jaxon was taken from the room. Something did not feel right, and she vowed to keep a close eye on him. The red-haired woman was also conspicuous in her absence yesterday, and their explanation felt contrived and, frankly, weak. During her preparations there was no mention of randomly selected individuals being pulled from the group on entry, which seemed like a big oversight. The intelligence had been meticulous before her insertion was forged, and her training concluded that anomalies are rarely coincidental or accidental.

She would have to keep an eye on them both. This first phase was critical to the success and it was important that she qualified every stage and made that final flight. She was not scared. There was glory in her mission, and Gaia would reward her sacrifice.

For now, she would need to put such thoughts from her head, though they inspired her. Phase one of training was a series of aptitude tests that she would need to complete in order to advance. She focussed her thoughts on the mission, revelling in the opportunity.

I joined the class after lunch, where we sat through a training exercise on maintaining our equipment, using pressure-test devices, and soapy water of all things. The oxygen masks in our kit belts could be inflated without being worn, so they taught us to fill them, dunk them in the soapy water, and then check for bubbles. I could tell I wasn't the only person who was less than gripped by the task, but they continued to drum into us the importance of our rebreathers, and our flight suits and kit belts and bags, checking and re-checking daily. The way Harris bleated on about safety you'd think they had some serious issue with the space station, but I figured he was just overplaying it so we'd remember.

A couple of hours later we were released for the day. I headed straight to the dorm to get showered up. I was contemplating an hour's kip before dinner when Hennessey entered the dorm and announced we'd all be having short individual assessments before chow time, so I went back to the rec room and grabbed a coffee, and parked myself on one of the sofas. The tall guy sitting opposite had already introduced himself as Mark Hanson. He was an engineer from Bedfordshire, and had previously worked in the Coalition Air Force as a flight mechanic. By all appearances he was quite the alpha, but turned out to be very softly spoken and, it seemed, relatively shy. We talked for a little while, and then Hennessey appeared and asked Hanson to follow her.

I turned my attention to the room as he walked away. Most of the crew were out here, with the exception of one of the women. I assumed she was in the dorm, but I didn't like the fact that she was the only one not present. The rest of the group were chatting between themselves. Leon had regained some of his swagger after the verbal beating he got this morning, but it looked to me like everyone was keeping him at arm's-length.

One by one, we were all taken into one of the training rooms for ten minutes. I sat and watched each of them come and go, and they all returned unwilling to talk about what the assessment was. I assumed they'd been told to keep it to themselves until everyone had been through the process. The missing woman turned up about halfway through, hair still wet from the shower so I gave her the benefit of the doubt, although she must look like a prune if she'd been in the shower for the last half an hour. I shook that thought from my head and looked up to see Hennessey approaching. She motioned for me to follow.

She took me into a smaller training room. It was more of a large office I suppose. She asked me to sit at the desk.

"It was a good idea, Jaxon, but unfortunately we struck out."

"Nobody saw him?" I couldn't believe it.

"Quite the opposite; everybody saw him."

"Crap. I thought you'd eliminate most, but not all. It was always a likelihood though. He was hardly inconspicuous. So what's the next step?"

"Well, we're working under the assumption that it's not you or Mr Prouse—he's far too up his own arse to be covert in any circumstances."

"I agree. I would doubt it's Hanson either. We only had a brief chat, but he seems quite genuine. Used to be a flight engineer in the CAF, and doesn't strike me as someone that takes the difficult path if there's an easier one open to him."

"That was my assessment too, but we can't quite discount him yet. On balance, he's an unlikely candidate, but then how often do you hear about a terrible crime being committed, and the neighbours are all shocked and saying 'he seemed such a nice quiet man, always helped me with my bins...'" She put on an old lady voice for that part, and I must have smiled because she looked at me and laughed.

I couldn't see Hanson being a real suspect, but she did have a point. I'd taken a number of people at face value in my life and ended up paying for it later.

"It's much more likely to be one of the women. There are only six, and one of them is Laura, so five potential candidates. It's obviously easier for Laura to keep an ear out in the shower block, without drawing attention to herself, so you'll just have to get to know them all and see how that plays out."

I nodded. It made sense. It wouldn't sit well for me to hang around while the ladies were showering—that's more Leon's game, and I suspected he'd alienate himself from the group relatively quickly, which would only leave myself and Mark as approachable members of the opposite sex. Given Mark's apparent shyness, I was wondering how I'd figure into this equation. The thought terrified me.

We chatted for a couple of minutes more to drag it out to a plausible length and then wrapped things up, and I headed back to the dorm.

The next few days were more of the same. Harris and Hennessey were having briefings every morning with Grealish and Cooper, but I got the sense that little progress had been made. Both made excuses to talk to me each day, but we had to be careful so as not to look like we were collaborating on something. For my part, I'd gleaned nothing of any real significance, although I was still wary of one of the women, Amanda, who seemed much more on the periphery than the others. I didn't voice this concern to Harris or Hennessey just yet, because I didn't want them to focus on one person and miss something, but there was a definite feeling in my gut about the other blonde.

Laura moved into Hennessey's chosen bed, so we were only a few feet apart. We'd chat about everything and nothing before lights out, but were careful to keep the conversation light. She seemed pretty switched on—maybe a little intense, but without doubt very focussed. What private moments we did have together she'd tell me about university and her grandparents—never straying towards her recruitment into the ICP. I sensed some internal struggle. She told me how quickly she'd gone from being an outside operative to inside Compression. She lacked family, but I could hear her throat catch when she talked about her friends and neighbours. I felt for her, and for the first time I felt a little out of sorts because I'd spent most of my life alone, keeping everyone at arm's-length.

As suspected, it didn't take long for people to stop worrying about the communal bathroom facilities, although Leon made a habit of timing his showers to coincide with whichever of the women had taken his fancy that day. Not until day four did we get a shouting match between one of the women and Leon. I say 'match', but really she was just bawling him out for walking into her shower cubicle. He protested his innocence, but nobody believed him—he'd shown his true colours from day one, and I wondered how long before he was inevitably extricated from the program.

When the shouting started everyone ran to the bathroom only to find Leon, face down, naked as the day he was born, with his arm twisted up behind his back by an equally naked woman—Amanda. She seemed completely unabashed, and it was only when Laura stepped in to separate them that she grabbed a towel and covered herself up. There were cold lines of fury across her face and her whole body was coiled, ready to lay into him again. She could look after herself, clearly, and I found myself wondering where she'd learned to put those moves on anyone. I definitely needed to keep an eye on her.

An hour later, once everything had calmed down, we were all on the sofas with coffee and toast, except Leon who was sulking in the dorm. Harris walked in and beckoned us to join him in a room in the far corner we hadn't been in before. I went to fetch Leon, and then headed to the room. As we entered there were some audible groans—it was a fully fitted out gym, with some serious tech in the gear in front of us. Cue the pep talk.

"You are all going to be living in space. It is paramount that you are in peak physical condition for your journey to the Bertram Ramsay. Whilst astronauts no longer suffer the rigours of G-force in space flight, thanks to modern technology, it is imperative that you begin conditioning your bodies for the increased gravity on the Bertram Ramsay. The entire facility rotates at one hundred and four per cent of the required speed to produce Earth's gravity, and so your bones will feel heavier, and you will fatigue more quickly. Four per cent may not sound much, but if you do not condition your muscles to handle it, it will have a significant impact on your ability to function aboard. So, starting from today, you will be doing daily workouts in here, with structured exercises designed to increase your muscle tone and fitness."

Harris asked us to take our hollopads from our kit bags and load them up into the docks on the far wall. Each of us had an assessment program to get through, each identical, to determine the course of our conditioning over the next three months. We were each given gym clothing, training shoes and bio-monitors that linked with our hollopads via our bracelets. We had a ninety-minute program to complete, across various different machines, including a ten-metre-long hydrotherapy pool with underwater treadmill.

I admit I was pretty confident in lasting out the ninety minutes, having spent half my life running up and down stairs and walking to and from the commune, and I got to work without complaint only to end up flat on my back, barely able to breathe after just eighteen minutes. I wasn't the only one either, or the first to drop. But I wasn't the last, and to my great annoyance Leon managed almost fifty minutes before he found himself in a heap on the floor, gasping for oxygen to fill his lungs.

We were each handed a carton of fluids to rejuvenate, some special cocktail of minerals and modified water, whilst Harris collected up the hollopads and redistributed them to each of us.

"While you all recover, allow me to give you the good news. Firstly, nobody ever completes that workout in their first eight weeks. It is designed specifically to break both your will and your body, which it clearly has. And now the bad news—each and every one of you will be expected to complete that workout by the time we finish Compression. This is not a negotiation.

"You will shortly receive an assessment of today's performance and a program to build your muscle mass and fitness. Once a week, you will do the entire program and will be assessed as you were today. There are eleven assessments remaining, so you will need to stick to your program. These are not supervised activities. You will be expected to come to the gym daily, at your own leisure, to complete your daily program."

We were dismissed and given two hours of recovery time before our next session. Looking at the faces of the crew, I could see more than a few were considering bed as a credible option right now. Emotions were still high, and the feeling that we'd abandoned our homes and anyone we ever knew or loved weighed heavily throughout, so the intensity of the last few hours had wrung out what little resolve any of us had maintained. I headed for the showers, exhausted and spent. My gym clothes were soaked through with sweat, so I lobbed them into the laundry chute and soaked for ten minutes under the steamy jets in the shower room. My muscles were still screaming at me for the punishment I'd just given them, and that was only twenty minutes. I seriously wondered how I'd ever get to the ninety-minute mark.

I grabbed myself a change of clothes, pulled some shorts on and wandered back into the dorm.

CHAPTER EIGHT

GREALISH PACED THE room, thinking and waiting for Cooper, Harris and Hennessey to show up. He was agitated at the lack of progress despite only being a few days in. There'd been no contact from the agent inside AoG since the last, and the silence was deafening him.

Cooper entered her office and jumped slightly when Grealish walked into view.

"Andrew, Christ, you scared the crap out of me! What are you doing here?"

"Waiting for you—sorry I'm early, but there are people in and out of my office every two minutes and I can hardly hear myself think. Where are Harris and Hennessey?"

"On their way, Sir. They'll be here in a—" She broke off, at a knock on her door. "Come."

Hennessey stepped in, followed by Harris, and they took their seats on the far side of the desk.

"What's our latest, Tyrone?" Grealish asked as he finally stopped pacing and sat down.

"Very little to report. We had one incident yesterday before the conditioning program—Mr Prouse and his wandering eyes got put on the floor by Amanda Barclay. According to Jaxon and Laura, there was a shouting match and by the time they'd rushed into the bathroom, she had his arm up behind his back and his face flat on the floor."

"Is Prouse going to be a problem here?" Cooper raised her eyebrows.

"He absolutely is, and there's no way we want a creep like that on a space station. I recommend we pull him out before he gets too far into the process." Hennessey was decisive, with just a small hint of anger.

"Is that your assessment also, Tyrone?" replied Grealish.

"It is, but also it isn't." He rubbed his face, as if trying to clear his thoughts before proceeding. "I agree with Sara—he absolutely has to go, but not yet. He's pretty much alienated himself from Crew 41, and they're all keeping their distance, but his presence almost forces confrontation, and I wonder if this added irritation might not be a good way to stress-test the candidates."

"How so? If he's so antagonistic, how is it going to do anything other than distract them?"

"Well, it won't. But it's not just distracting candidates, it's distracting the AoG infil. We're working on the assumption that it's a she, given our understanding of the current male Occos, and to be honest, Ms Barclay just went to the top of the list with those moves she put on Prouse—clearly she's had training of some sort, despite no official records of service, which makes me more suspicious. We're about to make Jaxon the Crew Leader, and then he'll pair off the other eight for daily crew tasks. Might be an opportunity to create some tension and see what happens." He shrugged.

Cooper's brow furrowed. "Given what's already occurred, won't the other candidates be expecting Prouse's departure? I mean, if he can't be trusted in a crew of nine, how can he work with a crew of nine million?"

"Granted, I expect they'll all be delighted when we get rid of him, and we will get rid of him, but his very presence lowers the odds on Jaxon becoming a confidante of the other crew members. Most crews run an even number of female to male candidates, and our experience shows that whilst the women bond, they also tend to seek the friendship of a male counterpart—just part of our genetic make-up, regardless of sexual orientation. With Prouse out of the picture, that just leaves Jaxon and Mark, and Mark is painfully shy, so odds on Jaxon becomes the alpha and they all look to him for leadership as well as friendship. With Prouse still on site, they're much more likely to see these bonds sooner rather than later, if for no other reason than to be on the right side of this when the axe drops on Prouse."

"Sounds like a lot of psychobabble bullshit to me..." Cooper held up a placatory hand before Tyrone could respond and continued, "... but you've got me convinced. From my own personal perspective, I'd probably react the same way in those circumstances."

"Sara?" Grealish looked at Hennessey for a response.

"Tyrone's right. We see in most groups that the females will create a bond between themselves but will also seek out male company in a more one-to-one scenario. Probably worth pairing them up accordingly."

"Exactly that," said Tyrone, sitting forward. "If we pair off Laura with Mark, she can eliminate him from our investigation sooner rather than later, so we can concentrate on finding the infil. I'd put Prouse with one of the other women to see how she copes, and then pair up the remaining women together. Jaxon will float between groups on tasks. They usually rotate pairs each week, so it would only take four weeks to get Prouse paired off with each of them before we boot him."

"Five weeks, Tyrone. There are five women in the group that are unknown quantities."

"No, just four. We can't pair off Prouse with Barclay, or she'll break every bone in his body in the first day. Plus he'll be fucking useless to anyone if paired with her because he'll spend the entire time trying not to get the shit kicked out of himself. For now, she's our number one focus, so let's see if she cosies up with Jaxon. If I were an enemy agent, I'd want to keep the alpha closer."

"Or further away. He's shown himself to be capable and observant, and it might be a better tactic to keep him out of reach." Sara looked at them all. "If I had a secret mission, I'd want to blend into the background, and draw no attention to myself, but that's just me." She shrugged.

"Okay, let's go with this for now. You two find a way of communicating this to Laura and Jaxon. Laura is the priority as she is one of our own, and despite our feelings about Jaxon, he's still a relative newcomer and has yet to be really tested. Back here tomorrow at 6am."

The BRMC Captain Hennessey took the woman into a room away from the others. It was explained to her that everyone was undergoing this particular assessment, and in light of recent events, this would be a test of her observations.

She placed the hollopad on a desk and sat to one side, gesturing for the woman to sit down. She noticed that Hennessey stayed far enough to the side that she could see the screen and the woman's reactions.

The screen lit and projected a series of images which the woman dutifully watched. She asked if they could be repeated. "Yes," she said, "that was our bus driver, and this was one of the guards on the bus. That man was in the crowd. I remember him because he stared at me as I came through security. He was very still compared to the rest of them."

She went through the remaining photos but was unable to identify anyone further. Captain Hennessey thanked her for her time, made a note on her hollopad, and dismissed her.

The woman left through the door, trying not to smile to herself. If they had any idea who that man was, she thought, they would close this program right now.

The following morning I was up early again. My legs were stiff and aching from the previous day's assessment, and honestly, I felt a bit wobbly as I stood up. I stretched by my bunk, just wearing my shorts as nobody else was awake except Laura whose bed was empty and made. I headed for the shower block. I grabbed a towel from the rack and a change of clothes, and stepped into one of the shower cubicles. I put the water on full pressure, letting the heat steam up for a couple of minutes, and was about to step into the shower when Laura walked into my cubicle.

She held her finger up to her lips and stripped off her underwear, motioning me into the shower. It was quite an odd moment—I'd never been naked with a woman I wasn't intimate with before, excepting one instance a long time ago where I was robbed. It had been a while, so I was trying my hardest not to let her body have an effect on me. She was clearly fit, and despite being quite petite she had 'more than a handful' as we used to say when we were teens. We were both under the hot water when she leaned into me. Her scent was quite intoxicating, and suggested she'd already been through the showers this morning.

Laura checked behind that the room was clear, quite oblivious to my surprise and whispered, "What did you make of Amanda putting Leon down yesterday?"

I went to reply but Laura held up a hand to stop me, and motioned for me to get closer to her head. I leaned around to her ear. "I'd say she had some training. I didn't see her actually take him down, but she's tiny compared to him, and he was locked in place when I walked in."

"I completely agree. That's the sort of thing they teach us at the Academy. She could have snapped his arm completely if she'd leaned in a bit harder, but it looked like she was controlling the position. I had a quick face to face with Hennessey after lights out, and they're concentrating on all five women, but have a special interest in her. She's told me you're going to be made Crew Leader today, and you'll be pairing us up."

"Me? Why me?" I was genuinely surprised.

"Never mind that now, it's you, done deal. This is important though—you need to put me with Mark, and Amanda with either Jennifer, Eloise, Aoife or Libby. Put Leon with one of the girls, and pair the other two up. And make sure Amanda gets security detail—on balance, giving her better access is a risk, but also makes it easier to track her movements and watch her. Got it?"

I nodded. She grabbed my towel and walked out without so much as a backward glance. Great, I'll just parade across the bathroom naked to get another. I stayed in the shower for another five minutes, assuming Laura had left by then, and headed back to my bunk to get dressed.

Laura wasn't in the dorm, so I towelled myself off, got dressed and headed to the rec room for coffee. The time on my bio-band said it was just after 6.15am. When I entered, I saw Laura sat over on the sofas, loading the news on to a hollotab. There were four others, presumably another crew, at one of the tables, eating.

I grabbed a coffee and headed over to the sofa. As I sat down, Laura looked up and smiled.

"Sorry about that, but it's going to be difficult for us to meet here without being noticed. I knew you'd be up early, so I waited in one of the cubicles for you. I think that's a routine we'll also have to be careful with, but we'll think of other ways to communicate as things happen."

Her voice was barely above a whisper, although as she spoke one of the four at the table looked over at us for a moment, before returning to his breakfast.

"I understand—it did make sense, you just caught me slightly unawares." I was almost whispering too, but mindful that whispers can carry further than low-speaking, so I was currently flip-flopping poorly between the two.

We continued to chat normally for fifteen minutes, talked about the process so far, and laughed about getting dunked in freezing oil for a bit.

"Why does it have to be so fucking cold? And it's disgusting... I got a total mouthful when it dropped and thought my lungs would burn from the fumes. It's a good job it didn't stick in my hair or I'd have been putting the drop on whichever bastard pulled the switch." She was so animated when she spoke, that her hands looked like they were signing. I tried not to imagine her being naked and dunked in oil, but the thought did cross my mind once or twice.

At that point, Mark and Aoife walked in together from the dorm. He'd relaxed a bit since the first couple of days, and she seemed to be coming out of herself a bit too. About the only thing I'd heard her say in the first day or two was "It's pronounced 'EE-FA'—my Irish parents wanted a traditional Irish daughter, so I get a funky name and spend my entire life correcting people that call me 'ay-off-ee' or some similar ridiculous pronunciation." She seemed quite good-natured, though I suspected there was a coiled cobra inside just waiting to be unleashed.

They joined us on the sofa, coffee in hand, and we talked a bit about the previous day's assessment. We all agreed it was brutal, and most of us were genuinely concerned that we'd ever make it to ninety minutes. The conversation was just getting going when all hell broke loose.

Seven klaxons sounded in quick succession, followed by flashing lights and a monstrously loud wailing from the ceiling. The immediate reaction was pandemonium. Jennifer and Eloise came flying out of the dorm, followed closely by Leon, who was still only partially dressed, and Amanda, as we all scrabbled about looking for the source. Half the group didn't have their kit belts on them and rushed back to grab them, whilst I grabbed mine off the floor and flung it around my waist. I found the release button and pressed it, waiting for the mask to drop out, only to realise I had it on back to front and was pressing the inflate button. I pulled it around to the front and pressed it manically until it released, which it did after the third press. I grabbed the bubble and pulled it over my head so the hose was running down my front and right side, getting right in my way, as I tried depressing the yellow button on the left of the belt, which was nigh on impossible to find when you're half suffocating and unable to see through a wrinkly plastic bag on your head. I did find it eventually, and the mask inflated. I felt like I was being strangled by a weak child. It was very uncomfortable, and I struggled to catch my breath. The seal around my neck felt like a silicone bag filled with fluid, and was cold to the touch. I tried to relax and looked around at the others. Amanda had hers on, but everyone else was in a shit state.

The lights suddenly stopped flashing, and the alarm fell silent. I looked up to see Harris walking into the room with Hennessey at his heels. The four members of the other crew were just sitting there, masks on, conversing normally as if this happened all the time, which it probably did.

"Masks off and listen up!" barked Harris as he approached the sofa. We complied, which took a couple of minutes, as most of us were in various states of chaos trying to get the gear off or back into the kit belts. Two or three hadn't gotten as far as to take it out in the first place.

"That was your first oxygen drill, and as expected, you're all dead, having frozen in space and suffocated on your own incompetence. The good news is that you can be defrosted and sold for dog food."

There were a couple of laughs at this, but Harris's face was stern, and it appeared he hadn't finished his little pep talk.

"These rebreathers will keep you alive. You were told to keep your kit with you at ALL times. This includes when you are sleeping, although you are not expected to wear them in bed. What we just simulated was decompression in space. Those seven warning sirens were telling you of an oxygen breach, and you should have been able to extract your mask, put it on and pressurise it in under thirty seconds. We will work on this after breakfast. Put your gear away, and I'll see you over there," he said, pointing, "in thirty minutes."

The group as a whole looked utterly bedraggled as we stowed our gear and composed ourselves for the day ahead. I grabbed another coffee and perched on the end of the sofa as the others followed suit. We looked around at each other, and there was an outbreak of laughter. We must have looked such a mess, and clearly in no fit state to interpret sirens and lifesaving equipment. I did make a mental note to myself to practise, so as not to look like an idiot when it inevitably happened again.

The tone sounded at 07:30 and we all headed over to the training room. The desks were in the same places as before, and I took my favoured seat on the left in the second row. Laura sat next to me, and to my surprise, Leon sat in front of me. I'd expected him to shrink back into the shadows after his humiliation with Amanda, although clearly he was a classic narcissist, so probably didn't think it had diminished his credibility at all. It had.

Harris pressed a button on his hollopad, and the holloscreen behind him lit up. On it was a list of what I assumed were jobs, though I wasn't sure whether it was for the Bertram Ramsay or here. The list had: security, engineering, maintenance, canteen and BRDF.

"On the screen behind me are just a few of the jobs available to you on the Bertram Ramsay. The jobs begin today, and whilst they may not be the final jobs you undertake upon the station, you will be expected to give them one hundred per cent whilst you are training in this facility. Failure to do so will lead to your early departure, which will likely be a fusion-bus rather than a space shuttle."

"Sir?" Aoife had her hand up.

"Sergeant or Harris or Tyrone will be fine, Aoife. How can I help?"

"What's BRDF?"

"An excellent question. The BRDF is the Bertram Ramsay Defence Force, which is a culmination of the Marine Corps, Navy and Air Force. This facility is manned by BRMC because we are the foot soldiers, and we also provide security on the Bertram Ramsay and all shuttle flights. Some, like myself and Captain Hennessey, have been through the astronaut training program as civilians prior to our military contracts, which is why we run the training programs in this facility and others like it around the world. The navy and the air force only operate from the space station itself. The navy is in charge of the space station flight, and all away missions on manned shuttles. The air force is purely combat, and until we discover hostile little green men, generally just escorts the shuttles and patrols the space around the Bertram Ramsay. To all intents and purposes, I am a BRDF NCO, but while I am here I am BRMC. You can tell by the patch on my arm which has crossed swords and an atom. Navy patches have an anchor and an atom, and air force have wings and an atom. Okay?"

"Yes, Sergeant."

"You are about to be paired off into different subgroups, where you will operate under one of these occupations. Your Crew Leader has been chosen and is, as yet, unaware of this fact, and it is he or she that will pair you off and assign you to one of the occupations on the board behind me. You may change occupations at each stage, if your Crew Leader deems it so, and we may even change the Crew Leader if he or she does not perform to our expectations. Is that clear?"

"Yes, Sergeant." I half-expected him to repeat the question in order to get a more assertive response, but Harris clearly didn't have high expectations at this stage of proceedings.

"Your new Crew Leader is Jaxon Leith." I tried to remain impassive. Faking surprise would have unravelled me there and then—I'd never been a good actor. The crew looked around at me. I wasn't sure if I should expect applause, but I didn't get any, so I kicked my ego to the curb and said, "Thank you, Sergeant."

"Jaxon, please join me up here." I got up and walked to the front of the class, feeling my face burning up as I did. Harris reached behind him and produced a white flight suit, with my first name on the front, identical to the BRMC fatigues he was wearing, but with an insignia patch that had an atom with the words Echo 41 below it.

"This is your Crew Leader suit, and you will be joining me in BRDF training for the duration of your stay here. In the meantime, you need to select a deputy to manage Crew 41 while you are otherwise engaged."

"Laura," I said, without hesitation. I got more than a few disgruntled looks, particularly from Leon who clearly thought he had the chops for leadership.

"Very well, Laura, here is your new flight suit." He handed her an identical one to mine, but in her size, clearly indicating that this had been predetermined, but maybe that was just me being paranoid. Nobody else seemed to notice.

"So, the next step is to pair up your crew into four teams of two, and after lunch, you will divi out their jobs. Okay?"

"Okay."

He pressed a button on his hollopad and nodded towards my seat, indicating that I should sit down, then turned back to address us all.

"That debacle we saw this morning will not happen again. You will, all of you, keep your kit belts with you at all times, including the shower block. They are waterproof so you need not worry. The kit bags with your hollopads in are not waterproof, so they should stay in your dorm while you are in the bathroom. When you go to sleep, you are to lay your kit belt on the floor by your bed. If you sleep with your left side facing the room, you will have the yellow button end nearest your head, so that should the alarm sound, you can reach it with your left hand, like so, and bring it to your left hip." He demonstrated in one fluid movement placing the belt against his hip, and reaching behind for the free end with his right hand, bringing both ends together at the front where the magnetic bonds connected.

"For those of you who sleep with your right side facing the room, you will put the blue button end nearest your head and follow the same procedure in reverse."

The next hour consisted of going through the kit belt procedure again, and practising putting it on and activating the rebreather, plus a refresher on the different alarms that may sound. He made us practise putting them on four times before calling time and giving us a couple of hours break before the afternoon sessions began. He instructed Laura and I to get into our new suits before the break, which I thought was a bad idea considering we'd be eating soon. I had visions of ketchup stains and must have looked dubious, because Tyrone looked at us both and said, "Don't worry—it's wipe clean," grinned and left.

CHAPTER NINE

LAURA AND I headed to the dorm to get our new kit on. The white fatigues were much lighter and more comfortable, and had bio-monitors built in which sync'd with our bio-bands automatically. The room was empty except for the two of us, so Laura told me what Hennessey had said last night.

"They're training you up as a BRDF Counter Intel officer. Apparently you flagged as an excellent candidate before you got your ticket, and your actions so far have proven those assumptions. I've already been through the first two stages of training as an ICP officer, which is why they want me in the group getting a feel for the other candidates, but once we hit Stage 3, I'll be joining you. We've got a week left in Stage 1 before we move on, so plenty of time for us both to get to know the crew."

"What about Leon? I'm surprised he's still here, to be honest."

"Don't worry he's already on the chopping block, but they want to keep him in for the time being to raise tensions."

"That seems like a terrible idea. If everyone is tense, how can we possibly identify this infiltrator? Surely there's..." I broke off as Libby walked into the room.

She looked at us both and said, "Don't mind me. You two can carry on with your conversation. I'm just grabbing a shower, as I missed out in the middle of the pandemonium this morning." She laughed and wandered through to the shower block.

Laura gave a slight shake of her head, which I took to mean "no more talk", before zipping up her fatigues and heading for the rec room.

I finished up putting my kit belt on, grabbed my bag and followed her out.

The rest of the crew were sitting on the sofas. I'd barely sat down when Leon cosied straight up to me.

"Hey, Jax. Could I have a word about my job? Only I think I'd be the right fit for BRDF, like you. You saw me in my first conditioning assessment. I'm at my peak, mate. You should use that. I'd fucking die if I had to do maintenance or catering. Come on, mate, do me a solid."

I wasn't a great one for platitudes, especially with a steaming pile of shit like Leon, so I remained non-committal and told him I hadn't given it any thought. I also made a mental note to make sure I put him in catering or maintenance. He no doubt felt like he'd got the right stuff for BRDF, and for a man like this a bit of power must seem like wearing a crown. I wasn't even sure I deserved leadership, let alone BRDF, so I was absolutely certain Leon didn't. The rest of the group had lowered their voices to listen to our conversation.

"What is there to think about, mate? Come on, you know it's the right thing to do. I'm the right guy for the job."

Aware that I had an audience, I decided that honesty was the best policy. "Leon, Amanda put you flat on your face for us all to see for being a total creep in the shower block. Seeing as you're almost a foot taller, and about twice the width, I'd say that security isn't your strong point. And so far you've managed to piss everyone off at some stage, so I don't think you're in a position to ask for any favours." It was brutally blunt, but people like Leon make my skin crawl and honestly, it felt good to put him in his place. I saw Aoife and Eloise exchange looks and smiles. Amanda remained impassive, despite being mentioned, and shrunk back into the sofa. I definitely needed to keep an eye on her. She was far too cool a customer for my liking.

Leon looked like he was going to retort and then clearly thought better of it, taking himself off to one of the dining tables where he sat alone, throwing furtive glances at the group.

We milled about for another hour drinking coffee and just chatting, mostly about the process so far, but with lots of speculation about life on the Bertram Ramsay. None of us knew what to expect, so it was quite enjoyable to hear everyone's theory on the life that awaited us.

Soon enough the tone sounded, and we grabbed our kit bags and headed to the training room. As we entered, Tyrone was standing in his usual spot with Hennessey sitting behind him. I wondered what she was doing here, but figured I'd find out soon enough. I took my usual seat, as did most others. Leon decided to sit as far away from me as he could. Suited me just fine.

"Jaxon, I need you to make a decision on the work pairings so we can send you all off to begin your training. Have you given it some thought?"

I nodded.

"Very well then, let's have it."

"Laura and Mark are pairing up. They'll be going into engineering, as Mark was CAF in his former life. Libby and Eloise will take care of catering for now. Aoife, you're with Leon." I almost added 'sorry' to that sentence, but felt it was best to just continue. "And you'll be taking care of maintenance, and Amanda and Jennifer on security."

There were definitely a few sighs of relief from the crew, but equally a couple of people looked ready to boil over. Aoife looked furious, and I decided to have a private word with her at the earliest opportunity.

"Excellent. Okay, well, Libby, Eloise—please head over to the kitchens. Crew 40 are in there and they'll get you trained up. You'll be keeping us fed and in supplies for the next couple of weeks. Off you go. Aoife, Leon, I need you both to go through to the demonstration area where you first came in through the airlock. Someone from Crew 40 will be there to meet you too. Mark, Laura, you're going with Captain Hennessey, and the rest of you are coming with me."

There was a scrape of chairs as everyone made a move towards their instructed places. Leon went straight to Harris, presumably to protest, so I took the opportunity to grab Aoife as she left the room.

"Aoife, wait."

She glared at me, and it reminded again me of the suspicion that a coiled cobra lurked inside her.

"I'm sorry you've been lumbered with that idiot, but there's a reason behind the decision. I can't put him back with Amanda, obviously, and I have seen nothing in Jennifer or Eloise that suggests they could handle being in the same room as him. I needed someone with a bit of backbone, who won't put up with his shit. And I'm telling you not to put up with his shit. The sooner they get rid of him, the better as far as I'm concerned, but that decision is well beyond our reach, so we'll just have to dig in for the meantime."

"He's a fucking turd, Jaxon. Why should I be the one that ends up with him?"

"I hear you, and I agree. And I also promise it's temporary. I need someone strong-willed to keep him in check, and that's you. It's a shitty deal, but it was always going to be crap for someone. I'd rather put him in the hands of someone who can fight their corner than someone that he'll do his best to get his grubby little paws all over. Like I said, I'm sorry, but I appreciate you doing it."

She rolled her eyes and walked away. I suppose that was better than I expected. I walked back into the room to hear Tyrone with his voice slightly raised.

"You will do what you are told, Mr Prouse, or I will escort you from this facility right now, and you can bitch and moan about it to whoever you like. Understood? Now, I don't want to hear another word. Get your arse to the demo room." His face was about an inch from Leon's and I could see him recoiling. I couldn't blame him either—I wouldn't square up to Harris if I could avoid it.

He turned back to us as Leon skulked out, still muttering under his breath. Just me, Amanda and Jennifer remained.

"I'd love to know how that idiot passed our assessments." Harris shook his head and looked up. "You three, come with me." He walked out of the training room and turned left through the rec room, turning left again at a set of double doors. He held his bio-band against a pad on the wall, and the doors opened, leading into a long corridor. About fifteen yards up on the right was another door with a security pad, which he dealt with as before, and then motioned for us to enter. We walked into a room that was buzzing with activity. There were consoles around the walls, and a fire exit in the far corner. Half a dozen people were in here with headsets on, staring at holloscreens, and talking to unknown persons at the end of the line. It was way darker in here, with thin blue mood-lighting nestled under the cornicing. The entire room oozed 'operations centre', like a glossy TV spy headquarters or something.

"This is SECO 2. For you two," he said, gesticulating at Amanda and Jennifer, "this will be your place of operations for the next few weeks."

"What do they do here, Sergeant?" asked Jennifer.

"SECO 2 maintains security for the first two stages of this complex. They have hard-wired, closed-loop cameras in many of the communal areas, but due to the nature of this facility, they are only on an internal network and not connected to any outside lines. You'll monitor cameras in the training rooms and workrooms, in the airlocks, and the corridors leading up to them. There are no cameras in dorms or DECON 1 for privacy reasons. Plus you've got bio-pads on all security doors, which we will give you access to, and you will join the other crews' two-man teams in monitoring and patrolling this facility. We take this responsibility seriously, so you will train hard with the other crew and learn from them, because I will expect you to train the next crew when they come in. Is that understood?"

"Yes, Sergeant."

"Okay, you two find Corporal Patel in the corner cubicle. He's expecting you and will take you through your training. Jaxon, come with me."

Harris headed back out of the door we'd just come through and crossed the corridor to a set of double doors opposite. He swiped his band and pushed through the door into a long corridor that ended at a frosted glass screen. The carpet stopped six feet before the screen and gave way to what looked like a metal sheet.

"You need to watch what I do and then follow me in. Get it right, or they'll fry you where you stand." He smirked and stepped onto the sheet, turning to face the wall to his right, which had a floor-to-ceiling mirror. He lifted his hands over his head, with his feet about twelve inches apart.

A low growl permeated the walls, and a light emitted a single sweep from ceiling to floor, illuminating Harris with a thin stripe. I assumed he was being scanned for weapons or something equally unwelcome.

A lofty tone sounded, and the glass screen to his left lifted and closed behind him as he stepped through. I stepped onto the sheet, turned to my right and did exactly as Harris had, then followed him through into a small room about the size of an airlock, with another screen at the opposite end. As the first screen closed behind me, the one opposite lifted, and I passed through to where Harris was waiting.

"This is the control centre for the BRDF Earth Operation—Opps. This facility is dedicated to training new operatives prior to departure to the Bertram Ramsay. Here, you will train in counter-intelligence, combat, flight and security. You will have twice-weekly conditioning assessments, and will spend two hours every day in physical exercise to build your muscle mass and stamina."

"Is there enough time to train me fully while in Compression? I always thought you guys trained for months before becoming operational."

"We do, and your training will continue once you are on board the Bertram Ramsay, but you'll complete the basic training in eight weeks, and will be operational before you pass through Compression. You will not talk to your crew about this, except Laura, as she'll be joining you here in a few weeks, but we are training you to be a counter-intelligence operative, not a foot soldier. To your crew, you'll just be another grunt like me, but you're destined for a much higher clearance than I, and a much more important role on board the space station. Okay?"

I nodded, not really sure what to make of it all.

He motioned for me to follow him through a door in the back corner, which I did.

"And this," he added, sweeping his hands outwards in a grand gesture and looking back at me, "is what you are training for."

My jaw dropped. The full length of the far wall was a floor-to-ceiling window, overlooking the external areas of Echo. The view was incredible. In all my years, I had seen nothing quite like it. There was a myriad of glass-fronted buildings, spanning my full view, with the ground level open-fronted, and housing an extraordinary assortment of military vehicles. Covering the buildings was a honeycomb-patterned metal exoskeleton. The buildings must have been a hundred metres away, and stretched up around ten floors, although they were all different heights. In the centre, between us and the buildings, sat a raised, circular metal platform, with steps and a ramp leading up to it from the right side. On the platform sat three, what I could only describe as 'space ships'—one huge one, that looked to be about the size of several buses, and two smaller ones, more like the size of a mag-tram. To the left was a raised gantry—a bridge, really, that looked like it spanned between Echo and the buildings opposite.

"This is launch command. That's the crew shuttle. It flies every other day with a new crew to the Bertram Ramsay. Those small craft flanking it are Sigmas. Flown by BRAF to escort the shuttle and its crew. Armed to the bloody teeth and capable of Mach 9 inside Earth's atmosphere. You'll be learning to fly one of those as part of your training."

I must have looked utterly stunned, because he followed up quickly.

"Don't worry—we're not training you to be a pilot, unless you show an extraordinary aptitude for it, but all BRDF Counter Intel operatives have to learn how to fly—it's the rules. Have you ever flown before?"

I shook my head. I'd never even been in a cyber-car until a week ago. It was extraordinary to look at. The shuttle was unlike anything I'd ever seen, although I'd never left The Bleeds before so I'd seen bugger all, truthfully. Looking at the main body of the shuttle, it vaguely resembled a metal wasp. Instead of wings it had four stanchions extending upwards at forty-five degrees, one on each corner, with a metal sphere at the end. The spheres were encased in a honeycomb mesh that looked like it was floating six inches from the surface.

"It's about to go up. Want to watch the launch?" Harris was grinning his head off. As if I was going to say, "no thanks". I mean, really?

I settled for, "Fuck yes," and then, remembering myself, I apologised.

Harris laughed. "Don't worry. My face was exactly like yours the first time I saw a launch."

I watched as the spheres emitted a blue glow, and the honeycomb mesh began to spin, though it was impossible to tell in which direction. There were people still climbing the rear-loading ramp, and a forklift was hauling a pallet onto the ship.

"What's with the blue glow? Can you see them in space? Those spheres are bloody bright."

Harris looked at me and pointed at the nearest sphere. "No, they're not visible beyond the stratosphere. The glow comes from oxygen burning around them, and millions of little forks of lightning between the mesh and the spheres, as they power up and the static discharge intensifies. The mesh channels the energy back into the nucleus."

It was almost possible to see the millions of little lightning strikes. The way the light swirled and pulsed was extraordinary.

Harris continued, clearly enjoying himself. "I heard a story, once, about the first test, before they knew they needed the mesh, back when fusion drives were in their infancy. They powered one up, and everyone within a hundred feet got wiped out by lightning. Not a good day at work, I shouldn't imagine. Once they're high enough, there isn't enough oxygen to burn, so it stops. Impressive to see though, isn't it?"

I nodded. Unbelievable for a city boy like me, who'd barely seen more than a tram since the day I was born.

I could hear an electronic sound, like an amplifier being turned up, but way, way louder to the point where I could physically feel it pulsing through me. As the last of the pallets ascended the loading ramp, the two Sigmas lifted off the metal dais, hovering ten metres above the Launch Bay.

The pair rotated slowly in place while the shuttle bay cleared, and then suddenly shot vertically upward at an astounding speed. They stopped just as suddenly, frozen in mid-air, hovering imperiously above the shuttle like metal predators, circling slowly, in absolute synchronicity.

The Sigmas were much smaller, and even 'waspier' than the actual shuttle. They had two stanchions each, that were more like blades, extending upwards from the rear of the fuselage. Both had glowing blue spheres with that crazy mesh spinning around and were visibly weaponised.

The electronic noise grew louder as they retracted the loading ramp into the shuttle. The spheres at the ends of the stanchions stayed exactly where they were, as the body of the shuttle lifted. It was as if the spheres themselves were doing a huge push-up until the shuttle body was above them and the stanchions were angled down by twenty degrees. The spheres glowed much brighter for thirty seconds, and then as quickly as the Sigmas had launched, the shuttle launched too. It remained in view for about another five seconds before I lost it to the clouds, flanked by the two smaller aircraft.

It was an unbelievable experience. I could feel the energy of the spheres pulsing through the walls, which led me to a question. "Tyrone, why can't we hear these shuttles taking off from inside the rec room or the dorm? Christ, I could feel it taking off in here."

"You can. Your crew will all have felt it back in Echo 41. We just haven't had a launch since you arrived because of the intel. No choice today though, or we'll be backed up with crews and this entire facility will get bottle-necked. Echo is the only Compression site with a launch pad, so the surrounding sites use it too."

He turned on the spot and gave my shoulder a squeeze.

"Come on, let's get you started."

Harris walked back through the door into the operations room, turned left and headed through another door into a room that looked a lot like SECO 2. Wall-to-wall holloscreens, what looked like a flight simulator, and a hive of activity with a dozen white-fatigued officers manning their stations. He continued through to another room, through a door on the south wall. It was another conditioning room, but decked out with much more hi-tech gear, and a decent-sized pool. There were a few people working out and one swimmer throwing weights in the deep end and retrieving them one by one.

"Changing facilities are on the right, as well as a sauna and steam room. Membership has its privileges." He gave his eyebrows a quick wiggle, as if to say, "What a treat, eh, sunshine?" before continuing.

"Everything you need is in the changing rooms. Before you leave today, see the quartermaster and get yourself the full kit. You are to keep it locked in the cupboard next to your bed, which is activated by your bio-band. I shouldn't need to impress upon you the need for security, or what may happen should any of this gear fall into the hands of the infiltrator."

I nodded, wondering what on earth someone would do with my gym shoes. Harris wandered back into the ops centre and I followed. We spent the next hour coding my bio-band for all the security doors and gates, and running through the functions on my suit's bio-monitor. Then back into the sim room, where I parked at a holloscreen and went through the Stage 1 assessment programs. I put my headset on, adjusted my seat, leaned back, and hit "start".

She sat panting from the exhilaration. Finding him beaten and placid had made things easier. But she needed to be quick. Someone had gone

to get the medical team. Not that he deserved the help, but that would be irrelevant now. He would be dead before they could do anything.

The past few days had been eye-opening. She'd had no plan to strike this early, but her training conditioned her to see opportunities for what they were. This man needed disposing of as part of the mission, but his wandering eyes and hands were torturous, and so he had sealed his own fate, regardless. The blonde woman, Amanda, had dealt with him decisively, and needed to be watched. She was obviously trained, but had not managed to disguise it. The woman wondered if she was another operative. She doubted the connection, but nevertheless it pays to monitor someone so small that could overcome a man so much larger than her.

Having been assigned to the kitchen, they took the woman through the procedures. The bio-dock, the med kit, how to use an EpiPen, and the codes for storage access. Then an hour on safe handling of chemicals, where they were deployed and stored, before being taken through into the kitchens and cold stores and put to work. She worked diligently, looking for any window of opportunity that may present itself. She knew it would eventually, over the course of the next few days, but had not expected it to come so soon. Her co-worker was learning to do the cold-storage stock-take, which left the woman alone whilst she was on cleaning duty in the kitchens.

Her bio-band was in the dock when the man from the other crew walked through and headed for the exit. She followed him to the door, careful to make sure her sleeves were covering her wrists. He had opened the door for her, as she knew he would, enabling her to leave without her bio-band. Getting back inside would be a problem, but she'd worry about that when the time came. Nobody would suspect her.

Walking cautiously through the rec room, she looked for her target. She knew she shouldn't draw attention to herself, but using the bathroom was an excuse everyone used, so it wouldn't raise suspicions.

Her co-worker was in the cold store, so nobody would notice her absence for at least ten minutes. As she walked to the dorm, the Irish girl was just walking into the rec room, and looked like she'd been crying. Staying towards the edges of the oval room, walking slowly but purposefully, avoiding eye contact so as not to attract her attention, she blended into the background and the Irish girl passed by, maybe six or seven metres away without noticing her. As she entered the dorm, she could hear voices in the shower block.

Changing direction, she turned towards the toilet block and checked it was empty before tip-toeing slowly back to the dorm. There were footsteps getting louder, so she receded into the shadows, holding her breath. The tall man, Mark, was entering the shower block, his fists clenched by his sides. The blonde girl, Amanda, was leaving through the tunnel. She waited a few minutes until she heard footsteps retreating towards the exit.

The woman crept back around to the showers where she discovered him, laying there, sobbing, holding his arm and his ribs, blood smeared everywhere. She walked to him and he looked up, defeat all over his face, tears leaking from his eyes, his skin red and blotchy, and his hair matted with sweat and blood. She knelt by his side as he lay on the floor, careful not to disturb the pooling blood, and quickly, surely, pushed the needle under his arm. He barely winced, still cradling his broken ribs, mucus dripping from his shattered nose. She stepped back, stowed the syringe, and walked slowly back to the kitchen, leaving him soaked in his own pity.

She waited in the doorway, looking out into the rec room whilst staying in the shadows, until she spotted the other crew member leaving Crew 40's dorm. She walked quickly to time her arrival at the kitchen door, just behind him, and as before, he opened it with a smile and she walked inside and back to her station.

I spent the next four hours staring at a screen, doing reaction tests, aptitude tests and several other modules, presumably designed to make me better at something, or discern my flaws. There were manuals to read on site security, protocols in case of fire, attack, depressurisation and evacuation, and a ton of documents to sign. I was eventually interrupted by another officer, who escorted me to the quartermaster where I received fresh fatigues, better boots, a holdall full of gym stuff including swim shorts and goggles, a belt communicator, and an upgraded bio-band which linked to my bio-monitor and showed me the whereabouts of all non-BRDF personnel in Echo 41. I could tap in a name and it found them in the complex, which was disconcerting, but at least now I understood why Harris was twitchy about me locking stuff up.

Most of the crew were in the dorm or the rec room except Libby and Eloise, who were both in the kitchens still presumably sorting dinner out. I wondered if they'd had a break, or whether I was going to get it in the neck when I got back. Only one way to find out, I suppose.

I stuffed everything into the holdall except the new boots which I put on. The QM took my old ones off me, and I headed back through the screens to the tunnel. This time, they both lifted without me having to get scanned and I made my way back to the double doors, turning right into the rec room.

As I entered, most of the crew were sitting around the sofas, laughing. It was good to see them in decent spirits. Aoife was in the thick of it and smiling, which was ominous. I wandered past them, towards the dorm, and as I walked down the passage I heard someone moaning. The dorm room was empty, so I followed the sound to the shower block where I found Leon covered in blood, as was most of the wall and floor around him, his entire body wracked with sobs.

"What the fuck happened here? Leon?" I grabbed a towel, and ran it under the cold tap, and handed it to him to clean his face up. He looked like someone had given him a proper beasting.

"He picked on the wrong girl." Laura walked in behind me, with a wry smile on her face. "Didn't you, you little gob shite?" she almost spat at him.

I turned to face her. "You did this?"

"God, no. I wish. The little prick got a bit handsy with Aoife after the shift, and then Amanda walked in. The pair of them taught him a valuable lesson I expect."

I looked back at the pitiful mess on the floor of the shower block. "What is wrong with you, Leon? Are you incapable of being in a room with a member of the opposite sex without doing something that ends with you bleeding heavily?"

"I didn't TOUCH her!" he screamed, and pointed out of the room. "They just," he sobbed, "fucking came in and started smacking me about."

At that moment Harris walked in, took one look at Leon and nodded at the door. "You two, with me. Now."

I looked at Leon, and back at Harris. "Don't worry, the med team are on their way to take him to the infirmary and patch him back up."

"We'll try our hardest not to worry." Laura's reply was dripping with sarcasm.

We left Leon in a sprawling mess on the floor without a moment's guilt, and followed Harris back to the rec room. He continued to walk to the double doors I'd just come back through, and up the corridor past SECO 2 and the entrance to BRDF Opps, to another airlock on the right. He took us through it, and onto a skybridge over to the ICP Command centre. We headed along another corridor to the lifts, which took us back up to floor two, and walked down to Cooper's office.

Colonel Grealish was there, with Lieutenant Cooper and Captain Hennessey.

"Come in, take a seat. We won't be long." He was all business, and I wondered what had happened.

I sat in the corner, and Laura sat next to me. Harris stood by the door as the office was getting decidedly crowded.

"Jaxon, I understand you've been in Opps all day, and signed all of your paperwork?" I nodded. "Your clearance is now the same as the rest of us, so may I remind you that these conversations are for the ears of the people in this room only?" I nodded again.

"First things first. I want you all to listen to this. I've only heard it once, as has Sara." He touched his hollopad, and I could hear speaking.

"*Are you okay?*" It sounded like Amanda.

"*I'm fine,*" replied Aoife. "*This idiot just needs to shut the fuck up. He's done nothing but bitch and moan all fucking day, then he follows me in here to moan some more.*" Her Irish accent broadened considerably when she was angry.

"*I didn't follow you. I was coming in here anyway to shower up.*" Leon being his usual defensive self.

"*Where's your washbag then? You didn't come in here to shower. No fucking way. You came in here to perv on me, or kick off because you've been stuck doing a shite job that actually requires you to work all day, with someone who won't put up with your creepy fucking comments constantly. You don't get to say whatever you like because you happen to be carrying a bag of knickers from the laundry. You sad, sad little man."* Aoife sounded in total control.

I could hear footsteps and a door closing, and then the unmistakable sound of Leon screaming.

"Now listen here, you little fuck. I have more important things to do while I'm here than put up with your shit." It was Amanda, and by the sounds of the struggling she was putting her moves on Leon again. *"We're not all fucking tourists, and we didn't all get chosen for our aptitude tests. They put me here for a reason, and if you get in my way, I'll break every fucking bone in your body. I've had training that you can't imagine, and if I get the urge to slot you and make it look accidental, it'll be easy. And it wouldn't even be the first time. So I suggest you shut your fucking mouth, because I'm dying to practise on someone, and you're at the top of the list. Got it?"*

"Yes, YES. Just let go of my fucking arm. You're going to break it, you evil..." Leon stopped as the dull sound of a punch landed, presumably on his face. Then more footsteps, then the door closing again, much louder this time.

Grealish tapped the hollopad, and it lit green for a moment before switching off.

There was a brief period of silence, and then Cooper let out a breath. "So, are we to assume that it's definitely her?"

"Wait a minute," I interjected. "Doesn't it seem just a little strange that she'd blurt all that out with Aoife listening?"

"Aoife wasn't listening. She'd left the room," replied Grealish. "You can hear her footsteps and the door closing. We have the locator feed from the bio-bands to corroborate."

"I thought there weren't any cameras in the private areas? Or microphones? How did you get this?" I was certain that's what Harris told us.

"Your bio-band records everything," Grealish continued. "We almost never access the feed though, as it isn't often necessary, but we switched on monitoring on Amanda's bio-band this morning after you allocated her to security. One of the guys in SECO 2 was listening when it happened and alerted us immediately. You walked in about five minutes after the fireworks started."

"Something's not right," I said. "Something about this isn't making sense." I shook my head, trying to clear my thoughts, but every fibre of my being was lodging a protest at the assumptions surrounding that recording.

"I think it makes perfect sense," said Cooper.

"Look, I agree with what we've just heard. It's definitely Amanda's voice, and definitely Leon's, and Aoife was definitely not in the room when it kicked off properly, because you said you've got the bio-location feed, right?"

Cooper nodded. "Right."

"Okay, so why, when I walked in five minutes later, did Leon say 'I didn't touch her. They just came in and started smacking me about'? Not 'she', 'they'. Plural."

"Heat of the moment? Perhaps it was a royal 'they'," replied Grealish.

"I don't think so. He was pointing out of the room when he said it. He meant 'they'. And I'm no detective, but there's only one punch on the recording, and Leon's face is an absolute fucking mess. No way one punch did that. No way."

"Okay, but we've got the bio-locator feed, and there wasn't anyone else in the room with Amanda and Leon," said Hennessey. "Hanson walked in shortly afterwards, and left again a minute later, but the damage had already occurred. The recording proves that."

I wasn't convinced. "If there wasn't anyone else wearing a bio-band in the room. Who's to say someone wasn't wearing theirs?"

Harris piped up. "When you unsnap the mag-lock on your band, it sends an alert to us, in SECO-2, in Opps and in the infirmary. You were told only to take them off in a medical emergency, because taking them off alerts us to that so we can act quickly and decisively. Sorry Jax, but there's just no way."

Everyone else seemed placated by this rational, but not me. Nothing is foolproof, and I've taken a fair few punches in my life. There's no way she could have done that amount of damage with one punch, training or not.

"We need to get Leon in a room alone and ask him. Ask him who was there." I was sure it needed following up.

"He'll be in the infirmary being patched up. Hang on." Hennessey reached for her belt comms. "I'll call them and ask them to keep him there. Harris and I can have a quick chat. You two," she said, looking at me and Laura, "need to maintain your cover." Hennessey put a call in to the infirmary. The rest of us sat there waiting for her to finish when she suddenly shouted, "WHAT?! When? Lock it down. I said lock it down, NOW." She jumped to her feet.

"Leon's dead."

CHAPTER TEN

THE NEXT TEN minutes felt like an hour. We rushed back to the complex, Laura and I having to endure DECON 1 whilst Harris and Hennessey went straight to DECON 4. Once we were both through the airlock, still spitting out the foul-tasting oil, we headed straight through to the rec room where we found everyone exactly as we left them, and in exactly the same mood. Clearly they didn't know about Leon. The alarm lights were flashing all over the complex, although they'd switched off the sirens now. There was a visible presence of BRMC patrolling the site, and they'd sealed the airlocks. Nobody was entering or leaving this facility.

We walked past the crew into the dorm and through to the shower block, where we found an empty room, still covered in blood. Laura searched the cubicles while I checked the toilets. We found nothing. I walked back through to the dorm and checked out Leon's bed. Nothing here either, except a couple of personal items he'd brought with him.

"We need to go to SECO 2. Something isn't right here."

Laura nodded, and we walked out.

As we walked past the sofas, I stopped and walked back to the crew. "Nobody is to go into the dorm or the toilets or shower block until I return. Understood?"

There were a few nods, then Libby asked, "What if we need the loo?"

"Use the loos in Crew 40's dorm if you need to go. They're rotating through at the moment, so I suspect they're virtually unused."

"Who put you in charge? You can't tell us where to go." Aoife clearly felt she still owed me some stick after this morning.

"Harris did. And I can. See those bio-bands on your wrist? They track your movements everywhere, so unless you want to become a murder suspect and be out of this facility tonight, you'll stay out of that dorm. Got it?"

With that I turned and walked away, Laura close behind. I'd mentioned murder, loud and clear, and I could hear volume increase behind me as the crew digested the bombshell I'd just dropped on them. I held my bio-band up to the pad and opened the double doors, ushering Laura through, then up the corridor and into SECO 2.

Harris was inside, but Hennessey was nowhere to be seen.

"Good timing. We're just going back through the bio-band feed to see who went in after we left earlier. Hennessey is with the infirmary, while they figure out what the cause of death was."

"It wasn't obvious? He took a hell of a beating." This from Laura.

"It wasn't the beating that killed him. Scans revealed a swollen throat and closed trachea. He asphyxiated. Doc's first guess is anaphylactic seizure, but that's yet to be confirmed by the bio-scans."

"Jesus Christ! So this might have been an accident?" Laura looked between us both.

I looked at Harris and motioned for them both to follow me out of the room. As we entered the hallway, I turned to Harris. "Is there somewhere in the Opps centre we can talk without interruption or being overheard?"

"Launch View is usually empty. Come on."

We walked up the corridor opposite, to the scanner, and took it in turns to be scanned and walk under the glass screen. Once through, Harris took us through Opps, and into the Launch View room.

"Spill. Whatever it is you're thinking, let's have it."

"Look, this wasn't an accident. There's just no way. If Leon was allergic to something, he wouldn't have gone anywhere near it. He had far too high an opinion of himself to forget something that could cause his throat to swell and suffocate him."

"If it's accidental death, Jaxon, I've seen weirder," said Laura.

"And I would probably agree with you, if he hadn't just taken an epic beating, and if he hadn't specifically said 'they'. And I don't think it was Amanda. If she could have done this and make it look like an accident, why land a few punches? Or even one punch? Why not just get him in contact with whatever he's allergic to and leave him to die?"

"How could anyone know he's allergic to something? Who would have access to those kinds of medical records?" replied Laura; she was asking Harris.

"It's coded into your bio-bands, in case of a medical emergency. But no way to read those without having a bio-dock. There's two in the facility outside of this Opps centre—SECO 2, and the kitchens."

"Why would the kitchens have a bio-dock?" I asked.

"Because they're handling food and drinks on an industrial level, and some of the chemicals, detergents, sanitisers and other things they'd be in contact with would eat through the band, not to mention all the bacteria they're carrying around on their wrists being a pollutant to food and drinks."

"But you said you can't take the bands off without setting off an alarm."

"Unless you have a bio-dock. They have a huge one in the kitchen for about six bio-bands. People place their hand inside the dock, and the magnets attach to the casing, keeping an uninterrupted signal flow across the bands."

This was getting confusing. "So, just to clarify, anyone working the kitchen can take their bio-band off?"

"That's correct."

"And wander around this facility completely unchecked?"

"Not exactly. They can move freely around in the kitchen and stores, but they can't leave the room without scanning their bio-band. You can't unlock the security door without one." Harris shrugged.

I was getting the feeling we were looking in all the wrong directions for this infil. We were doing exactly what I was trying to avoid doing: focussing on one person, leaving the actual infil to operate without scrutiny.

"Look, Jaxon, I agree something isn't right here, but I've been through the bio-locators, and none of the crew were anywhere near the shower block, except Leon and Amanda, and we know Amanda left because of the recording, and the bio-feed. Hanson came in for less than a minute and left again. Nobody else came in or left except the med team, a few minutes later. He was still breathing when they got him in the HolloDoc, but he succumbed very quickly."

I sighed. "I'm telling you, he took a proper beating. That one punch we heard on the recording—no way it did that damage. So it couldn't have been Amanda. Can we get the recording from Leon's bio-band? Maybe that'll have the killer on it?"

"No can do. We only switched Amanda's to record because we suspect her of being our infiltrator. They only record if we ask them to, and they're on a twenty-four-hour loop, so they overwrite themselves continuously."

"What would we hear anyway?" said Laura, looking between us. "Someone smothering peanut butter on his face?"

"You'd hear the other ten punches that he took. And I suspect he'd have bruised his ribs too, judging by the way he was leaning over. Looked like someone gave him a kick to the kidneys while he was on the deck."

"There's just no evidence, as yet, to support further blows, Jaxon. We've got a recording with one punch on it."

"Look, I'm not arguing with you or the available evidence. He'll bruise up in minutes, I promise you. I grew up in The Bleeds—I've taken my share of beatings. I know what a single punch can do, and it can't do that. Evidence be damned."

I was getting fired up here. As much of a turd as Leon was, nobody deserves to die just for being an arsehole.

I took a deep breath. "We need to separate the crew, and interview them one at a time, find out their movements, and piece this together. I can't do it on my own, and in all honesty, I'm in over my head here. This is more Laura's domain, or yours. It's the very minimum we need to do to satisfy ourselves that we don't have a murderer in the crew. I don't know about you, but I'll struggle to sleep at night with someone in the dorm capable of killing."

I turned and walked out, back through Opps, through the security screens and down to SECO 2. There were still several people analysing data, and still no sign of Hennessey, so I left and went back through to the rec room. Everyone was there and, it seemed, they were talking about Leon.

"Jaxon! What the fuck is going on here? You talk about murder and then just walk out?" Aoife again. Her tone had certainly improved, even if her language hadn't.

"Look, I don't know what I can and can't tell you right now. Leon is dead. We don't know how yet."

"But he was alive when they wheeled him through on the gurney! Has someone in the infirmary killed him?" She wasn't going to let this go.

I was a bit startled by this. That was one scenario that I hadn't even considered. I'd already been told that he was alive when he arrived at the infirmary. Could a doctor have administered something that caused his death? I had to concede that it was a possibility, but that still didn't explain the beating, or the comments made by Leon to my face an hour ago.

I tallied up in my head all the possible suspects—Eloise and Libby both had access to the bio-dock, and many chemicals and foodstuffs in the kitchen. The med team that collected Leon from the dorm. Aoife was definitely in the shower block with Leon, and the doctors in the infirmary were with him when he died. Then there was also the timing to consider—did he ingest something or come into contact with a substance during the day that took several hours to react? If so, everyone was a suspect.

My brain was about ready to explode when Hennessey walked in with Harris and Laura at her heels, and a team in coveralls, masks and gloves just behind. Hennessey asked for everyone to assemble in Training Room 1, as the masked team headed into our dorm.

We all filed in and took our seats. Harris sat in the corner, whilst Hennessey addressed the crew.

"Leon Prouse is dead. The ME is still working on an autopsy with the HolloDoc, and we'll have more information about this shortly. He was ferociously beaten, and suffered two broken ribs, a ruptured spleen, a broken nose and a fractured jaw. Someone in this facility caused these injuries. We don't believe they were the cause of death, but I want to talk to all of you individually, except for Jaxon as he was with Sergeant Harris at the time of death. You will stay in this room, and you will not talk until I call you through into Training 2 for your interview. Laura, can you hold the fort here for two minutes? I need to talk to Jaxon and Tyrone outside."

"Yes, Ma'am."

I followed Hennessey out of the door, with Harris close behind. As we reached a reasonable distance from Training 1, Hennessey turned and faced us both.

"We have a problem here. We cannot tell Amanda that her bio-band was being monitored in case we are right about her and she is the infil, so do not mention it to anyone and be careful who's around when you are talking. I would recommend you save all such discussions for Opps. Clear?"

We both nodded.

"Tyrone, you're with me. Jaxon, tell Laura to watch the group—we'll come and get them one by one. Then head back to Opps and enjoy a steam room or sauna—you can't enter the dorm for another hour while it's processed as a crime scene and then cleaned. And pop your head into SECO 2 and ask them to cancel this bloody alarm, please. No release on the lockdown though, until further instructed."

"Okay."

I walked into Training 1, had a quick word with Laura, and headed out to Opps. I wasn't massively impressed with being on the peripheries, but I understood its necessity, and honestly, a sauna sounded awesome right now. I still had my holdall from earlier, so I made my way through the barriers and straight into the conditioning room.

I spent the next ninety minutes soaking in the pool, sauna and steam room, until my skin looked like a pale prune, withered and wrinkly. It had been nice not to do anything that required thinking, although my brain had been working overtime. I just couldn't get it out of my head that we'd been looking in the wrong place all along. If Amanda was our infiltrator, I could think of no better way of drawing attention to herself than showing everyone her capabilities. And there simply wasn't a good explanation for Leon's death that involved her. The bio-band recording and tracking gave her a cast-iron alibi, even if her choice of words was rather incriminating.

On balance, I concluded she was just intimidating him. Making boasts he might believe, given the damage that she'd already inflicted. But that just opened up more questions than it answered.

Someone had beaten Leon to within an inch of his life, but the beating hadn't killed him—the preliminary findings contradicted that.

No, someone had found a way to kill Leon without violence. But even that made no sense. None of the crew had access to medical records that would have showed Leon's allergies, and even if they had, what were the chances of them finding that very weapon on site? I concluded that it had to be someone from the kitchens. Whilst Amanda and Jennifer had access to a bio-dock, they also had eyes on them all day, by far more qualified people. And there was a minimum of two security doors between SECO 2 and the dorm, which made it improbable for either of them to have done it. Plus, we had Amanda's bio-feed, so she hadn't even attempted to disguise her whereabouts, although I'd only just found out that bio-bands were traceable. There was no reason to believe the rest of the crew were aware of this.

It had to be someone from the kitchens. They were the only other crew members with access to the bio-dock, and by all accounts it was accepted that you would remove your band in the kitchens at all times. So, as far as I was concerned, our new suspects were Libby and Eloise.

I towelled off and dressed, and headed back to the rec room through the screens and the two sets of security doors. When I entered, Harris was leaving the training room, and to my surprise Mark followed, his hands cuffed behind his back and two other marines flanking him. He looked up at me as he passed by, a sad smile on his face. I walked up to the training room, knocked and entered, to find Laura and Hennessey inside. They looked up as I came in, then exchanged a look between themselves.

"What's going on? Why is Mark being frogmarched out?"

Hennessey raised her hand to quieten me down. "Not here. Go back to the dorm. I'll come and get you both later for some 'training'." She made quote marks with her fingers.

Laura got up, looked at me and gave her head a little shake. We left the room together and walked back to the dorm. There was nobody from 41 in the rec room, so we headed straight up the tunnel into the dorm. The five women were all in there, in deep conversation.

Jennifer looked up as we entered and said, "Ask him," pointing at me.

"Ask me what?"

"What's going to happen to Mark?" Aoife this time.

"I don't even know why he was arrested. I walked in to see him being escorted from the rec room in cuffs. What the fuck happened?"

"He gave Leon a proper thumping." Jennifer again. "Aoife and Amanda saw everything, didn't you?"

Aoife glared at her as if to say "thanks for that", while Amanda just shrugged, and then Aoife turned to me and Laura. I sat on my bunk as everyone else was sitting. Laura went over and lay down on hers, hands behind her head, staring up at the ceiling and listening.

Aoife kicked things off. "We had about half an hour left on our shift, and I'd been listening to that arsehole piss and moan all day about you, and your white fucking uniform."

I sat upright. "Me? Why?" Stupid question, probably.

"Because you tore him a new one when he asked you for the best job"—I wondered silently how they'd concluded it was the best job, since none of them had had any of these jobs before—"and then saddled him with the one job he didn't want. And while we are on that subject, it is a shite job—he was right about that. We'd been clearing air filters, running to the laundry, cleaning out the dorms, mopping the fucking floors—it's crap. But all he did all day was fucking whine about it, and then I decided to get washed up and leave him to it, and he fucking storms into the shower block after me just as I'm getting undressed. I mean, it's not like he's targeted me specifically—all of us have had to deal with him perving and making crass comments all the time, but this was one time too many. He got right up in my face and I shoved him away. He shoved me back into the shower block, and that's when Amanda walked in. She did her kung fu shit and put him to the floor again. That's when I left. As I left the dorm, Mark was walking in." She looked over at Amanda.

"Okay, so I punched him. Just once." There was a ripple of laughter through the dorm. "But it was only a tap, really. I left just as Mark was walking in. He didn't say a word, but I looked back through that little window in the door and Mark just went mad. Started kicking him in the stomach while he was on the floor. Then punching him repeatedly in the face. And then he walked out and joined us like nothing had happened." She shrugged. "Then you two turned up and you know the rest." She shrugged again.

It was more words than I'd heard her say since she'd been here, besides the incriminating recording.

"So what's going to happen to him?" asked Jennifer. "It's not like Leon didn't have it coming from someone."

"I don't know. This is all news to me. I guess they'll be asking Mark why he gave him such a beating." My turn to shrug. "And whilst I agree that he deserved a slap—well done, Amanda—nobody deserves to die for that."

I lay down as well, deep in thought. I hadn't taken Mark for the violent type, but then everyone has their trigger. I was more worried about Eloise and Libby, though. I was convinced one of those two was responsible. They were the only ones with the means and access to make it happen. The bigger question was how? How did they kill him? How did they get out of the kitchen unnoticed without a bio-band?

I must have drifted off, because they suddenly woke me with pandemonium mark-two. I jolted upright to see the others scrabbling to get their masks out and over their heads.

I heard Aoife shout "Motherfuckers!" at the top of her voice as we all jogged out of the dorm with our masks on.

CHAPTER ELEVEN

HARRIS WAS STANDING in the rec room as we assembled by the exit to the demo room. It seemed quite odd now, being the only man left in the group. He spoke into his belt comms and the klaxons stopped, and the sirens faded along with the flashing lights.

"That was sensational, Crew 41. Two minutes and nine seconds for your second attempt is very impressive. We'll need to get it down to thirty seconds for you to be in your masks, and a minute for you to assemble, but this was still an exceptional attempt. I know some of you must be wondering why we ran an oxygen drill after today's events, but it is my belief that any circumstance that requires your rebreathers is going to be tense and confusing, so there is very little benefit in sounding an alarm when you're all poised and ready, and in good spirits. By far a keener test is when you are under strain."

I considered pointing out to Harris that we were all lying in bed chilling, but the crew needed a win, so I let it go.

"You are all free for the evening. We are also opening up the back room. In there you'll find a games room, books, music and a couple of fridges of drinks and snacks. Please enjoy yourselves. You usually wouldn't have the privilege of the games room until Stage 2, but we felt that you'd had a trying week, and so better to let you relax a bit. I'm afraid Jaxon and Laura, you won't get to enjoy it just yet. We have a training module for you to complete first."

"What, now?" Laura flared up a little. I agreed completely. I'd had more than my fair share of action today.

"I'm afraid so. Get your kit and meet me in SECO 2." He nodded and walked off towards the doors.

Laura and I exchanged looks and walked back to the dorm. She seemed genuinely peeved at being called back, but then I expected she knew more about what was going on than me. I wanted to know where we were at.

We walked in silence back to SECO 2; Harris was in the hallway waiting for us, and motioned for us to follow. We headed through the airlock and the skybridge, and back up to Cooper's office on the second floor. Grealish, Hennessey and Cooper were waiting for us.

Grealish stood by the window as we sat and then addressed the room. "Busy day, then?" It wasn't really a question.

"What's going to happen to Mark?" I couldn't be arsed with small talk.

"Well, he's in the custody suite air-side at the moment. I have made no decision. I wanted to discuss this with you all prior to that, and to catch up on other happenings."

Hennessey spoke. "Hanson gave Leon a hell of a beating. He said little at first, but his hands were black and blue and covered in scratches, so he was very much caught. He realised this quickly and then just spilled his guts. A decade ago, a man stalked and killed his sister. We've checked it out, and his story adds up. It's actually in his file. Reading between the lines, Leon reminded him of the guy—his behaviour, the comments, the leering. And when he saw Aoife leave the dorm close to tears, he must have seen red. Walked in through the door Amanda opened for him, and you know the rest."

"So that's why he's not on the recording?"

"You've got it. He didn't actually speak, and we carpeted the dorm in the sleeping areas, so no footsteps, and no doors opening or closing because he walked through the one already opened by Amanda."

"Sounds like someone we need to keep." I wanted to shake the man's hand, if I was honest.

"You think it's wise to keep a man that almost beat another man to death?" Cooper now.

"I thought we'd agreed that Leon was not beaten to death?" I looked around at each of them. "Look, I'm not saying what he did was clever, but given the backstory, and that Leon was a nasty little prick, I'd say that Mark's instincts were protective, not aggressive. I'd rather have someone like that in the crew than someone like Leon, that's for sure."

"Leon tested off the charts in the aptitude tests." Cooper looked up, as if that settled things.

"Well then, the tests were crap. The guy was a lecherous arse, at best, and at worst a total predator. I don't think he deserved to die, but he still should never have been in a closed dorm with six women and a communal shower block that has no doors. Men like that think it's an invitation."

"Well, it's a moot point now. Mr Prouse is no longer with us. Which brings me to the ME prelim report. They're still to do a full autopsy, but the bio-doc has narrowed things down significantly. They found a puncture wound under his armpit, and the toxicology scan revealed a lethal level of chlorhexidine in his blood." Grealish looked at Harris and Hennessey. "He died of anaphylactic shock as a consequence of poisoning. You two are going to have to find out where the chlorhexidine originated, air-side, and how a syringe of it got into that facility."

"I know how it got in. At least I think I do." I ruffled my hair and breathed out heavily. "We've been looking at the wrong person. It's not Amanda."

"We're going to need more than that to close off the investigation, Jaxon. What do you know that the rest of this room apparently does not?"

"Okay, look. Let's take it a step at a time. Firstly, for anyone to have done this, we all agree that they cannot have been wearing their bio-band, correct?" I didn't wait for an answer. "So whoever did this had access to a bio-dock, and since there are only two, that narrows it down to Eloise, Libby, Jennifer, Amanda and me."

"And me," said Laura.

"Okay, and Laura. But we also know that Amanda was wearing hers, so she's out of the picture. Has anyone checked Jennifer's feed?" I looked up.

"Err, no. Not specifically, but she was in SECO 2 all day, surrounded by BRMC and other crews, and the bio-dock was unused. So we will check, but I would say that she's probably clean."

"Which leaves only two people who had access to and used a bio-doc that day. Libby and Eloise. I would put money on the chemical that killed Leon being in the kitchen. And they've probably got a med kit with syringes. Has anyone checked them yet?"

Hennessey spoke. "There are EpiPens in all the med kits. And there are med kits air-side of the airlocks, and in the training rooms as well. I don't know about the chemical, though. We'll have to speak to one of the QMs or crew that work the kitchens."

"You can't leave it until morning. Not when Libby and Eloise are in there. This has to be done quickly and quietly." Cooper's business-like tone gave a sense of urgency to the situation.

"In the meantime, can we make an excuse to split up the two women in the kitchens?" Grealish asked.

"To what end, Sir? The deed is done. We can't very well interrogate either of them without first getting some evidence, and I thought we'd agreed not to tip our hand to the AoG infil?" Harris had a point. "I don't see that we'd achieve anything by splitting them up, unless we're going to use it as an excuse to monitor them, but since only Laura and Jaxon are aware of what's going on, and both are currently training for BRDF, it would look strange to put them in the kitchens or on maintenance to replace Leon."

"I don't like it, Tyrone, not one bit. Leaving them to it seems like a risk to me. Especially considering Leon's death."

"Well, it may not have been them," I volunteered.

"I thought you just said it was," said Cooper.

"No, I said if it's one of our crew, then it has to be one of them. But they weren't the only ones who had access to Leon. You've got the med team, and the infirmary team to consider as well. They would absolutely have all of the following: access to Leon's medical records, access to syringes, and access to Leon. Probably to the chemicals, too. If a doctor says you need an injection, then you need an injection. In many ways, it fits better that one of the med team did this."

"But you don't think they did?" asked Harris, looking at me quizzically.

"It doesn't feel like it's the right solution. They may well be heavy on opportunity and means, but they are very weak on motive. Unless of course they've all got boobs and Leon displayed his usual charm the moment they wheeled him in." This drew a few laughs.

"May I make a suggestion?" Laura spoke up. Grealish nodded for her to continue. "I agree with Jax—Mark was protecting us from Leon, not being an aggressor. Why don't you reinsert him, but pull him out of engineering as a 'punishment' of sorts, maybe a probationary period, and stick him on maintenance with Aoife? I don't know if engineering needs him right now, but we're a man down here, so it would fill the gap. That would give me time to float between them and get my Stage 3 training done. He can do his time and be back on the engineering program in a few weeks, if he pulls his weight and we don't have any further incidents." She opened her hands as if to say 'Genius, huh?'

"Sara?" Grealish looked over enquiringly.

"Well, given what we know, it certainly makes more sense than kicking him out. But I also think we should rotate the crew weekly and give them different partners, which will be an easy excuse to split Libby and Eloise up and monitor them."

"A lot can happen in a week," said Tyrone.

"Tell me about it," I replied. They all laughed, and Grealish dismissed us.

That evening we had some fun, playing pool and darts and Hexalion, listening to music (although this caused arguments) and just generally chilling. I stayed in the room for a while, but the music was doing my head in so I grabbed a book and headed back to the sofas in the rec room.

Nobody stayed up too late. It had been a challenging week for sure, and I desperately needed a good sleep, so after reading the same paragraph eighteen times without taking in a word I took myself off to the dorm and hit the sack.

The next few days were certainly calmer, apart from our conditioning assessment which had me on the deck and out for the count in only sixteen minutes—two less than I managed on the first attempt. I was going to have to take this a bit more seriously. Three of the five women outlasted me, and I spent the rest of the weekend being teased about how I don't last long.

They reintroduced Mark to the crew for the assessment. He got a ripple of applause as he walked in. He said little, keeping his head down and avoiding eye contact, but it didn't take long for all the women, including Laura, to give him a pat on the back and thank him for doing something about Leon. "I didn't mean to nearly kill him, though," was all he said. The rest of the crew knew he wasn't the cause of death, and given their collective animosity towards Leon, they quickly placated him.

Laura was splitting her time between the kitchen and maintenance crews, as well as putting some hours in at the Opps centre.

I was still mired in procedures and operations training, along with several physical training 'classes' where they were teaching me hand-to-hand combat and defensive strategies. The entire program seemed to be centred around diffusing problems rather than tackling them head-on, and I wondered if they had drawn it up because of incidents on the Bertram Ramsay. I made a mental note to ask Harris when I saw him next.

Nobody had mentioned the launch last week at all. The day's occurrences had driven it from their minds, but a couple of days later we had another. I grabbed Laura from the kitchens twenty minutes before it happened and dragged her into the Launch View to watch. I saw her face utterly mesmerised when the Sigmas took flight, prior to the shuttle taking off. There was a lot more activity outside this time, with crews hauling pallets, and hundreds of people climbing on board.

We headed back to the rec room, where the conversation was all about the shuttle noise. Laura mentioned that we'd just watched it take off, and we spent the next hour answering questions about it from the rest of the crew. I think Laura enjoyed all the attention and she certainly went into some depth, talking about the blue spheres and the mesh. She nodded to me occasionally for affirmation, but otherwise kept up a steady dialogue which the rest of the crew lapped up. Tensions amongst us had eased considerably, and by the time it came to change the crew patterns, everyone was getting along famously and I was wondering how one of these women could possibly be an infiltrator.

We continued to practise putting on our masks, and by the end of week two we were forming up by the demo exit within sixty seconds of the alarm sounding. Harris and Hennessey kept Laura and I up to speed on developments, under the guise of "personal assessments", but things had been quiet and there'd been no need to reconvene in Cooper's office since Mark had been "arrested".

I was visiting the BRDF conditioning room daily, and working hard in the hydrotherapy pool, which they had advised me was the best way to build my leg muscles, and also on the rowing machine. I'd never actually seen anyone row, ever, so when I first got on it the sliding seat took me by surprise and raised a few chuckles with the guys in the room. I was progressing though, and that was important. I was just finishing up and about to get showered off, when Harris walked in.

"Jaxon, good to see you getting some work in. You should probably turn in now though—I've got you booked on the flight sim at 6 am tomorrow. You're in for a fun day." He did a weird finger-pointing thing while clicking his tongue and then left. Very odd.

I grabbed my bag and headed back to the dorm. I was going to shower in Opps but the room was filling up, and honestly the showers in the dorm were better. I weaved my way back around through the complex and into the rec room, said hi to a few of the guys on the sofas, and continued through to the dorm where I stowed my kit bag, fatigues and bio-monitor, stripped down to my shorts, grabbed my kit belt and walked through to the showers. Eloise was in one of the cubicles and she gave me a wave as I walked in, stared a bit too long before she realised what she was doing, apologised and turned away. I grabbed a towel and wrapped it around my waist, stripped off my shorts and lobbed them into the laundry bin before heading into the shower cubicle, one away from Eloise.

The water, as always, was powerful and hot, and I could feel the day's grime washing off me. Someone, I assumed Aoife or Mark, had left a bottle of cleaning liquid in the corner of the shower. I picked it up and flipped it so I could read the label and almost shouted out loud. There, in the list of ingredients of the industrial cleaner bottle, was chlorhexidine. I couldn't quite believe what I was reading, and I knew I had to report this immediately. I'd had no word from Harris or Hennessey about their investigations into the kitchen, but I'd found the very chemical that had killed Leon.

I showered as quickly as I could, grabbed my towel and the bottle and left. I picked up some fresh boxers and a tee, and went into the dorm to get changed.

Eloise was already in there, with a towel tied around her chest. I'd never really paid much attention to her before, but now that I looked, it was difficult to ignore her. She had a naturally curvy body, plenty of top and bottom to boot, a dark bob and brown eyes. Whether she'd deliberately or accidentally chosen a small towel, I wasn't sure, but it was only just covering her backside and she was either oblivious or an exhibitionist. I couldn't decide.

I shook my head and reminded myself to focus on the task in hand, grabbed my fatigues from the cupboard, attached my bio-monitor, pulled on my boots and left hastily, bottle in hand. I went straight to SECO 2 to find Harris or Hennessey, but neither of them were there. Laura was nowhere to be seen either. I'd finished early for the day, so most of the crew were still on task. I headed to Cooper's office in their absence, but the entry door by the airlock wouldn't let me through. Clearly, I only had access to internal doors.

I walked back, turned right into BRDF Opps and looked everywhere, but there was no sign of Harris or Hennessey so I headed back to the rec room, only to find both of them coming out of the conditioning room. I headed over to them and motioned for them to go back inside, which they did.

"Look what I found in one of our shower cubicles." I held up the bottle. "Check the ingredients."

They leaned in to read the label, and both of them opened their eyes wide in surprise when they got to the chlorhexidine.

"And you picked up the bottle without gloves or a towel or something? Jesus Christ, Jaxon." Hennessey shook her head, and I felt like a scolded child.

"It hadn't occurred to me that this might be the actual source of the chlorhexidine. I was just showing you because now we have at least one substance on site known to contain it." I probably sounded like a child too.

"Didn't you ever watch detective shows on the holloscreen? You never handle the murder weapon. Or move it."

"Never had a holloscreen at home, so can't say I did." I shrugged. I was expecting a bit more positivity for finding it if I was honest, and getting my head bitten off was unnecessary, given the circumstances. I must have looked like I was about to kick off, because Harris chose that moment to pipe up.

"You did the right thing showing us, Jaxon. We've been waiting for the QM to come back to us with a list, but this is certainly a starting point. We'll need to get this to the ME for analysis."

Hennessey reach out her hand. "I'll take it. There's probably too much DNA on it now to make any reasonable assumptions."

"If it's been there a few days, it's been handled by half the crew already, plus whoever packed it at the factory, loaded it onto transports, unloaded it here, put it on the shelf, and since it's almost empty, I'd surmise it's been extensively handled by every crew that's worked maintenance. So whilst I'm certain the true-crime channel would probably have educated me, I would doubt very much it would have proven useful in this situation, especially since I picked it up without knowing what was in it. Should I assume everyone else handled it with gloves, or the severed hand of a burns victim?" Boom. Back in the room. Sarcasm overload.

Hennessey rolled her eyes at me and stalked out, muttering to herself. Harris grinned and told me to go chill.

"Early start for you, Jax. I'll have your bio-band wake you up at 5.30am. Is that enough time for you to get showered, dressed and over to Opps?"

"Sure, if I decide not to have a coffee or breakfast."

"Trust me, you don't want either before getting in the simulator." He laughed and walked off, leaving me wondering just what I'd got myself into.

CHAPTER TWELVE

MY BIO-BAND VIBRATED me awake at 5.30am. I'd slept pretty well, although it took me a while to nod off thanks to my brain being on overdrive.

I could hear the rest of the crew sleeping, with the occasional noise emanating from someone's backside, and I headed through to the shower block, had a quick soak, dressed and grabbed my kit. I wandered through into the rec room, which was dimly lit in an orange light from the dawn sun coming through the skylights. I took the usual route through to Opps, peering into SECO 2 en route just to see if anyone was about, but there were only a couple of people in there and I didn't know either of them, so I turned about and headed into Opps.

Harris was waiting for me in the control centre and waved me over as I walked in.

"You're early, well done. We need to get you chipped and then I'll hand you over to your Sigma Wing for the day."

Nothing in that last sentence made any sense to me, so I just nodded and followed Harris into Launch View, and then left down another short corridor to another room that looked about as futuristic as you could imagine. Down the left wall were several reclined seats with metal hoses coming out of the backs. Each seat had a central dock with an empty cavity that looked a bit like a miniature coffin. The seats were connected to six or seven holloscreens and a couple of hollotabs each. The right wall was floor-to-ceiling holloscreens, currently filled with a kind of swirling paint that just floated around all the screens without stopping. There was a uniformed technician sitting in Bay 2 on a stool next to a reclined seat, and he was fiddling with something until he heard us behind him.

"Ah, Harris. Is this your man?"

"Wing Commander Nile, this is Jaxon Leith. Jaxon, Wing Commander Addison Nile." So, not a technician then.

"Nice to meet you, Jaxon. I'll be your horror show for the day." He held out his hand and laughed, as did Harris.

I took it. "Jax is fine. Looking forward to it." I smiled, trying not to make it look like I was suddenly nervous, which I was.

"Give me a minute, Jax. I'm just installing your Armadillo."

The conversation was getting stranger by the second. In his hand he held what looked like a small silver coffin, presumably to fit into the dock in the back of the seat next to him, with purple scallops down the curved back much like those of an armadillo. The other side of it looked like it comprised thousands of pins, and I could see them forming to the shape of Addison's hand. There was a disc in the centre with five tiny spikes arranged around the middle. He placed it into the back of the chair, needle side facing out, then punched a few keys on his hollotab. I could hear the machine whine as it powered up, though it was pretty quiet.

Another tech walked in from behind us. "Wing... Sim is up and ready for you."

"Thank you, Flight," he replied without turning around. The tech left, and Addison looked up at me. "We need to get you into a flight suit, young man. Lockers opposite, grab one that fits. I've had the QM bring all sizes."

He nodded to the corner where there was a rail of flight suits and four lockers. I grabbed a medium suit off the rack, stripped out of my fatigues and put the flight suit on. I detached my bio-monitor from my fatigues and slotted it into position on my flight suit. The flight suits were black, and criss-crossed with tiny tubing, like a hex weave covering every inch. There was a padded area in the back, with a metal clip the same shape as the Armadillo.

Harris put a hand on my shoulder. "Put your kit belt on for now. You won't need it in the Sim, but keep it with you in between rooms. I'll be leaving you in Wing's capable hands shortly."

Addison waved me back over and asked me to take a seat in the chair, which I did. Harris was grinning his arse off, so clearly this wasn't going to be pleasant. Addison pushed me firmly back and then pressed something, and I felt a pressure on my shoulders from a restraint. Out of nowhere I felt a sharp pain in the middle of my spine, and then just as suddenly it was gone.

I must have gasped as the spikes jabbed into me, because Addison put a hand on my leg and said, "That's as bad as it gets, I promise. And it's only for the Sims. Come, let's get you started and I'll explain."

He stood up, put his hand out and pulled me out of the seat, before turning and walking back towards Opps. I followed him through and into the sim room. Harris patted me on the back and headed back out through Opps to SECO 2.

"The Armadillo is a neural transmitter and receiver. In order to simulate the effects of flight accurately, the Armadillo will send signals to your nervous system and your brain, simulating the inertia on your body. Your flight suit has a network of conduits that will apply pressure in conjunction with the Armadillo, so you'll feel some elements of it physically, and the rest will be your brain tricking you into thinking you're moving. They used to use simulators with huge hydraulic pistons to move the cockpit around to simulate flight, but somewhere along the line someone invented the Armadillo, and now we can actually experience proper flight without leaving the room. The funny thing is, modern Sigmas and shuttles employ 'sonic quinoid inertia impedance drives'—I know, it's a bloody mouthful—so you'll barely feel anything when you're actually up there, but we have to train with all the effects so you can learn to operate it if the SQIIDs fail."

He pronounced it like "squids" which was a lot easier for a simpleton like me to remember. I could already feel my brain overloading, just from trying to remember all the technical terms for things. I must have looked confused because Addison put a hand on my shoulder and said, "Don't worry—you'll pick it up pretty quickly. I had the same look on my face when I first took to a Sim."

Addison definitely knew how to put me at ease. He looked to be about forty, trim and fit, clean-shaven, with short spiky hair with flecks of grey coursing through the dark brown. His well-spoken manner was jovial, confident, and oozed experience and wisdom. I could see why he was an instructor.

"So this is your job—to teach muppets like me how to fly these things?"

"Good lord, no. We all rotate through Opps, but spend most of our time up on Berty, flying sorties, patrolling the immediate area. The BRAF is a combat division primarily, but since there are no known enemies, we are largely redundant. We also defend against asteroids and meteors that stray a bit too close for comfort."

"What about planets? I've heard there's one about to stray a bit too close to Earth for comfort."

He leaned his head back and laughed loudly. "You and I are going to get along just fine, Jax. Come on, let's get you started."

Addison got me strapped in to the 'mockpit' as he called it. I had a five-point harness with magnetic bonds that were synced with my bio-band and released when I touched it to the central disc. He took the seat next to me and ran me through procedures.

"You will call me Wing. And I will call you Flight. This is a standard protocol during training, as we record all training sessions for use in classroom training centres. There are cameras all over the place, but just ignore those, speak normally, and try to keep your focus on what's happening around you. I'm going to take you for a spin first, and talk through the checklist and everything I'm doing. I do not expect you to remember any of it immediately, but repetition will force it into your brain and your memory will do the rest."

I looked around. There were three holloscreens in front of me. Addison had explained that these would give me the same visual as the windows on the Sigma. They were littered with data and target sights, graphics and a ton of numbers. Between us was the flight console, and above us another. In front of me was what looked like a steel sphere, about six inches in diameter, with moulded grip-handles on either side. There were levers behind each hand, and an array of touch-buttons on the front surface. There was also a fine pattern of lines criss-crossing the entire sphere, though they were barely visible. I picked it up, and looked across at Addison, eyebrows raised.

"Yes, that's your controller. Every flight control you need is on that. Made a lot more sense to put everything in the palms of your hands, so that's what they did. But that's not even the cool bit. Drop it."

I did, and it stayed exactly where it was, floating in mid-air, absolutely still. I looked around it and saw an incredibly fine thread trailing from the back of it to the console in front of me.

"EM silk. When you run a current through it, it locks into place. Has the tensile strength of steel cable and yet weighs almost nothing. The controllers pass a current through it when you're not touching them. For now, put it back in the dock and leave it there. You won't need it just yet."

I pushed it back into place and looked over at Addison. He placed his hand on the central console, and the whole simulator sprung to life. Everything lit up, but it was all a diffused blue light. It was bright enough to illuminate the switches and dials, but not so bright as to distract.

"This is your power bank. These two switches power up the fusion spheres. There's a tiny reactor behind the mockpit, which we need to get started, but once the fusion spheres have lit up, the gyro-shields around the spheres channel the energy back into Quirillium Nucleus. The Quirillium is almost ninety-eight-point-nine per cent efficient, so all the time the spheres are powered up, you can pilot this craft for millions of miles before the reactor kicks back in."

He had me at "Quirillium".

"This capped switch is the main start-up. The fusion spheres need to be switched on or this switch won't function." He pushed up the red cap, and flicked the switch, letting the cap spring back into place. "Following so far?"

"Yes, Wing. Two switches for the fusion spheres, they get turned on first, then lift the cap and power the reactor."

"You've got it. Now, see the red button with 'VOX' on it on your controller?" I nodded. "That leaves an open channel if you switch it up. Anyone listening on that frequency, including the towers here and on Berty, will hear every word you are saying. We only use vox when we're in trouble, and need our hands free to fly the Sigma, so bear that in mind. If you wish to speak to the tower, just press and hold, and release when you're done."

He pressed the vox button on his controller and said, "Tower, Sigma 242. Request clearance for launch." Then he looked across at me. "That's the actual tower—our call sign tells them it's a Sim, but they'll treat it like any other departure, so we time our sessions for when the dock is empty or not in use usually. Same with the tower on Berty."

"Sigma 242. Skies are clear. Proceed when ready."

He picked up his controller and brought it towards him, stopping when it was at a comfortable distance I guessed. The handles were on exact opposite sides to each other. Wing gripped them and then turned them downwards until they were sitting at four and eight o'clock respectively.

"Set the position to whatever is comfortable for you. Certain positions trigger different control responses, so don't stray beyond the side aspects. Somewhere between eight and ten o'clock for the left handle, and two and four o'clock for the right one. You can reach the vox button with your left thumb. The handle on your left rotates forward—that's your throttle. It'll stay in position until you pull the lever behind it—don't pull it too hard. It moves through two stages—the first disengages the drive, and the second engages the reverse thrust. Once you've disengaged the drive, you'll need to rotate it forwards again for thrust. Okay?"

I nodded, not sure I was okay.

"Jolly good. Shall we?"

He didn't wait for an answer. I watched him rotate his handle forward, and I could suddenly feel the vibration of the craft, which was bizarre since we were sitting in a box in a room. He pressed another button and the screens showed what looked like shutters lifting, illuminating us in the dawn light. It was so realistic. I could see the shuttle and buildings, and the Launch View room over on my left. It genuinely looked like we were outside, about to launch. He pressed a blue switch by his right thumb and looked over. "This is the VTOL button. Switches power to vertical take-off and landing."

He rotated his left hand forward a couple of notches and I suddenly felt pressure on my back. We lifted off the ground just a couple of metres, rotating left as we did. He leaned over and pressed another button on the central console, marked 'Gear', grinned at me and then rotated his left handle ninety degrees forward.

We shot up at an absolutely unimaginable speed. I could feel my entire body being pressed into my seat. Outside was just a blur for a few seconds, and then we cleared the tops of the buildings and the whole of England swept into view. I had never seen anything like it. We were still travelling up at a ridiculous speed, when Wing pulled the left lever and we stopped dead in the air, instantly. I felt the faintest moment of weightlessness, and some pressure on my shoulders from my harness. I could swear we were actually flying.

He looked at me and laughed. "You should see the look on your face, Flight. And you haven't seen anything yet. I'm going to show you what she can do, and then if there's anything you want to see, just let me know."

"Can we see the Bertram Ramsay?"

"No problem. If this impressed you, that's going to blow your mind."

Wing pulled the console towards him another six inches and then grinned at me. We shot forward at an outrageous pace. The HUD on the right screen showed 1,600 knots, but it might as well have been a million. I could barely take in the view. Wing climbed for a minute or two and then pointed out of the left side. We were above the clouds, and just on the horizon I could see a dark shape looming.

"Tyrone tells me you're from The Bleeds? Ever seen them from up here?"

As if. I shook my head, and he rolled us left a little. Within twenty seconds I could see the tops of the metal monstrosities that I grew up in. Eight hundred storeys high, and a hundred of them above the clouds. It was a view I never could have imagined. They once touted the top apartments to the wealthy professionals, but that fantasy had died when the first mag-lift failure occurred. To walk up eight hundred flights took a couple of days, and it wasn't long before they'd found bodies in the stairwells, of the thrill-seekers who wanted to climb them. The top hundred floors had long been abandoned, and the buildings looked decayed and fragile. The Bleeds stretched all the way to the horizon. We almost never saw the sun as kids, except reflected at the ends of the row in the mullioned windows.

Wing banked right and took us down through the clouds. “Technically, we’re not allowed below the tops of the buildings for safety reasons, but since we’re both sitting in Cheltenham, I think they’ll let me get away with it.”

We briefly entered the clouds, and the holloscreens switched to a digital rendition of the landscape below and back to windows as we broke through the white carpet overshadowing the streets of London. It was incredible to see where I grew up from this altitude. I mean, I got to see it a lot from six hundred floors up, but I could only view the buildings opposite and look down on the street. Now we were flying between the top floors of the buildings and looking down at the throng below.

“Shall we have a little fun?”

I nodded. This was already blowing my mind.

Wing pulled back on the controller and we shot vertically upwards at an incredible pace. I watched the HUD pass 1,900, 2,000, 2,100 knots and suddenly the blue sky above me dissolved into a deep purple, darkening with every passing mile until I felt the Sigma shudder slightly as we broke through into space. The stars were brighter here than I had ever seen them.

When I was a kid, my dad would take me to the edge of The Bleeds on a clear night, and we’d look up and see the stars. Back then I thought it was the most amazing thing I’d ever seen, and I’d beg him for weeks on end to take me back, until he finally relented. It was nothing like this, though. This was like a black velvet sheet with a billion holes punctured through it.

I looked over at the HUD; we were gaining speed at an astonishing rate. The gauge had switched to kilometres, and we were passing 15,000 kph.

"Bertram Tower, Sigma 242. Entering orbit and requesting permission for Orbital Recon."

"Sigma 242, that's affirmative. Enjoy your fly-by."

I looked down at Earth. I could just about see England fading behind us to the left. We were somewhere over Asia from what I could tell, but I was never much of a geography geek, so I was just guessing. Wing pointed out ahead. "There she is."

I could see the station just on the horizon. The darkness partially obscured her, and the earth below us was dark and full of specks of light—cities illuminated. We were now travelling at 17,500 kph and gaining altitude all the time. I could almost see the whole of Earth through the left window. It seemed like we were barely moving at all, watching the Earth slowly rotate below us.

It took us another twenty minutes to reach the Bertram Ramsay. I could see it in the front window as we approached. From here I couldn't figure out how they were going to fit nine million of us on board. It was only as we got closer that I started to get a genuine sense of her size. I was getting nervous about how close we were. There were thirteen spheres, twelve of which were connected by a huge, circular, metal tunnel with the largest sphere in the centre, connecting to each of the spheres by tunnels, like spokes on a wheel. I felt like we were going to collide any moment. It was huge and getting closer fast.

I must have tensed up, because Wing looked over and said, "Don't panic, Flight. We're still forty miles away."

Forty miles? Forty? It didn't seem possible. I could see tall buildings crammed together in the sphere nearest to me. There must have been twenty or thirty, all at least a hundred storeys high. There were factories and fields, farmland and roads. It was unfathomable. Wing took us for a circuit around the nearest one, and that took almost eighteen minutes at an altitude of three kilometres above it. He pointed out to me the docks where the shuttle launches and lands, and the command structure. I had quite forgotten about learning to fly.

As we completed the circuit, Wing broke away from the station and back into Earth's orbit, before communicating with the tower to re-enter Earth's atmosphere. We slowed down as the front of the ship glowed blue.

"That's the forward shields—they used to have physical heat shields to protect us from burning up on re-entry, but now we have electro-magnetic shields powered by the Quirillium Nucleus. It means we can pass through more quickly than we used to, but we need to keep the same trajectory or we'll bounce off the atmosphere."

My mind was completely blown, and by the time we cruised into land at Echo, my head was about ready to explode.

For the first time in my life, I felt like I had something worth working for.

CHAPTER THIRTEEN

THE NEXT WEEK flew by, quite literally. I was spending two hours a day in the simulator, and ninety minutes in the conditioning room in the Opps centre. By the time we'd got around to the next fitness assessment, I was aching but feeling more confident. They'd advised me to take a couple of days off to allow my body to rest, so on those days I just sat in the steam room, soaking up the heat. Laura joined me on one of them, and quite honestly it was difficult to stand up without embarrassing myself, after an hour of sitting in the steam with her just in a towel, opposite me. I got the distinct impression she knew exactly the effect she was having on me, and there was a definite uplift in hair-flicking and coy looks.

On the morning of the third assessment I was up early, as usual, and made my way to the shower block. There'd still been no further news on the chlorhexidine, and I'd put it to the back of my mind.

There had been an awkward moment in the middle of the week when a brigadier from the BRMC dropped into our training room and explained there would be a small service for Leon, followed by a cremation, and should any of us wish to pay our last respects we should join him in the demo room at 5pm. I watched Harris's face as the brigadier spoke, and I swear he was cringing for the world. Needless to say, none of us attended. The only other time it was mentioned was later at dinner, when Aoife decided to give him a proper send off by saluting with her middle finger as they carried his casket back through to the infirmary. Class.

In the shower block, I grabbed a towel from the rack and walked into the shower. The water pummelled me, and I was just getting used to the steaming jets when I heard a small sob from the cubicle next to me. Listening for a moment, I could definitely hear crying from next door. Leaving the water running, I wrapped a towel round my waist, grabbed another from the rack, and walked tentatively round into the other cubicle.

Eloise was sitting on the floor, completely naked, back against the wall, hands wrapped around her knees which were drawn up to her chest, water cascading on to her. Her head was down so she didn't notice me come in. I crouched beside her and laid the towel over her arms, preserving her modesty. I shuddered to think how this would have played out if Leon had found her. She flinched at the towel's touch and looked up at me, startled, tears pouring down her face, which was red and blotchy. I held my finger to my lips and put my palm face down in front of her to indicate she should be calm, leaned into her ear and said, "What on earth is the matter? Are you okay?"

Her face crumbled, and she dissolved into tears. I left the water running so the crew wouldn't hear us in the dorm, and put my arms around her. In seconds the shower soaked the towels, and water was now running freely from the hemmed edges. She was in absolute pieces. It took me probably ten minutes to calm her down enough to talk.

"Tell me what's going on. What's got you in this state?"

"It's just everything, Jax." She sobbed through almost every word, drawing her speech out to about three times the normal intonation. "I'm not going to pass these assessments. I've been trying really hard to work in the conditioning room, but I feel like I'm going backwards. And the other girls are all finding it much easier. And what happens if I fail? They'll leave me here and I'll die with everyone else. And I left my family, and they'll be so disappointed in me, and I miss them all." She broke down again, her eyes welling up and big tears falling down her puffy cheeks. "I don't want to die, Jax."

She was someone I'd had only a brief interaction with since we first entered Compression, so this was an odd moment to engage in our first meaningful conversation. The torrent of water had plastered her dark, bobbed hair all over her face. Eloise didn't have the same confidence or charisma as Libby or Laura, but she had a quiet, unassuming manner that endeared her to everyone.

"Nobody here is going to die. You heard them on the first day. They chose you for this—they assessed you, and you passed all the aptitude tests. It's still early in the process, so give yourself a break, eh?"

I thought Eloise was being unnecessarily hard on herself.

"What am I going to do, Jax? I'll never make the grade."

"Look, these people know what they're doing. This is the most important mission that humanity has ever faced. There's not a chance that you would have been selected if they didn't have absolute confidence that you could make the grade. I tell you what—I'll work with you a couple of times a week to help you get up to speed. But you know I've been struggling too. You were all calling me 'Egg-timer' last week, or have you forgotten?"

I'd finally extracted a smile from her face. "Come on, let's get you wrapped up and dry, and we'll go grab a coffee."

She nodded her head, and I turned around so she could wrap the towel around herself properly when she stood up.

She tapped me on the back, and I turned round. Towel-less and drenched, she threw her arms around me and buried her head in my shoulder.

"Thanks, Jax. I'm sorry for being such a mess. Don't tell the others, please?" She looked pleadingly up at me, her face very close to mine. Her eyes darted down to my lips, and I wondered how they'd feel pressed against mine. I gave my head a shake; this wasn't the moment. I didn't know quite how to hug her back. She was totally naked, her ample breasts pressed against my chest, and our thighs touching.

I settled for a light hug and pulled her head to my shoulder, careful to keep my hands out of the no-zone. "Of course I won't. It's all good. Come on."

I tried to wrap the soaked towel around her, but she pushed it down and tied it around her waist. I put my hand gently on her bare back, and coaxed her out of the cubicle, turning the water off as we went, and followed her out.

"OH. MY. GOD. What the fuck is going on here then?" Aoife was standing, knickers on, bra in her left hand, hands on hips and glaring at the pair of us. I didn't know where to look, with topless Eloise to my left, and topless Aoife in front of me. When I was a lad in The Bleeds, I'd fantasised about moments like this. Now I willed for a localised earthquake to open beneath my feet, plunging me into its depths.

I could imagine what it must look like, the pair of us stood there, soaked to the skin, dripping water from drenched towels, leaving the same cubicle together.

"Aoife, it's not what you think." I held my hands up in a desperate attempt to quieten her before the whole dorm walked in to investigate. Too late though, as Laura and Jennifer arrived right behind her, still in their underwear, clearly wondering what all the noise was about.

"For fuck's sake, Jaxon." Laura just shook her head, her eyes taking in the entire scene and walked out. Eloise broke out laughing.

Jesus fucking Christ.

I left the block, between Aoife glaring at me, and Jennifer smiling at me. At least she'd kept her top on. I wondered what my nickname was going to be this week…

Laura refused to look me in the eye at breakfast and made absolutely certain that I wasn't in her direct line of sight. I wondered why she'd got her knickers in a twist over nothing, unless she thought all blokes were like Leon. Then Eloise came out, looking considerably better than when I'd left her in the shower block, and plonked herself next to me.

Laura made a noise, somewhere between an animal growl and a tut, and left the table, heading for SECO 2.

Aoife came and sat down opposite me and Eloise, grinning at us both. "How are you two lovebirds?"

I started to protest when she burst out laughing. I looked at her and then at Eloise, who also had a smile on her face, but with an expression a lot more reminiscent of the looks I had been getting from Laura in the steam room.

"It's fine, Jax. I believe you." She laughed again, and so did Eloise.

Wondering what I'd got myself caught up in this time, I nodded at the pair of them and left them to it. I could hear Aoife cackling from the other end of the rec room. I presented my bio-band to the door panel and headed through towards SECO 2. I could hear Laura and Harris talking, so I pushed through the doors to join them. Laura took one look at me and turned on her heels, banging my shoulder as she barged out of the room.

"What was that all about?" asked Harris. Clearly they hadn't been discussing it, and I wondered why I thought they might have. I explained to Harris about Eloise, and her crying in the shower, and everything that had been said and happened afterwards. He listened attentively, nodding, and then broke into a grin at the end. "Fucking hell, mate." He laughed. "That'll be round the base by lunchtime." Then, seeing the unimpressed look on my face, he said, "Don't worry about Laura. She'll get over it."

"Get over what? What exactly am I supposed to have done wrong?"

"Jaxon, for an intelligent bloke you really are an idiot." I must have made a face because he continued. "Isn't it obvious that she likes you? You're taking steam room sessions together, and the pair of you are on the inside of an investigation that only you and her are privy to. Then she sees you leaving a shower cubicle, bollock-naked with another one of your crew—an equally naked, attractive female crew member at that..." He opened his palms as if to say, "You're lucky you've still got a nut-sack, sunshine." He laughed again. "She'll come around. Come on, I want to talk to you about something."

I followed Harris out of SECO 2 and up the corridor to Opps. He walked me round to Launch View, and then took a seat by the window, gesturing for me to join him.

"Jaxon, you are excelling in your training. I'm not the only one that's noticed either. Addison is telling anyone in earshot that you're a natural. Rumour has it you landed your Sigma on the Bertram yesterday, first attempt?"

I shrugged. It was true; I had made my first landing, both on the Bertram and back at Echo, but it was more by luck than judgement. The entire station is rotating constantly, to produce the gravitational pull necessary to walk freely around inside, so the launch tubes are side-on to the rotation. You have to accelerate to keep up with it, and then a touch more to coax the Sigma inside. I'd put too much throttle on, and shot inside at speed, hit the reverse thrusters and just literally stopped dead, wheels down. Addison fawned over me, telling me that my skills were "instinctual" and that I should consider Flight as a pathway once I'd got myself on board. I tried to tell him I'd bodged it, but he waived it off and told me to stop being modest. I felt like protesting to Harris would elicit a similar response, so a shrug would have to do.

Addison then made me take us all the way back—it was the first time I'd done a complete flight without hearing the words "my aircraft" and letting go of the controls. Bringing it back to Echo is easy once you've got past re-entry, and even that isn't a massive effort. I was learning the maths of navigation and doing modules on meteorology, but Wing had already told me that the Sigma was designed to fly completely autonomously and has controlled safety functions, so it was difficult to crash even if you tried. I dropped it onto the dock at Echo at hypersonic speed, with the AI switched on, and twenty feet off the deck Sigma took over and parked it. A ten-year-old could have done it.

"Jax, look—you've got skills you didn't realise you had when you joined us here. You're a natural leader, and Command is already looking at you as the new poster boy for BRAF, so what is it you want to do? I'm asking, because I suspect nobody has."

I didn't know what to say. I can't imagine that anyone would struggle with the flight training, but I'd been told some horror stories by Wing whilst we were skimming the ground at 1,600 knots. Before Compression, I'd never experienced flying before, and technically speaking I still hadn't. It was easy to admit that it was exhilarating, and that I wanted more. I had moments where I daydreamed about tearing over treetops, weapons ready, chasing little green men and wondering if I could stop the White House being blown up, but that's all they were—daydreams. Still, in my head, Will Smith was a comparative amateur.

"I don't know, Tyrone. I have to admit I love flying, or at least pretending to. But I'm also enjoying the connectivity with the crew, and watching them go about their daily routines, excelling in their own jobs. You know me—I'm quite happy with my own company, so for sure, stuff me into a Sigma and let me loose. But only if you think I'm good enough."

"I figured that's what you'd say, and I'd say it was a superb choice. That being said, we have an issue with infiltration at the moment, and probably more so on the Bertram, so whatever division you end up working in, Command wants to keep you as an operative inside the network. So do I, and, as it happens, they're discussing Laura in the same breath, although no decision has been made there. I haven't told her, so you're not to either. Okay?"

"How am I supposed to tell her and keep my gonads attached?"

Harris laughed. "That's the spirit."

I went back to the dorm and grabbed my gym gear. I got changed, picked up my kit bag and hollotab, and headed back to Conditioning. Everyone was already there, and as I walked in Aoife wolf-whistled, which almost everyone laughed at. I joined in, only because I already looked a dickhead, so I might as well play the part. Of course, if I'd wolf-whistled at one of the girls I'd be immediately vilified and cast out as a sexist pig. What was good for these geese definitely wasn't good for this gander, and alarm bells were ringing. I'd been with a few women over the years, but this level of attention was almost cloying.

I looked up and Hennessey winked at me from behind the group.

Fuck's sake.

"This is assessment number three, Crew 41. I am expecting a step-change in your individual performances from this point on, but today we are going to collaborate to build your stamina, and help you learn to work effectively as a team. There are four activities in this room that you would usually undertake during your conditioning assessments; hydro-pool treadmill, cross-trainer, exercise bike and floor work—push-ups, sit-ups and jumping jacks. In a minute, you will discuss your relative strengths and weaknesses, and then Jaxon, you will allocate four of your crew to the four different modules. The other four will be there to take over from their teammates, as and when you deem necessary. There are some targets on the screen behind me—you will hit these today, and you will not leave until you have managed the entire program between you. Understood?"

"Yes, Sergeant."

"Okay, you have two minutes to discuss. Go."

I got straight down to it. "Laura, what's your best module?"

She glared at me, letting me know I was a long way from forgiveness for something I hadn't done. I tried again. "Laura, whatever is going on in your head, now is not the time. Your crew needs a strong start from a strong candidate. Now, are you up to the task or not?"

"Hydrotherapy pool." She didn't even look at me.

"Okay, that's yours. Anyone else feel particularly strongly about the pool?" Everyone shook their head. I didn't blame them; the hydrotherapy pool seemed fun to begin with, but it was a brutal assault on your stomach muscles, thighs and calves.

"Great. Who wants the cross-trainer?" Eloise, Libby and Jennifer all put their hands up.

"Rock, paper, scissors, on three—one, two, three."

They shook their fists three times and then Eloise and Libby both chose rock, whilst Jennifer opted for scissors. "Eloise, Libby, you're on the cross-trainer. Decide between you who goes first."

"Exercise bike? Thank you, Amanda." Her hand had shot into the air at once.

"Floor work—Aoife, Jennifer, it's all yours."

"What about you, Jaxon?" This from Eloise.

"Actually, Mark is next on the list." He was so quiet and so reserved that it was almost impossible to remember he was there. "Mark?"

"I'll back Laura up if that's okay? I'm crap on the bike."

"Sure. So I'll back Amanda up on the bike, okay?" They all nodded, but without conviction.

Harris chose this moment to call us to order. "Okay, Crew 41. Start positions please."

Everyone parked their hollotabs in the docks and scrabbled around to their machines, and I tasked those of us watching in the first cycle with monitoring efforts and milestones as they occurred.

It took us almost three hours to complete the task, by which time we were exhausted. First to complete was Amanda and I on the bike, which we managed in just over ninety minutes. We switched around every twenty minutes, which gave us enough time to recover before the next stint, and kept the pace optimal. Jennifer and Aoife completed theirs about ten minutes after me and Amanda. I jumped into the hydro-pool next to Mark, just as he was finishing his stint, and then Laura clambered in beside me. She looked absolutely wiped. With two of us in there we were covering twice the distance in the same time period, so as my stint ended, I organised Jennifer to come to the hydro-pool and take over from me, and then Mark took back over from Laura. Eloise and Libby were really struggling on the cross-trainer, and both complaining about the pain in their arms and shoulders rather than their legs, so Aoife helped them for fifteen minutes, and then I joined her for a stint. It was brutal going—the hydrotherapy pool was the hardest physically, without doubt, as you're pacing on a treadmill through a metre of water, but the cross-trainer was agonising on the backs of my thighs and my upper arms.

Laura took the last few steps in the hydro-pool, and the buzzer sounded for the last time. The entire crew lay back on the floor, panting, drenched in sweat and physically spent.

"Very well done, Crew 41. That's a decent effort. Final time of two hours and forty-nine minutes. You've got nine weeks to get that down to two hours flat, but that's a great time for your first attempt at it." Harris's words washed over me to be honest. I wasn't really listening. Every muscle in my body felt like it was on fire.

"Get yourselves cleaned up, and have a couple of hours' rest, and then we'll open up the games room tonight."

We all pushed ourselves slowly to our feet, retrieved our hollotabs from the dock, and trudged wearily back to the dorm. It was the first time we'd all completed our day simultaneously, so there was a rush for the showers and the inevitable offers from all the girls to let me join them, whilst they winked at each other and laughed about it. Even Laura joined in, although I didn't get the impression that her offer was a joke. God help me.

CHAPTER FOURTEEN

IT TOOK US all a few days to get over the assessment, and it hadn't escaped any of us that we were due another in four days' time. True to form, Harris ran an oxygen alarm at 05:00 the morning after the joint assessment. He didn't make many friends that day, but we formed up in under ninety seconds. Nobody even bothered to dress. We all just lined up in our underwear, eyes bleary and limbs screaming in protest.

Everyone climbed back into bed. Even me. Usually when my brain wakes, it's game over—might as well grab a coffee—but I was beyond exhausted, mentally as well as physically.

My flight performances were improving, but I was struggling to grasp the basics of meteorology and air navigation. I was spending two hours a day in Sim, just working the charts and numbers and studying the Met Office data. Wing was being very patient with me, but I couldn't help thinking my lack of progress on the written stuff had dampened his enthusiasm for me. I redeemed myself slightly later on, during a simulated shuttle launch. As one of two Sigma pilots, Addison charged me with taking the lead and maintaining security around the shuttle. As we entered orbit, a meteor alert triggered on my heads-up display, and I successfully headed it off and destroyed it before it could reach the shuttle. It was the first time I had deployed my weapons, and whilst I'd been taught how they operated and how to use the targeting system, I basically just lined it up and obliterated it with my plasma cannons. Wing was absolutely delighted, and thereafter it seemed I had restored his faith in me.

"We'll have to change your surname from Leith to Lethal."

Hilarious.

That afternoon Hennessey paid us a visit. I hadn't seen her for over a week, and Laura and I were summoned to Cooper's office for the first time in a while. When we arrived, Grealish and Cooper were already in the room. I let Hennessey and Laura sit down in the chairs, and Harris and I stood back by the far wall.

"We've got a lead on our infiltrator. I want you all to see this." Grealish's tone suggested it was serious, so we all focussed on the hollopad, on which he placed a ring.

"They've killed someone in Compression. I don't have any details, but they're celebrating it here. You need to check out your company, as someone is no longer there."

The screen flicked off and Grealish turned back to us.

"This came in last night. In and of itself, it doesn't tell us much that we didn't already know, but it confirms we have a leak outwards as well. Given that we eliminated all but eight ICP personnel for the fraudulent documents given to the infil, we've cross-referenced these with those that had access to information on Prouse's demise last week. The only people with external access to that data are in this room, and in the infirmary, so we're looking closely at the two medics and the HolloDoc operator, and watching the eight suspects from our own team, to see if their paths collide at all." He looked over at Cooper.

"Thank you, Sir. That's not all we've discovered. Thanks to Jaxon finding the chlorhexidine on a cleaning solution bottle, we've been through the entire chemical inventory and found four other solutions that contain chlorhexidine. We've also replaced all the med kits in Echo, and the lab has been analysing the EpiPens. Both of the ones from the kitchen were still full, but one of them had traces of chlorhexidine on the needle. No prints, no DNA. Professional job. Whoever did this dumped the contents of the EpiPen into another container, refilled from one of the chemicals, did the hit, and then refilled the EpiPen with its original contents."

"So, are we still looking at Amanda as a suspect?" I'd made my views on this clear, but it needed asking.

Grealish looked at me. "We can't discount her just yet, Jax. We've seen what she's capable of, and whilst we know for certain that she isn't responsible for Prouse, she is still a person of interest."

"Okay, so are we looking at Eloise and Libby now? They were the only two with access to the kitchens," Laura asked, looking over at me and then back at Grealish. "Sir?"

"They are the priority, yes. We're not recording their bio-bands, though. Too many questions being asked in SECO 2 from people who don't need to know. Not that it would have made a blind bit of difference if we had been recording this whole time, since both of their bands were docked at the time of Prouse's murder. We are still tracking all movements."

The meeting finished up and Laura and I headed back to DECON 1 but were diverted to DECON 4 by Harris.

"Can't go through DECON 1 with those scrubs. They'll incinerate them. Come with me."

He led us back around the building under the fire escape on the skybridge and left into an alley that opened out onto a courtyard.

There were four lots of razor wire fences with electronic gates that we had to pass through one at a time, surrounded by armed ICP for the first two, and BRMC for the last two, scanners on the other side like the ones leading up to Opps. Eventually we entered DECON 4, which was essentially a carbon copy of DECON 1. I stripped off and put my fatigues in a box on the side, which was then passed through some sort of microwave process to kill any and all foreign entities. I gritted my teeth through the freezing oil for a third time and then passed through where Laura was waiting for me by the airlock. We waited out the familiar squeeze and exited into a short corridor which led us to the end of the corridor that housed SECO 2.

We headed back to the dorm, just chatting away. Laura's attitude towards me had improved considerably over the last few days, and I suspect Harris had said something, or maybe even Eloise. That moment of calm passed in an instant, though, as Eloise collared me in the rec room.

"Hey Jax, you offered to give me some help in Conditioning. Any chance we can get an hour in now?"

"Err, sure. Let me get my gear. I'll meet you in there in five." I could have done without it, but I didn't have an excuse not to, so I headed for the dorm.

Laura walked beside me, although she'd gone deathly quiet. As we walked into the dorm, she rounded on me.

"So, you're giving private gym lessons now, are you, Egg-timer?" The renewed use of an expired insult didn't go unnoticed.

I'd promised Eloise not to say anything about what happened, so I just played it straight.

"Not 'lessons', no. She asked me for some help, and I said yes. You were here on the first day in the classroom. You heard Harris tear Leon a new one. We're a crew, and we look out for each other. So yes, I'll help Eloise, and anyone else that asks for it." I was probably a bit defensive, but my patience with her mood swings was wearing thin. I'd always thought the whole 'fiery redhead' thing was just a generic label with zero evidence to support it, but I had to admit, I was starting to see the truth.

"And what if I want some lessons? Will you help me too?"

"Of course. But you're probably the strongest candidate here. How could I possibly help you?"

"I'll think of something." She did that coy smile and flicked her hair, then completely stripped off right in front of me and walked to the showers without a backwards glance.

Jesus fucking Christ.

I grabbed my gym bag and headed back out of the dorm to the conditioning room, where I found Eloise waiting for me. She was still in her fatigues.

"Shall we get started then?" she said, and proceeded to undress in front of me. My head was spinning. I peeled myself out of my fatigues and pulled on my shorts.

"It's warm in here. Don't feel like you have to put your shirt on." She put a hand on my shoulder and bit her lip. I was feeling like a cobra in a room full of mongooses. Mongoose? Mongeese? That needed some thought.

I put my shirt on, more as a kind of 'barrier-to-entry' than anything else. She was right though, it was ridiculously warm in here.

"Straight in the hydrotherapy pool then, Eloise. The best way you're going to build up your core strength is in there. Stick your hollotab in the dock and let's get cracking."

She jumped in and I followed. I set the timer for half an hour—no way we'd last longer than that in one stint. The treadmill was set up for a steady walking pace. It was like trying to wade through treacle. We got on with it though, and she turned out to be decent company. I'd barely spoken to her in the first couple of weeks. I suspected that was more my fault than hers, being that I liked to sit on the periphery rather than get stuck into the chat, but she was easy to talk to and it made the going a bit easier.

"So what have they got you doing in BRDF? You haven't really talked about it."

She's right, I thought, I hadn't. I had two problems here. Firstly, I didn't know what I could and couldn't tell the crew, and secondly, she was one of two people we were actively investigating for murder, and for being a credible threat to the Bertram Ramsay. Of course, she didn't realise that. It hadn't gone unnoticed that she'd started to cosy up to me, and more than once I'd wondered if the bathroom scene was a performance. I couldn't see it though. She'd seemed genuinely distraught; but then, if she were an AoG terrorist and spy, she'd probably have trained for this situation. I figured it would be easier just to let her build her confidence and get to know me, and see if it led to more penetrating questions, so I told her about my flight training and flying up to the Bertram Ramsay in the Sim, and how I was struggling with met and navs. She was attentive, and injected the odd question, but mostly just listened.

"And what's your story, Eloise? How have you ended up here?"

"There's not much to tell. I've had a quiet life, really. Parents died when I was twenty, just as I'd started university. I went to Oxford to do Politics and Law, despite there being zero hope for either profession, but you know what it was like back then—half my peers bleating on about fate and inevitability, and the other half living in hope that it would all just fizzle away. Uni was more about having a purpose and distracting myself from the constant reminder that I only had a decade left to live. After that, much the same as everyone else, really." She shrugged. "Struggled to find a job, let alone a career. Tried to join ICP, but I was turned down after the second assessment—that was two years ago, and then I got my invite, totally out of the blue. I couldn't understand why, and if I'm completely honest, I thought it was all some sort of sick prank."

I could relate.

She talked a bit about her past, growing up on the outskirts of Windsor. Windsor wasn't far from The Bleeds—less than ten miles from where they stopped. She hadn't seen a sunrise until she was ten, because The Bleeds blocked out the light until late morning, but she talked about playing in the fields and climbing trees with her friends, and her face lit up as she remembered those precious moments in her life.

It was a pleasant session. She was easy to like, and I found myself surprised at how well we got on.

We pounded on until the timer went off and then clambered out, legs wobbly from the exertion and utterly drenched from head to toe. It was virtually impossible to keep your footing the entire thirty minutes, so we'd both taken at least one tumble each.

"Come on, Jax. Let's grab a shower. I promise not to cry this time." She giggled and then walked out of the room, hips swinging.

Pool puns aside, I was well out of my depth here. Romance wasn't something I'd had much luck with. I wasn't particularly sociable, and I didn't have any money, so the opportunities afforded to me were brief and inconsequential. Those fleeting moments of intimacy did little to prepare me for the kind of attention I was getting from more than one person, and I wondered about the wisdom of letting anything develop beyond where it already had. We were only going to be a crew for three months, of which there were nine weeks left, and that seemed like a long time to be in a cauldron like this.

I was beginning to realise why they called it Compression.

The man walked down the cobbled alley to where a grand old building stood, a relic from a time when architecture was a social statement, and a reflection of wealth. There was an air of decay about it, and the man wondered how long it would continue to stand in the shadow of The Bleeds.

He knocked on the heavy wooden doors and waited. They were expecting him, and he was nervous. This was a gathering of very high-ranking Acolytes, and it was prudent not to linger in doorways when so many of them, sworn to the righteous cause, were assembled in a single location in High Holborn.

The door was answered by a sallow-faced man with heavy eyebrows and pitted skin; the calling card of a heavy drinker. He was ushered inside and pointed towards an opulent oak staircase, which wound its way upwards around the edges of the hallway. He ascended purposefully and confidently, passing the antique paintings of past masters that stared imperiously down upon him, reminding him that the origins of this building extended well beyond the foundation of the New Order. The light was warm and low; the windows had long since been covered, with no sun filtering through from the eight hundred storeys of condensed housing that dominated the sky above.

The second-floor landing was tiled like a chessboard; black and white squares alternated through the length of the hallway, and it was edged with walnut parquet. The door at the end of the hallway was closed, and so he knocked and waited. It was answered quickly, and he was announced into the room and shown to a seat at the high table.

It was a magnificent table. Polished mahogany with seats for twenty people, all of whom were present. Sixteen men and four women. The chairman raised his glass and turned to the man who had just entered.

"Thank you for joining us. Are our plans in motion and on schedule?"

"Good afternoon, Sir. Thank you for inviting me to speak at this meeting. I am humbled."

The chairman waved his hand impatiently. He had always despised sycophants.

"The operatives will shortly move into Stage 2. The unfortunate incident with the other candidate is behind us, and I have been assured no loss of control will re-occur. The two of them are unaware of each other and are proceeding with their individual plans."

"Very well then." He stood up and leaned his enormous frame on the table, making eye contact with all of them. "Acolytes of Gaia. Sworn protectors of our Mother Earth. Our operatives are inside. There is a plan in place to cause maximum disruption over the next few weeks, and a single event that will cause the evacuation to halt. Our work here is progressing as planned, and despite the unfortunate incident, our operatives remain undiscovered inside Compression. You have all done well, and we will be rewarded when the time comes."

PART 2

CHAPTER FIFTEEN

I WOKE UP AND looked at my bio-band. 05:55. It surprised me to wake so early after yesterday's assessment. I'd managed one hour and nine minutes, which was a significant improvement from where I was just two weeks ago. Between the extra sessions I was putting in with Eloise, and the physical requirements of my training, I was finally seeing results in the assessments.

The whole crew seemed buoyed by their performances, and spirits had been running high last night. I'd spent some time talking to each of them, although Mark still seemed very quiet and remained on the peripheries of the conversation. I honestly felt sorry for him. He'd only done what we all wanted to do at some point, but I suspected he still felt responsible for Leon's death. For most of us, the intensity of Compression made Leon's demise seem like ancient history, but not for Mark. He'd lost control in that room, but he hadn't killed Leon, and I decided to spend a bit more time with him to see if I couldn't get him to relax again.

I showered up and headed out for a coffee. Harris and Hennessey were on the sofas drinking coffee and chatting. They looked up as I approached.

"Morning, Jax. Come and join us. We were just talking about you anyway." Harris grinned.

"Sara, Tyrone." I nodded. "Give me a minute to grab a coffee." I filled my mug and went back to the sofas, parking myself next to Harris. Hennessey gave me a reproachful look, like I should have sat next to her, but there was already too much drama in my life without her complicating it further.

"Today is an important day for you all. Are you looking forward to it?"

I couldn't say I'd given it much thought. After the assessment last night, Hennessey called us into Training 1, just before dinner, and announced that we would move to Stage 2 tomorrow.

"We're advancing you early, given that you are a small crew. We also have two crews arriving tomorrow afternoon, so better that we shift you across rather than have half of you move to a different dorm and walk back to Stage 1. You were due to move over on Monday anyway, and weekend duties are usually light, so you'll head over to Stage 2 tomorrow and can spend the weekend relaxing before we start the second process."

We'd been dismissed, and that had set the stage for the conversation that evening.

"To be honest, I just want to get up there now. I've been to the Bertram and back four times in the Sim, and I'm eager to just crack on."

Harris laughed. "Everyone has to do Compression, mate. You've done the hard part—the first stage is always the most brutal. Everyone is new, everything is new, and it takes some time to acclimatise."

Hennessey looked at her bio-band. "Tyrone, we'd better get ourselves to Opps for the meeting. Jaxon, you'll get up there soon enough. Keep doing what you're doing and you'll have a bright future on the Bertram."

They both got to their feet, bade me a good day and left me to my thoughts. Over the next hour, the crew appeared one by one, looking as knackered and stiff as I was. The conversation was low and lacked energy. There was a definite sense of lethargy clouding us.

Harris returned at 08:00 and assembled us in the rec room on the sofas, which was a first.

"You are moving to Stage 2 now. I want you to grab your gear and meet me back here in five minutes."

Everyone headed back to the dorm to grab their stuff, filling their mini-holdalls with whatever knick-knacks from home they'd brought with them. I didn't bother moving. Everything I had was on me already, as I'd been planning an hour in the steam room this morning.

The crew formed up inside five minutes, and Harris walked us through to SECO 2, where those of us that hadn't had access granted beyond the rec room were given the access to Stage 2 areas, excluding SECO 2 and Opps. That only took a minute, and then he walked us back up the corridor to a set of double doors opposite DECON 4. We entered a long, rectangular room, which was a huge upgrade from our first digs. I could see everyone's eyes widen, and there was a rush for the far corner where we had floor-to-ceiling windows overlooking Launch. The chattering intensified as everyone got excited. It was their first view of the Launch Bay, and whilst empty, it still represented the pathway to our departure. Even Mark was showing signs of interest.

Harris called our attention back to the room. It was much larger than the previous rec room and had a lot more in it. There were sofas and chairs assembled in the middle, like before, and a dining area close to the mullioned windows. There were a dozen skylights in the ceiling, and so the room felt twice as bright as our previous accommodation. In one corner was a huge, wooden bookcase, stacked with books, and a couple of desks to work at. In the south-west corner was a pool table. There were two lots of double doors on the east wall, one set at the north end of the west wall, next to a long hatch—I assumed this was the kitchen—plus another set on the north wall, near the corner.

"Stage 2 is where we train you for your life on board the Bertram Ramsay. You will undertake proper jobs here, and your Crew Leader will announce these on Monday." He nodded at me. "The kitchens in here are manned by staffers, as are the maintenance teams. You are not to discuss your training with them, and we trained them not to talk to you beyond the platitudes of daily life. The conditioning room is beyond those doors on the north wall. The facilities are virtually identical to the ones you are used to, so you are to continue your daily workouts in there. I expect no less than ninety minutes a day, and I have updated your hollotabs with the schedules for training. Your dorm is through those double doors in the middle of the east wall, and the doors a little way up from that are for the training room. Get yourselves settled and familiarise yourself with the facilities, and I will see you all later."

Harris walked out, and the crew headed straight for the dorm. It was basically the same as the previous one—windowless, but well lit, and the shower block was identical, except this one also had a bath in the corner with a low wall around it. There was a moment where they all looked up to see which bed I'd choose, so I made life easier by choosing the bunk again. They weren't laid out quite the same because of the position of the entry door, but otherwise very similar. My bunk was in a corner, and I stowed my kit in the locker next to it, coding the door to my bio-band.

I left the crew and wandered back to the mullioned windows in the corner of the rec room. It still fascinated me to look out and see the tall buildings opposite and to the right, the sunlight dancing across the surface of the hexagonal exoskeleton that shrouded them. I was joined shortly by the rest of the crew, who were all equally fascinated by the view.

"I wonder what that hexagonal frame is for?" said Aoife.

"It's a conduit for static discharge, should one of the aircraft malfunction." Everyone turned to me. I explained about the shuttle and the spheres, and how the gyro-shields captured the escaping energy and recycled it back into the Quirillium Nucleus.

"So you've been out there already, Jax?"

I spent the next half an hour explaining about my training, keeping it vague so as not to give away anything that I might get in trouble for. I told them I hadn't been out there, but I had seen a couple of shuttles launch. Everyone then drifted to the sofas and drank coffee and talked for a while. I tried to get Mark to open up about his days as a flight engineer in the CAF, but it was hard going. He answered most things with as few words as he could and seemed more intent on sitting quietly and watching the group.

We spent the rest of the weekend milling about, with all of us getting some time in the conditioning room. I spent an hour a day over in Opps in the steam room and sauna, but did my training with the crew. Eloise continued to improve, and I joined her for another session in the hydrotherapy pool, which left both of us with wobbly legs for a few hours. By the time Monday arrived, everyone was refreshed and eager to get on with something. As nice as it was to relax, the facilities were limited, and the long weekend had seemed much longer by the time Sunday came around.

On Monday morning, the entire crew got up early. There was a lot of chatter in the dorm, in between people heading in to shower, and a month into the process all inhibitions were gone. Everyone just wandered around in their underwear or a towel and didn't give it a second thought.

I headed to breakfast where I was greeted by a smiling, round-faced woman who offered me everything from scrambled eggs to a full English. I declined, sticking to toast and coffee. I had no idea what was coming today, so felt that loading myself up with greasy food would likely be a mistake.

Laura and I chatted quietly through breakfast. She was keen to join me in the BRDF, but she'd been through the physical training element already, which I was about to face, and speculated as to what she'd be assigned.

We didn't have to wait long to find out. Harris entered and asked us all to join him in the training room.

"This is the second stage of your training, and this will be the most intense. You will take on the occupation you will continue to have when you board the Bertram Ramsay; it is essential that you learn as much as you can so when you finally get up there you hit the ground running. There is no room for inefficiency on a space station, and all of us must play our part. Your earnings from your time here will provide you with enough funds to enjoy your first month on the Bertram."

"Earnings?" Jennifer raised her hand. "You're going to pay us?"

"Sort of. On the Bertram Ramsay there is no physical currency. Your bio-bands have a digital vault, in which is stored our own crypto-currency called Lunar. It is an insular currency and has zero face value outside of the Bertram Ramsay. Even here, it is worth nothing."

"So, what's the point of it? If everything is free anyway?" Aoife had a way of making everything sound negative, even unexpected money.

"Once on board the Bertram Ramsay there are plenty of leisure facilities and bars. We have our own brewery and distillery on board, and several places to drink in each of the globes." There was a sudden increase in murmuring between us, and I could see not only excitement but also a bit of relief that there was an air of normality on board the space station.

"You are credited with a fixed sum of Lunar, monthly, which you can spend on these activities and leisure. You cannot buy anyone else a drink, or food, as the currency also acts as an exchange of information, tracking your diet and updating your nutritional needs constantly. Nobody goes hungry, and there's nothing to save for, so you may as well use it and enjoy it, but there are limits on certain activities because of the number of occupants in each globe wishing to use them."

It made sense. Harris explained that whilst drinking was okay, getting drunk was not, and so our alcohol intake was limited by our body mass to ensure that nobody got out of hand, or made themselves ill. "Space is dangerous enough, without people getting drunk and operating essential systems with a hangover."

There was a smattering of chatter following this, and I detected an air of defiance amongst the smaller women who clearly felt like their alcohol intake ought to be the same as everyone else's. If I had to guess, I'd say Aoife would likely drink us all under the table.

"So, today you are going to go through individual assessments and interviews to determine your occupation on board the Bertram Ramsay. There is an element of choice involved, although your assessments will ultimately take precedent. Jaxon, you'll be heading over to Opps—your routine remains unchanged. The rest of you, go back to the rec room and start reading the information we've uploaded to your hollotabs. You'll be called in one at a time during the course of the day."

I took my leave and headed to the dorm to grab my gear, before leaving for Opps. Addison was waiting for me as I entered and took me through to suit up and have my Armadillo installed.

"You're going to do one-on-one combat training today in the Sim. There's another crew in a Sim in California, and you'll be going head-to-head with one of their brightest, or so I'm told. The Sims are linked, so you will fly the same terrain at the same time, and you will navigate to each other, and then try to shoot each other down. You have a specific mission to accomplish, as do they, and their job is to hinder yours and complete theirs. And vice versa. Today's battleground is New York City, because that provides the most challenging terrain for combat—tight streets and tall buildings with lots and lots of places to hide and turn. It'll be fun."

I was sceptical about the 'fun' part. I loved flying, and it was good to feel like I had some sort of purpose here, but to pit me against another human seemed like a recipe for disaster. Wing explained my mission objectives.

"You have three primary missions. Your first mission is to park your Sigma on the forward deck of the USS Intrepid. The Intrepid is a floating museum on the Hudson River, but nearly three hundred years ago she was the pinnacle of wartime weaponry. She also assisted in the recovery of Mercury and Gemini spacecraft, which is why she has special significance to this programme."

"And I just have to land on her?"

"Yes, and no. You need to hold it for twenty seconds before you can release. If you lift off before the twenty seconds is up, the clock resets, so choose your moment wisely, as once you're in the thick of battle this will be a much harder mission objective to complete."

The words 'the thick of battle' made the hairs on the back of my neck stand up. Addison was being unusually serious, and I wondered what was at stake for him in this. He explained that my opponent had the same mission objectives, and that their designated LZ (landing zone) was the derelict Ravenswood Power Station in Queens.

"Your second objective is a simple seek-and-destroy mission. Find your opponent and blow them to kingdom come."

"And the third?"

"Bring your Sigma home. Preferably in one piece." How to inspire confidence, by Addison Nile.

"Jaxon, I'll be your RIO for this hop, but I can only offer communications that your first officer would in normal circumstances, and not give advice on how to do things, or answer questions to that effect. The flight recorders will get every word I say, regardless of vox, as they use these to check the validity of the win/loss and also as part of training Sims for new pilots."

"What's a RIO?"

"Sorry, old jargon. Used to stand for Radar Intercept Officer back when warplanes had a pilot and navigator on board. These days, they are totally redundant, but we use the term RIO to mean 'First Officer' I suppose."

"Okay, so what's the strategy? Do I attempt to complete my LZ mission first or do I attempt to prevent him or her from completing theirs?"

"I can't make that decision for you. The whole point of this process is to iron out mistakes, so you're allowed to make as many as you like as long as you learn from them. There is a right and a wrong way here, but there have also been occasions when the wrong way yields results and vice versa, although we've never had a definitive winner."

"Never?"

"It's a tough mission. Almost everybody completes at least one of the three objectives, and occasionally two. But not all three. Your number one aim should be to return home safely. I can give you that much. How you prioritise your other two objectives is entirely up to you."

"So if I feel I'm going to fail my missions, I should try to make it home?"

"Better to retire safely with an intact aircraft than to push a dangerous scenario and risk your own life. Obviously this is a Sim, so there's no real-world danger here, and so far we've never had an enemy in the history of space flight, so this is about preparing for the things we haven't conceived of, and honing your decision-making process, your skills and your reflexes so that if and when that day comes, you will be ready."

"Okay, let's do this."

Once my Armadillo was installed, I headed over to Sim with Addison. He was his usual jovial self, but I couldn't help noticing a slight edge to his tone. I had the distinct impression that this exercise was more important to him than it was to me, but I kept that to myself. The last thing I needed was him giving me some dire warnings that would increase my nervousness. Every time I stepped into the mockpit I could feel every sinew in my body tighten, and my breathing get shallower. It was always fine once I was in the air, but until now I'd just been cruising around and sightseeing. This was my first combat mission, and I was anxious.

Wing loaded up his hollotab and asked me to dock mine to the left side of the console. He explained that it would monitor my biometrics for analysis during debrief. I went through the pre-flight checklist, which, honestly, was short—once I was in an actual aircraft, I would have to do a visual inspection of the exterior, but it was pointless doing that here unless I wanted to inspect the outside of a room.

I spun up the spheres and then powered the reactor, feeling the usual thrill of anticipation as the vessel vibrated underneath me.

"Tower, Sigma 242, request clearance for launch."

"Sigma 242, you are clear to launch. Go get 'em, Flight."

I smiled. It was the first time that Tower had engaged with anything other than the standard protocols, and it made me realise there was a team behind me here.

I throttled up to hover, retracted the gear, told Wing to hold on to his knickers and took off vertically. I continued to rise well beyond the normal level of three hundred metres, and could feel Wing looking sideways at me. Usually I would stop and check the skies during an escort mission, but my scopes were clear, and I'd been told to do it my way. I figured if I had to come down over New York, better to enter from sub-orbit than to take the long route across the Atlantic. It would probably give me an extra two minutes at most, but that would be enough for me to complete my first mission.

As we approached the stratosphere, I took it out of VTOL and pointed us skywards, continuing to check the scopes for any sign of my target before bursting through into space and that wonderful view of the stars. I hoped this feeling would never get old. I cruised over to the US at a steady 15,000 kph just below our normal orbital pathway, and then started my descent as I crossed the southern tip of Greenland, making re-entry somewhere over Massachusetts.

I could see Manhattan Island in my forward view and decided now was the time to hit the deck and stay low. There was no such thing as flying under the radar these days. Satellite technology had changed the game totally. I couldn't even hide inside a building, as my reactor signature would glow like a beacon on their sights. But getting low would give me cover. It would also stifle my own view, but that wasn't important until there was any engagement. I brought the Sigma down to twenty metres off the deck, skimming the east shores of New York State, before rounding Staten Island and heading upriver to the Intrepid.

It was eerily quiet. Wing hadn't said a word since we left, but I could feel his gaze upon me every minute or so, as if he was assessing my mental state.

"Wing, bring the weapons system up, but leave the targeting array for now. I want an unobstructed view ahead."

"Weapons systems, aye, Flight. Systems online."

I could see the Intrepid ahead of me and slowed my approach to 500 knots, which was still breakneck speed this low to the ground. The forward deck housed several ancient warplanes, but there was space between the bridge and the bow to make my landing.

"Hold tight, Wing. Have my timer ready."

I stayed at 500 knots and brought myself up to fifty metres, my fingers extended out to the brakes, and my right thumb hovering over the VTOL button. This was going to be very close. I held on to my cruising speed until the very last second, and then pulled the kill switch, and hit the VTOL button, throttling forward in one seamless movement. The AI kicked in at five metres, dropping the landing gear, and lowered us onto the deck.

I couldn't believe how easy this had been so far, and I could feel the hairs on the back of my neck prickling. I could only conclude that my American counterpart had chosen to do the same thing and was currently sitting on their pad in Queens. So that's one mission failed already, I thought, but no point lamenting that. The timer ticked down, agonisingly slowly. As it passed five seconds, I readied the throttle and hovered over the VTOL. My hollotab lights went green, and I shot up to a hundred metres.

As I stopped to switch to forward flight, all hell broke loose. Six Sigmas broke cover from the buildings on my right and started firing upon me. I throttled forward and powered away.

"Wing, what the fuck is going on? Why are there half a dozen Sigmas shooting at me?"

"Flight, take a breath. Deal with it. That's what you're training for."

Fucking fantastic. Thanks for the pep talk.

"Give me my HUD. Left screen only." I needed my targeting systems, but right now I didn't need them clotting up my forward view.

"Systems up, left screen only, Flight."

I turned at extraordinary speed, under the George Washington Bridge, and right towards uptown Manhattan. The buildings flashed under me like bullets, and my proximity sensors were flashing red on the underside. I turned right onto Broadway and got myself down to five metres. The streets were littered with cars and pedestrians, and I was thankful that this was a simulation. I had no idea what I was doing here, and I'd hate for my incompetence to kill innocent people on the streets. I took a sharp left at 165th Street and headed for the East River. The abandoned Ravenswood Generating Station was just the other side of Roosevelt Island. As I went to turn right onto the river, the building on my left exploded and I had to pull up and right sharply to avoid being taken out with it.

"Wing, where are they? I can't look for them and fly this thing. Keep talking to me."

"Yes, Flight. You have three Sigmas directly behind, in close pursuit. The other three are over midtown. They look like they're heading to cut you off."

"Marvellous. It's almost like someone told them where I was heading." I gave Wing a sarcastic look, and he just grinned at me.

Six against one were impossible odds, especially for a rookie like me. I wondered if my counterpart was having to face similar odds.

The three Sigmas on my tail were staying glued. I couldn't shake them. I needed to fly into the maze of midtown and see if I couldn't use the buildings as cover. I pulled over right and then zig-zagged my way through the centre of town. My inertia suit was squeezing me everywhere, simulating the force of taking these corners at stupid speeds. I had to be careful—whilst the Sigma's manoeuvring capabilities were totally out of this world, flying at this speed through high buildings was going to get me killed quicker than I'd get shot, so I dialled it back to 200 knots, and continued to turn sharply, doubling back on myself, and then turning around again. Nothing was shaking them. I headed towards the Chrysler

Building to see if I could throw them off by circling it, but they just stuck to me like glue, firing their plasma cannons indiscriminately. I wondered if they'd been told to destroy as much of the landscape as they could, and whether my drawing them into it would count against me. For the next ten minutes, I battled with the terrain, pushing the Sigma hard around turns and under bridges, trying desperately to shake my pursuers, but they were clinging to me.

I needed a fresh approach. Albert Einstein once said, "*The definition of insanity is doing the same thing over and over again and expecting different results.*" I don't think I've ever really understood that expression until now. Time to change things up, and I had an idea.

"Wing, how do the Sigmas cope with water?"

"I'm sorry, Flight, repeat?"

"Wing, can I put this aircraft in the water or not?"

"I have no idea, Flight, sorry."

Fuck it. Only one way to find out. I turned about and headed down Lexington, keeping my speed to 200 knots, before turning into 59th Street and heading for the Queensboro Bridge. As soon as I made the turn, I powered the throttle forward to 1,000 knots, staying right of the bridge so as not to enter its frame. I broke free of the buildings, and the moment I flew over water I hit the VTOL button and shot downwards into the river. The impact felt like hitting concrete through my suit, but that didn't matter. The AI kicked in five metres from the riverbed and stalled us. I powered down the system and sat there, taking stock.

I could see all six Sigmas now on my HUD. The three behind me had continued over the river before stopping. They were circling the power station; I assumed, looking for me. Wing was just grinning at me from his seat. I must have done something right, or something idiotic. The other three Sigmas were circling the Intrepid.

I powered up and throttled forward, dead slow. The water was murky, and visibility was almost zero, and I had to be careful not to create a wake that would be visible from the skies, so I switched the screens to radar and navigated slowly through a wire-frame render of the riverbed. I wondered why the image quality was so basic, but then realised they probably hadn't bothered to render riverbeds for a simulator that was supposed to operate in space. That seemed like a flaw in the thought process to me. I cornered the southern tip of Roosevelt Island and turned northwards to the power station, keeping one eye on the scopes for Sigmas. The three that had been tailing me had broken formation and were running lanes across Manhattan Island searching for me.

The other Sigmas were coming this way at some speed, and it took me a minute to realise there were four of them. The front one was weaving left and right, trying to break free of the relentless chase. This was my US counterpart. I was sure of it.

"Wing, keep my weapons hot and ready. We need to end this thing now."

"Flight, weapons ready."

I pulled my controller closer to me and watched as the Sigma chase continued towards me. I would probably only have one chance at this, and I was going to take it. They were flying west up 41st Avenue now, towards Queensbridge Park. I waited until they'd just made it to Vernon Blvd before maxing my throttle and leaping out of the riverbed, all weapons firing. I rotated forward to concentrate my fire ahead of them, and then watched as not one or two, but all four of the Sigmas flew directly into my path of fire before they even knew I was there. They exploded in a fiery mess, littering the landscape with debris, and scorching the park before cascading one by one into the river.

I raised my hands to the air and shouted, "Yes!" at the top of my voice, punching the air with my fists. What a total rush. Then, remembering that there were another three Sigmas inbound, I hit the VTOL and the throttle, and shot into space. No sense waiting for them to come and get me. Wing had been clear—priority one is to return home safely. I'd destroyed my target, and half of the ones I wasn't expecting, and I'd completed my mission on the Intrepid. Time to take us home.

I was elated. For the first time in my life, I actually felt like I was good at something. We pushed through into orbit and came out about six minutes in front of the orbital trajectory of the Bertram Ramsay.

"Tower, Sigma 242. Request permission for Orbital Recon."

"Sigma 242, this is Tower. Congratulations, Flight. Enjoy your fly-by."

I laughed, and so did Wing who actually clapped me, and then took a short reconnaissance circuit of Globe 9 before heading back to Echo. My entire body was buzzing as I brought the Sigma to a standstill on the pad and powered down the reactor. Eighty-one minutes. That's all it had been, but it had felt like a week.

Wing grinned at me. "Fucking first-class, Jaxon. Come on, let's get you out of that suit. I've got a surprise for you." He walked me through to the flight room, removed my Armadillo, then asked me to follow him.

I wondered if I was about to be treated to a new part of the facility, or some sort of secret pilot room, but he walked through Opps without a backward glance, steering me left towards Stage

2. He opened the double doors and gesticulated for me to enter. "After you."

As I entered the rec room, I was met with a wall of noise. My entire crew was there, clapping me and cheering, along with Harris and Hennessey. I could feel myself blushing, and I must have been grinning my head off. Everyone was congratulating me and patting me on the back, and the girls were hugging me and kissing my face. Even Aoife kissed me on the cheek and said, "Fucking smashed it, Jax. Good for you."

Harris walked over and shook my hand, and I looked between him and Addison. "How do you all know about this?"

"It's my fault, Jax. I didn't tell you because I knew you'd get nervous if you knew they were watching. It's tradition for a crew to watch a first combat flight of a fellow crew member. Few of them get to experience it, because most crews don't have a candidate for BRAF. I'm genuinely proud of you, Flight." Addison clapped me on the shoulder.

Harris looked similarly joyous. "We've never had a victor, Jax. Neither have the Americans. Usually the first combat mission ends in everyone being blown apart, and it rarely lasts longer than about twenty minutes. That was absolutely superb." He did a mock punch to my gut, then patted me on the back and pointed to the training room. I walked across and saw the entire room was wall-to-wall holloscreens. On my left were visuals of the inside of the Sigma. In front was a bird's-eye view of the combat zone, and on the right was my cockpit view, and all of my screens. They'd seen everything from every angle.

"Better get back to your crew. They look like they have some celebrating in mind."

I partied with my crew for the whole afternoon and evening. Harris even chipped in a case of beer and wine for us, which definitely brought me some plaudits. They had really needed to blow off some steam after the intensity of Stage 1. It didn't take long before some smart arse decided my nickname should be Red October, for hiding my Sigma underwater, but I didn't complain. It was certainly better than Egg-timer.

The kitchen staff laid on a buffet for us for the evening, which made everything more relaxed as everyone picked at it and ate at the sofas. I was the centre of attention for the whole evening, with questions coming at me from all sides. The crew, whilst delighted with my victory, seemed most in awe of the Bertram Ramsay fly-by, as none of them had seen it before. I couldn't blame them—I'd felt exactly the same the first time I saw it. At 22:00 I was just about burned out, happy to sit on the peripheries and listen to the conversation, but I decided to get showered. By the time I'd come out of the Sim I felt like I needed an hour in a bath, but I hadn't had an opportunity since getting back to the rec room, so I decided on a hot shower, and then bed.

I stripped off and grabbed a towel, before climbing under the steaming jets of water, and letting the heat soak through me. About a minute later, Laura appeared at the opening to my cubicle, wearing only a towel. I was completely naked, and not sure whether to cover up as she'd already walked in on me previously, but before I'd had a chance to, she'd dropped her towel, walked straight to me, grabbed my face in her hands and kissed me full on the mouth.

"The crew were rewarded for your performance today," she said, leaning close to my ear, "so I thought you should be rewarded too..."

CHAPTER SIXTEEN

THE FOLLOWING MORNING I got up, still slightly dazed from the night before. I hadn't drunk very much so expected a clear head, but my memory of the evening's overture had other ideas.

I dressed and headed out to the rec room to grab a coffee and chill for a while before the entire crew woke, but just as I was about to sit down I heard a familiar pulsing noise. I ran back to the dorm and woke up the crew. They needed to see this.

Everyone jumped out of bed in various states of undress and followed me out to the mullioned windows. The shuttle must have arrived during the night and was being loaded up by the ground crew. I stood at the back of the group—I'd seen it before, and just watched them marvel at the size of the shuttle and the two Sigmas stationed either side of it.

"Is that what you were flying yesterday, Jax?" Aoife pointed at the Sigmas. They all turned to look at me.

"One and the same," I said, grinning back at them. We stood and watched as the shuttle began spinning up the spheres, and I talked them through the blue light and the spinning mesh. Laura crept up behind me and grabbed my hand, giving it a squeeze before letting go and stepping in front of me. She looked stunning this morning, despite looking no different than she had any other time, but her vivid red hair just glowed in the dawn light and I couldn't help looking over her body and remembering the night before.

Slowly, the two Sigmas lifted five metres from the ground, and we watched as they rotated through three hundred and sixty degrees, as they taught us to do before launch. Shuttle security was the principle priority of the BRAF, and both pilots were synchronous in their movements. The pair shot up three hundred metres, where they remained, rotating slowly, facing in opposite directions. The all-clear must have been given, because the next moment, the shuttle raised itself with the stanchions keeping the spheres level in its giant push-up. I could feel the pilot increase the power, and the pulses shook through us all as it quickly ascended from the launch pad, until it reached the Sigmas and they turned as one and shot off to the stratosphere.

The crew were energised and excited by what they had seen. Speculation about the uniforms on the boarding staff dominated the morning conversation, and how many people could sit on the enormous vessel. It wasn't until Harris entered at 08:00 that most of them realised they were still in their underwear, and rushed back to the dorm, laughing.

"I dunno how you cope, mate. Two blokes surrounded by six women. Must be a total mind-fuck."

"You've no idea." I didn't fancy going down this line of conversation though, and Harris must have sensed it because he changed the subject at once.

"I hear the crew have a new nickname for you, Jax. Or shall I call you Red?"

I laughed. "Jax will be just fine, thank you, Tyrone. They'll have thought of something else in a week, anyway."

"No doubt. It's going to be a busy week for your crew. Not much changes for you, although you've got some hand-to-hand combat training to start today, and you need to continue with your conditioning program. Next assessment is only a few days away."

"What have the crew got in store today, then?"

"Occupations assessment and allocation. Lots of written tests and interviews. They'll be wrung out by the evening. There are a couple of gimmes in there—we'll be putting Mark on flight engineering, and Laura will join you in a few weeks, so no point allocating her with anything long term. In fact, I recommend you put her in charge of the troops while you're over at Opps."

"I thought I already had?"

"Yes, and no. She's been named as your Deputy Crew Leader, but you haven't actually communicated to the team than she's in charge when you're not here. Best do that this morning, so they're all aware and on board."

"Why can't I just make her the crew leader? I'm not cut out for leadership, mate. Sure, I can tell them what to do, but it's out of my comfort zone."

"The fact that you don't crave the power of leadership is exactly why you'll be good at it. It's only a crew, Jax. They already look to you as their leader, whether you want it or not."

"But I don't want it."

Harris looked at me with one of his penetrating gazes. "Look, carry on for now. You haven't got to do much, but your crew has had a rocky ride of it so far, and they need a little consistency. If you really don't want it by the time you step up to Stage 3, then sure, we can make a change, but I think it'd be a crying shame."

I didn't know how to respond to that.

The crew drifted out one by one over the next five minutes until they were all assembled on the sofas.

"Crew 41. The speech I gave you yesterday was real, despite me using it to convince Jaxon here that you'd be spending the time doing assessments. Today, those assessments will begin, and we'll allocate you to your final occupations on board the Bertram Ramsay. Jaxon?"

I guessed that was my cue. Cheers for the heads-up, Tyrone.

"As Tyrone says, today is important. You're not being given a position for just three months—these will be your permanent positions on board the station, so give it your maximum effort. I'll be over in Opps all day, continuing my training. In my absence, as the Deputy Crew Leader, Laura will be in charge. If you need anything, or have any questions, she is at your disposal. Okay?"

They nodded, to my great surprise, and I took my leave, heading through to Opps for today's training.

Grealish, Hennessey and Cooper were all sitting in Cooper's office. The mood was grim.

"It's been confirmed. We definitely have two operatives inside Echo, no question about it. We know it's not Jaxon or Laura, which means that thirty-three per cent of the remaining crew are AoG spies. That's a tremendous problem, and we need to find a way to overcome it, and soon. They're also planning a big attack, which is designed to keep all future crews on the ground."

"Sir, what's the intel on this? Is it the same source?" Cooper looked at Grealish. He looked tired this morning, and his usual youthful vigour was replaced by anxiety and concern.

He pulled out his hollotab and a watch from his pocket, and placed it on the flat surface. A screen flickered into life, and the distorted voice reverberated through the room.

"They've just finished a huge meeting of all the top players in AoG. This was the last thing said in the meeting."

There was a click, and then a voice recording. *"Our operatives are inside. There is a plan in place to cause maximum disruption over the next few weeks, and a single event that will cause the evacuation to halt. Our work here is progressing as planned, and despite the unfortunate incident, our operatives remain undiscovered inside Compression."*

The recorder clicked off, and the distorted voice came back. *"I don't have an inside track on the plan, but I've no reason to doubt their capability or their resolve. Don't switch off."*

The screen faded, and Grealish looked over at Hennessey and Cooper. "We can't tell Jaxon or Laura about this, and I'm on the fence about telling Tyrone. This message clearly conveys three things." He counted off on his fingers. "One, they have more than one operative inside Compression. Two, they have a plan to attack the facility with an event large enough to halt the entire operation. Three, the reference to the 'unfortunate incident' also proves that they have a communication pathway out of the facility, which must lead us to conclude that a senior team member in Compression Echo is a mole for the AoG."

"Why wouldn't you tell Tyrone? You surely can't suspect him? You brought him in to this investigation yourself." Cooper looked between the pair of them, eyebrows raised.

"Andrew's right." Hennessey sighed and leaned back in her chair. "For all we know it could be Tyrone, or any one of our BRMC team." She raised her hand as Cooper was about to protest. "But I think it's unlikely. He's been a key component in this investigation from day one, and we've rotated him through this facility for almost four years. Why would he leave it until now? He could have sabotaged this operation from the inside at any point. It doesn't make sense."

"There's something else to consider," replied Cooper. "Well, two things really. Firstly, the words they used were 'cause the evacuation to halt'. Not the operation. The evacuation. So we need to consider what kind of event could occur that would stop an entire global evacuation effort."

"And the second?" Grealish looked thoughtful.

"They also said 'despite the unfortunate incident'. Why would they use that phrase, unless Leon's death was not part of it, and might have led us to one or both of the operatives inside?"

"What are you implying, Amy? That Prouse wasn't supposed to be killed? Or that the killer may have inadvertently led to us discovering the infil?"

Cooper shrugged. "Pick one. We'll never know, but it might give us pause for thought. For example, who did it implicate?"

"Well, nobody. We're no closer to finding out who did it," replied Grealish.

"No, I'm with you, Amy." Hennessey nodded at her. "It's not about who committed the act. It's about who it implicated. So let's go back through it—who do we know is not responsible or implicated? Jaxon, for sure. Jennifer and Amanda were both in SECO 2 the whole day, except for when Amanda fronted Leon up in the shower block, and we have every word of that recorded, and her bio-band tracked. So it wasn't her. Aoife is exonerated by Amanda's bio-band recording, and the tracking shows her in the rec room after she left the shower block anyway. Mark kicked the crap out of him, but implicated himself, so I'm not sure that fits unless he is the actual infil, in which case his actions were stupid."

"Or brilliant." Amy shrugged again. "Hiding in plain sight. He deliberately implicated himself, knowing that it would eventually unravel."

"That's a push. I mean, the guy is intelligent. We know that from his file and his aptitude tests, but that's a real stretch. Don't you think? Andrew?"

"I don't know what to think. We're left with Libby and Eloise, who we already suspected. We also suspected Amanda. We know she didn't kill Leon, but could she still be an infiltrator? What about Laura? Was she accounted for?"

"Yep. Laura's bio-band is her alibi. Besides which, we walked her into that facility. It would have to be a hell of a gamble for the AoG to place her in a position where we might just do that. No, that doesn't make any sense at all." Cooper was about to continue when Hennessey gasped out loud.

"What? Sara?"

"Where's the recording of Amanda confronting Leon in the shower block? Do you have it here?"

"It's on my hollotab, hang on." Cooper reached into her drawer and pulled out her hollotab, found the file and hit play.

First, the sound of footsteps and a door closing, and then they could hear Leon screaming.

"Now, listen here, you little fuck. I have more important things to do while I'm here than put up with your shit. We're not all fucking tourists, and we didn't all get chosen for our aptitude tests. They put me here for

a reason, and if you get in my way, I'll break every fucking bone in your body. I've had training that you can't imagine, and if I get the urge to slot you and make it look accidental, it'll be easy. And it wouldn't even be the first time. So I suggest you shut your fucking mouth, because I'm dying to practise on someone, and you're at the top of the list. Got it?"

"Yes, YES. Just let go of my fucking arm. You're going to break it, you evil..." It finished with the unmistakable sound of a punch landing, then the sound of Amanda leaving.

Cooper clicked off the hollotab and looked at Hennessey.

"We've got it all back to front. All of it." Hennessey stared at the floor, a strange look on her face.

"Start making sense, Sara." Grealish looked bewildered.

"Okay, we've made an assumption that her words implicate her as the infil. Specifically, 'We're not all fucking tourists, and we didn't all get chosen for our aptitude tests. They put me here for a reason, and if you get in my way, I'll break every fucking bone in your body. I've had training that you can't imagine...' But what if she isn't an infil? What kind of person would be 'put here for a reason'?"

"Jesus fucking Christ." Amy looked at Hennessey and then at Grealish. "Amanda's one of us, Sir. Got to be. Some deep cover unit, and of course they wouldn't tell us."

"Holy shit. This is becoming a nightmare." The three of them sat quietly for a minute, each contemplating the implications of Amanda being ICP.

"What do we do, Sir? Call the brass and ask the question?"

"Christ, no. For a kick-off, we're not even sure. She could still be the infil. And if Sara's right, we can't blow her cover to the brass. She'd be rendered ineffective and returned to unit. No, if she really is ICP then she's on our side, and doing a decent job of hiding her identity because we thought she might be AoG. We need to talk to her. Sara, we need to find a way to get Amanda, Tyrone, Jaxon and Laura over here together, without causing a scene. Can you make it work?"

"Andrew, is that the best idea? You'd be blowing Laura and Jaxon's cover to Amanda. What if we're wrong?"

"She's either a spy for us, or a spy for them. Anyone have another alternative? No? Right, so if she's a spy for us, and she doesn't come clean, we'll give her the boot, and then it doesn't matter what she knows about Laura and Jaxon. Sara, can you get them all over here?"

"Yep. Give me a couple of hours. We'll have to do this a different way."

"This better pan out, Sara. If it doesn't, I'm going to have to start putting together a failure protocol for the entire crew. The risks are becoming too great, and if we can't cut off the head of the snake, we'll just have to remove them all."

CHAPTER SEVENTEEN

IT WAS AN interesting start to the day for me. They ushered me into the conditioning room where they'd laid out some sort of sparring mat for a small group of BRDF officers. I was the outsider really, having only been given the opportunity a few weeks ago, but they were friendly enough, and a few of them made comments about my performance in the combat exercise.

We spent the next hour working on various techniques—aikido and shorinji kempo predominantly, and the focus was on putting people down quickly and effectively, using their body mass against them. More than once it reminded me of the sort of moves Amanda put on Leon, and it was clear to me that she'd done this training, or something very similar.

After this lesson they walked me through to a room beyond the Flight Readiness room, where one entire wall was a locked cabinet. My instructor, Jonathon, opened the nearest cabinet door and extracted a short baton—and I mean short. It couldn't have been much over six inches long, with a small sphere at either end—one blue and one orange.

"This is your Paroxysm Baton. It's a bit of a mouthful, but we call it the Proxy for short. Your Proxy is your only weapon or means of defence when you are Earthbound, so you need to learn to handle it properly and effectively, and deploy it with speed and accuracy."

So that's what it was called. I'd been on the receiving end in my youth. Back in The Bleeds we referred to them as 'Sleepers'.

He passed it over to me, and I gripped it in my fist. One end of it was stippled, with small bumps, and the other end was completely smooth.

"You'll notice the difference in feel at both ends. The stippled end is your weapon, and the smooth end is your shield. It is necessary to differentiate by feel, because in a combat scenario you don't need to be looking at your Proxy to see which way up you have it. To deploy either just requires a small amount of pressure at either end—you'll feel a slight give, almost like an inset button."

I squeezed, but nothing happened. I tried again, making sure I only squeezed at one end, but still it wouldn't deploy.

"You can only use this if it's coded to your bio-band or bio-monitor. You could apply pressure a hundred times and nothing would happen. Here, give it back and I'll show you."

I handed it over, and watched as he gripped it with his fist held vertically with the stippled end up, so that it pointed the orange sphere to the ceiling, and the blue to the floor. He applied gentle pressure, and an oval blue shield appeared in front of him, shimmering slightly.

"This is an EM shield. It's a scaled-down version of the technology used on the shuttle and the Sigmas for re-entry. Nothing can pass through it at all, and it is a natural repellent. Try to touch it."

I wasn't too impressed with the thought of trying to lay hands on the blue oval. I wondered if I was about to get zapped just for shits and giggles, but I did it anyway. As I approached it tentatively with my closed fist, I hit an invisible wall, a couple of inches from the shield itself.

"This same EM field also surrounds the Bertram Ramsay and deflects almost all collisions, from meteors to space debris. As you can see, you can't even touch it, which makes it very useful when projectiles are thrown or shot at you. And the shield itself extends beyond the edges of the oval by a full thirty centimetres in every direction, making it very effective at preserving life." He squeezed again, and this time the shield went out.

"And the other end?" I knew full well what it could do.

"Ah, well, that's the clever bit. The other end sends a pulse that will render your opponent inert. You need to point that end towards your enemy. Anyone in the direct path, friend or foe, will drop like a sack of spuds. It's non-lethal, and will put them out for between twenty minutes and twelve hours, depending on how long you hit them for. If you twist the top you can also reverse it and wake them up. We have lethal options on the Bertram, and a range to practise on, but that's not part of our arsenal here. We also have a medical intervention device that revives them should you accidentally take out one of your team."

I spent the next thirty minutes having my Proxy coded to me, being shown how to stow it so it was easy to access the correct way up, and practising deploying the shield. Jonathon offered to render me inert so I could feel the sensation, but I declined with thanks. I'd been knocked out enough times in my life.

We finished up, and I handed back my Proxy and wandered through to Conditioning.

An hour in the steam room eased my muscles after the morning's combat training, so I decided to get myself fitter and hit the exercise machines. My hollotab slotted into the dock and I got to work. Twenty minutes into being put through my paces, Harris entered. I was on the rowing machine, so he tapped his bio-band and held up five fingers, before pointing back out the door. I assumed he meant Launch View, as that had become the regular perch for our chats.

I pulled my sweats on over my shorts, grabbed my kit bag and belt, and navigated to Launch View where, sure enough, I found Harris waiting for me.

"Sara wants to see us. SECO 2. Let's go." He stood up and walked out.

"Couldn't you have just said that to me in Conditioning?" I said to his retreating backside. He completely ignored me and continued walking. Must be serious.

I followed him through security and back down the tunnel to the double doors, and through the second set to SECO 2, where we found Sara and Laura waiting for us.

"Yes, Captain," said Tyrone. "You wanted to see us?"

"There's been a development, but we have a situation we need to deal with, in a specific way. Tyrone, I need you to get Amanda; tell her it's her assessment time, and then take her through the exit airlock in Stage 1 and up to Cooper's office, through the main entrance." She then addressed all three of us. "Whatever happens, whatever is discussed in that room, you're to keep your cards close to your chests. Don't be emotional, or show surprise. I will explain all in due course. You two, you're coming with me across the skybridge."

We followed Hennessey out of SECO 2, turning right and then right again, to the airlock on the skybridge which we crossed and navigated our way up to Cooper's office. Laura and I exchanged a few looks, and I wondered what we were about to walk into. We entered the office to find Grealish and Cooper already there.

"Come in and take a seat. We've got a lot to go through." Grealish pointed at the seats in the corner. Whilst a decent-sized office, recently a couple of us had taken to leaning against the back wall, but today there were more chairs, and someone had centralised one in the room.

"We've had a big development, which I'll be taking you through step by step in due course. I need you all to contribute to the discussion afterwards. No ideas are bad. We have a serious issue to contend with, and we need a plan of action right now. Game faces on please when Tyrone—"

Grealish stopped mid-sentence as the door opened and Tyrone ushered Amanda into the room. She glanced around and her face looked almost relieved, although there was a flicker of concern there. Or was it fear?

Cooper stood up. "Take a seat please, Amanda." She pointed at the vacant chair in the centre of the room.

"You got my message then?" Amanda looked between Grealish and Cooper.

"Your message?" replied Cooper, puzzlement on her face.

Amanda's brow furrowed, and she scanned our faces for an answer. "Why am I here?" she asked. It felt like she'd made an assumption and was doubting herself.

"Amanda, is there anything you want to tell us? Anything you feel we should know?" Grealish's tone was gentle but firm.

"I…." She looked around again and then breathed out. "Fuck."

"Spill. Tell us everything." Grealish took a seat to face her. "If you choose to omit anything, you will be escorted from this facility immediately."

"You can't do that. You have no idea what's going on here."

"I assure you we can and we will. So why don't you tell us what we don't know? Or what you think we don't know." Cooper's tone was more confrontational.

Amanda grimaced and shook her head. "Fuck. I knew this would happen. Fuck fuck fuck." She looked up at Grealish. "Sir, I can't tell you anything. If you think you know who I am, then you'll know why. And certainly not in front of these guys." She motioned towards Laura and I with her thumb over her shoulder.

"Everyone in this room is actively involved in a serious investigation. Anything you have to say stays in this room, with this team. Understood?"

"Look, Colonel, I know Laura is ICP. It was obvious from the moment I got on the bus. But why is he here?" She pointed at me.

"I'm here because I identified Laura as ICP, and Captain Hennessey as a plant on day one. And I also identified you as possible infiltrator after you dropped Leon."

That seemed to take the wind out of her sails. She opened her mouth to retort, but the words wouldn't come, so Cooper picked up the slack.

"Amanda, we had you pegged as AoG from very early on. It's only in the last twenty-four hours that we've considered an alternative scenario, but we can't give that to you. You either come clean now, or you're out the door."

"I'm sorry, but you simply don't have the authority. And if I'm not in there, a lot of people are going to die."

"We're close to shutting Echo down and kicking everyone out, so start talking." Cooper bristled and was about to get right in her face when Grealish held his hand up to halt her. "Amanda, you need to give us an explanation. And you need to give it to us now."

"You shouldn't have pulled me out. That was a mistake."

"There wasn't a viable alternative."

"You're doing assessments. There's a hundred viable alternatives. Take me into a training room. Question me in Stage 1 demo room. Take me anywhere, but out of the facility and across the street for anyone to see was stupid."

"Laura and I have been over here several times and nobody noticed."

"Everyone fucking noticed." She scowled at me like I was a rank amateur, which I suppose was true. "You waltz back in with wet hair and reeking of that fucking oil. Do you really think your crew is that stupid?"

We all looked taken aback.

"I've had to start rumours about external assessments to cover for you twice now. It isn't fucking clever. And now you're going to have to drag them all out, one by one, to do an assessment in this office, just to hide your stupidity."

Grealish sat down and sighed. "Okay, okay. Let's take a step back here. Who are you and who are you working for? We'll get to the whys and wherefores in a minute."

"Did you drag me in here because of the conversation you heard recorded through my bio-band? Yes or no, please. This'll go much more quickly if I know what you know."

Hennessey spoke. “Yes, we did. How did you know you were being recorded?”

“I was working SECO 2. Those muppets know nothing about covert operation. I literally watched them switch my feed on. As soon as I knew you were monitoring me, I tried to see my actions from your perspective, and came to the conclusion that I was not looked upon favourably. So I sent you a message when I put down that cretin in the shower block.”

There was an awkward silence as we all digested this bombshell. Amanda picked up on it straight away. “Yes, that’s right. I told you who I was in that message, or at least what I was, assuming, foolishly, that you’d get it and back off. I’ve been deep cover for almost a year so that they could insert me into this facility as a civilian. But no, not you guys. You have to drag me out of the fucking complex to question me.”

“With respect, we thought you were AoG. It’s only in the last day that we’ve contemplated the alternative, and we had to make sure. There was no way we could continue to let you stay in there if you were our infiltrator.”

“Not to mention the fact that you’re operating illegally in an air-side facility that we run,” Harris chimed in. “An unsanctioned operation that you were obliged to inform us about.”

“Are you listening to what I am saying here?” She turned to look at Harris. “I’ve been deep cover. I can’t just phone you up and disclose my identity. If you haven’t figured it out yet, you’ve got a mole in the BRDF. Someone on your team is leaking information to the AoG. I know this for a fact, because we’ve got an intercept on the outside that’s getting all the communications. For all I know they could be sitting in this fucking room.”

"Okay, Amanda." Grealish held his hands up to placate her. "Assuming, of course, that your name is actually Amanda?"

"It is."

"Okay, I'm going to tell you what we know. Then you're going to tell us what you know. Then we're going to sit here and work the problem until we have a credible plan. Cooper?"

"Fair enough, Sir." She turned to Amanda. "We have a source in the AoG. Also deep cover. She's been inside for six years, and communicates to us sporadically, when she has something relevant to tell us. On the day your crew arrived, we had intelligence that an AoG operative was being inserted into the facility. We've since had word that there's more than one. Jaxon outed Laura and Sara on the first day, which is why we brought him in to the team. Laura was our ICP officer on the bus. She was never meant to be inserted. Sara was to take her place on the inside. But Jaxon blew that for us immediately, so we went out on a limb and actually inserted Laura."

"I guessed that when I saw her brought back in on the second day."

Cooper continued. "Since then, we've been investigating and trying to establish who is on the inside that shouldn't be. You came to our attention when you put Leon on the deck the first time. It was obvious you'd been trained."

"Have you asked yourself how that moron got a ticket in the first place?"

"That doesn't matter. He's no longer relevant, anyway. The point is, we kept a sharp eye on you from that moment. Then someone killed him, and your little dialogue with him proved it wasn't you, so we needed to focus elsewhere."

Amanda bit back her impatience. "It matters. He was an AoG defector. He joined their ranks years ago, and then convinced them to let him infiltrate the facility, and destroy the Bertram Ramsay from the inside."

"What?"

"Yeah, that shakes it up, doesn't it? Except that the moment they pulled the strings to get him on board, he cut them off and it wasn't until later that they realised he intended to take his place on the station and live happily ever after."

"Wait a minute." Grealish shook his head. "So, Leon was one of the infiltrators that our deep cover operative was warning us about? That's good news, surely?"

"I don't know for sure, but I think not. I think they had plans for an operative to go in and fulfil the mission Leon was supposed to undertake and then sent in a second to kill him. That's been my assumption, anyway. We've had eyes on Leon for months and months, because we suspected they would put a hit on him on the outside. The problem with Leon was that he'd boast about anything to anyone, so it didn't take long before he told someone in our network that he'd got himself a ticket. He didn't know it, but once inside this facility, my job was to cosy up to him and see how much information I could get from him about AoG. Except the little turd thought I was giving him a come-on. Usually, advances like that could pay dividends, but he'd already alienated himself from the entire crew, and if I'd let him get closer, it wouldn't have looked right to the rest of you. I needed to stay in the crew, so I put the cretin down. After that, I couldn't get a word from him."

"And when were you going to let us know?"

"I wasn't. If he'd made it to Stage 3, I'd have slotted him and made it look like an accident. No way he could be allowed on that station."

There was a stunned silence at this.

"Okay, so if what you're saying is right, we've still got two infiltrators in Compression, and now a third that died a couple of weeks ago."

"Yes, and that's the big problem. Three in one crew shouldn't even be remotely possible. There's a team working the external angle, but you have a serious problem between air-side and land-side. We don't think it's just BRDF—most of your crew are stationed on site, so someone has to be passing information to ICP land-side, which is feeding back. And someone is handing out tickets to AoG like biscuits. They have totally compromised this entire facility. Not to mention that you've got a murderer in there, and everyone is flouncing around like it didn't happen."

"I don't think that three in one crew is the big issue here." Honestly, I didn't. "If what you've just said is correct, then the plan was to only insert one. Then, when they realised Leon had defected, they sent another to replace him, and a third to kill him. No, that's not the issue at all. The issue is, why this crew? They could have taken Leon out and put someone inside a month later. Or a month after that. So why Crew 41?"

"Staff rotation." Tyrone opened his hands. "Every six months, the entire land-side and air-side crews rotate to different facilities. We've got a week until that happens. With the exception of Sara and I, almost every other BRDF officer rotates out next Wednesday, back to the Bertram or on to another Compression site. Which means after next Wednesday, the AoG lose their man on the inside."

"And we find ourselves with a traitor on the Bertram." Sara looked at Tyrone.

"We've still got to work out who the infiltrators are," said Grealish. "That's vitally important, as they have a mission to cause the evacuation to stop."

"Which is precisely what I was working on. You've got potentially three candidates in the crew. Jennifer was with me all day when Leon was killed, and honestly, she doesn't seem the type, unless she's some kind of super spy, in which case her cover is fucking flawless."

"We'd already discounted Jennifer, too."

"Good. So we agree it has to be one of either Libby or Eloise, or Mark?"

"I don't think it's Mark," said Laura. "He seemed really shaken up by Leon's death."

"Yes, but what if that's because it almost blew his cover?" My brain had gone into overtime. "There's been something off about Mark ever since you released him back to us after Leon's death. I thought it was some sort of shyness or fragility, but the more I watch him, the more he seems like the outsider in the group. Doesn't involve himself with anyone at all. Just sits back and soaks it all up."

"I agree with Jaxon," replied Amanda. Laura shot me a withering look. "Plus, there's some intel you're probably not privy to. Mark's parents were both killed on the Valiant."

Cooper gasped. "No fucking way!"

"Wait, what's the Valiant? Where have I heard that name before?" I'd definitely heard it somewhere.

Cooper pulled her hollotab out, found the file she wanted and pressed play. The distorted metallic voice spoke.

"They've infiltrated. I don't know who or where. What I do know is that their timetable says '4 pm, 5.15 pm, 6.45 pm final'. I got a look at it during a meeting. They keep mentioning the Valiant, but without any context. Then I heard, 'congratulations on the second'. I take this to mean that they already have one inside, and that this timetable is for their second infiltrator. That's all I got."

The whole room fell silent. Cooper clicked off the hollotab, and we just sat there, consumed by this revelation.

Hennessey spoke. "That message makes so much more sense now."

"Is someone going to explain what the Valiant is, please?" It obviously meant something. Something quite important, judging by the looks on the surrounding faces.

Grealish spoke first. "The Valiant was one of the first fusion-powered shuttles built for orbital transport, back when the Bertram Ramsay was still being built, twenty-five years ago. It had a reactor failure and exploded shortly after its maiden launch."

"Okay, so why is that of significance here?"

"I have no idea," said Grealish.

"I do," said Amanda. Everyone looked at her. She sighed. "The Valiant wasn't a fusion accident. It was deliberate. We shot it down. There were three senior AoG agents on that shuttle, and the intel arrived too late to stop the launch, and they couldn't recall it back to Earth, because the intelligence was that they'd smuggled a bomb on board and were planning on detonating it on the Bertram. Bringing it back here risked us taking out more than just the shuttle. We had no defences back then. Not in space anyway. So we shot it down, killing everyone on board, including the crew and two prominent scientists—Dr Mark Hanson Sr. and Dr Susan Hanson—Mark's parents. The problem is that it was a significant launch, so there were cameras on it everywhere, and I've personally seen several minutes of footage that clearly show a missile hitting the Valiant. They launched a huge operation to confiscate all the footage, but none of us believed it had ever been fully recovered. It wouldn't be unreasonable to assume that the AoG got their hands on it and are using it as propaganda to recruit."

"Jesus Christ." Cooper shook her head. "So you think Mark is avenging his parents' deaths? Is that what this is about? And why don't Command know about the missile attack? This is the first we're hearing of it."

"I don't know what Mark's motivation is. That was also my mission. Identify the threat and neutralise it, after extrapolating every microscopic detail that I could from them. I work in a subdivision of Command that operates at a different level than the basic command structure. We have military training for covert ops, subversion tactics and wet work. We're basically a black ops team. I won't give you our designation, but the senior brass funnel our funding through various legitimate fronts. We operate independently of the ICP."

"Jesus." Cooper's eyes were wide open.

"Okay, so why can't we just eject all three from the facility right now?" Laura asked.

"That wouldn't be fair," I said. "At least one of those three is totally innocent."

"So what? We're talking about one life ruined to save millions."

"Actually, if we don't get a handle on this, we're ejecting the whole crew. The risk of overlooking someone would be too great. So it's all of you, or none of you." Grealish looked sombre.

"We can't just throw everyone out," said Amanda. "Firstly, they now have an intimate knowledge of the facility. What's stopping the AoG from taking that information and using it against us?"

"But you said there's already someone on the inside—BRDF and/or ICP. Surely they've got that information anyway?" Laura wasn't going to let this drop.

"Okay, let's assume you're right. The bigger issue here is that if we don't identify the mole in BRDF, they'll end up on the Bertram Ramsay. We have to assume that they have a liaison on board the Bertram, and all intelligence suggests that the Bertram was infiltrated months ago. If you remove the crew, you'd be taking out our only lead. Is that a risk you're willing to take? I'm certainly not. My job is to continue investigating from the inside and to neutralise the threat. Now, I'll admit, I wasn't enamoured at being outed right here, but now there are at least five of us investigating internally, and you, Lieutenant, and Colonel Grealish investigating the ICP connection land-side, I'd say the odds of success have improved exponentially."

"I'm sorry, Amanda, but these risks are becoming too great. We can't leave a compromised crew in the program because they might eventually lead us to a cell on board the Bertram. We'd be knowingly swelling their numbers and compromising the mission."

"Listen, Colonel, I'm begging you. We are blind up on the Bertram. We have no leads at all, at least we didn't by the time I joined Crew 41. You're struggling to find two infiltrators inside a facility that houses, what, eleven hundred people? You know for a fact one of them is in Crew 41, and with only three potential suspects you still can't point the finger. The Bertram is a maze, with over six million people up there already. Kicking out Crew

41 isn't even a sticking plaster. You'd need to bin off every person in Echo, regardless of designation or rank. And then think about how many of those people were involved with previous crews. You are compromised. It's no longer a question of 'if'. Our only chance of finding these people now is to follow the breadcrumbs once we're up there, or everyone dies."

CHAPTER EIGHTEEN

THE MEETING WENT on for another twenty minutes. My mind was spinning with the revelation that Amanda was ICP, and about Leon, and Mark's parents. There wasn't much I could do about Mark. He clearly wasn't opening up to me, but I'd formed a relationship with Eloise, and I would continue that and find a way to form one with Libby too. As luck would have it, I didn't have to wait too long.

Laura and I walked back alone through DECON 4. We went through the process and then met by the airlock. Harris and Hennessey were working on a cover for Amanda when they brought her back, and arrangements were being made for brief excursions to ICP command for the rest of the crew, to deflect suspicion.

"I've got to do something, and you're not going to like it, Laura."

"I know. You need to get closer to Libby and Eloise."

"Eloise is less of a problem. We've already got conditioning sessions together. It's Libby I need to form up with. I need to figure out an approach."

"I could try getting chatty with Libby—see what her challenges are and maybe nudge her to talk to you. Worth a try?"

"Maybe. I honestly have no idea what I'm doing here. I'm concerned about Mark if he's about to be given access to the shuttle."

"Don't worry about Mark. I'll be working with him. He'll expect that, as you paired us up before. And you're not the only one that knows how to flirt you know."

I was about to protest my innocence, but she just winked at me and walked away. Fuck's sake.

I headed back into the rec room where I found most of the crew milling about. Mark was seated at the desk in the library corner, poring over some voluminous textbook and taking notes. Eloise was on the sofa, coffee in hand, scrolling through her hollotab, and I saw Laura's backside disappearing into the training room.

I headed for the dorm to shower after my workout and training this morning. Thinking I was alone, I stripped off and walked into the shower block, where I found Libby soaking in the bath. I ignored her and stepped into one of the shower cubicles. I was just getting used to the steaming water when Libby called out from the bath.

"Hey, Jax. Can I ask you a question?"

"Er, sure. What's up?"

"How do I choose my occupation on the Bertram? I don't even know where to start. You seem to be getting on with things in the BRAF. And that's one of the options open to us. Do you think it would suit me?"

My gut instinct was to say no, but in reality I knew nothing about her at all. "I was lucky with the BRAF. When I arrived, I was just another nobody, so I've no idea how I've wound up with this gig. I really don't know enough about you to answer that. I don't know what you like or what you're capable of. We've had so little time together since we got here."

"I know, but Eloise says you've been really helpful. She trusts your judgement. She told me about the shower in Stage 1 and you covering her up and not telling anyone. Big brownie points for you." I wondered what else she'd been told.

"That's good to know. She seems like a decent person. But what about you?"

"Am I a decent person?"

"No, sorry. I meant, what do you want to do? What did you do before?"

"I suspect I'm not much different from anyone else here. I went to LSE for a year before they closed it and then tried to earn my keep taking any job available to me. You know what it's like out there."

"I do. This process has saved me from myself, I think. I was drifting. It's nice to have a purpose."

"And to be surrounded by women who all dote on you can't be so bad, can it?"

"Well, I'm not sure..."

"I'm teasing you, Jax. Everyone likes you here. You're basically the only bloke that talks, so you have a captive audience."

"Yeah, it's weird how quiet Mark is. He wasn't this shy at the start of the process."

"I think he still blames himself for Leon's death. I've told him plenty of times already that even if it were true, he's done everyone a favour."

"That's true enough. Not sure Leon deserved to die, but I certainly don't begrudge anyone giving him a kicking. So come on, if they gave you the choice of any job in the world—forget the Bertram, what would you choose?"

"Anything? The world is my oyster and all that?"

"Sure, why not? Maybe it'll give us some insight."

"As a kid, I wanted to be a singer. I was desperate to front a metal band so I could daub myself in sinister make-up and wear ripped-everything."

"Really? You sing?"

"Not so much any more. Sometimes in the shower when you lot aren't hanging around."

"I'm not sure singing is a viable option for the Bertram." I was getting wrinkly. It felt a little odd talking over a wall, but this was the opportunity I needed to get to know her better.

"No, I think you're probably right. I quite enjoyed the kitchens in Stage 1, but not sure it's a job I'd want for life."

"What are the options you've seen so far?"

"Well, they have a huge manifesto loaded on a hollotab out on the table by the sofas. It's a bit intimidating, actually. There are literally hundreds of options, but all categorised into different subgroups. They do have hospitality as a subgroup, and I suspect that includes everything from entertainment to cleaning. What I don't want to do is select a subgroup, and then get the shitty end of the deal."

"That's probably one to discuss with Harris or Hennessey. They've been stationed on the Bertram, so they'll know it better. What were you doing at LSE?"

"Er, economics, Jax. It's literally called the London School of Economics. But like I said, I only did my first year and then they closed it. Not enough funding to keep it going. And half a degree is basically the same as no degree."

I was keen to continue the conversation but I was wrinkling up badly, so I rinsed and switched the shower off, wrapping a towel around my waist. I stepped out of the cubicle and Libby was already out, standing in just her knickers. She turned to face me and I didn't know where to look. Her body was the same light coffee colour as her face and her skin was flawless. The tiny upturn at the corners of her mouth suggested she knew exactly what I was thinking, so I averted my gaze and wandered back through to the dorm. I just needed Jennifer to pop her norks out in front of me, and I'd have collected the set. Fuck's sake. What is with these women?

Libby followed me, tying a towel into a knot on top of her head as she walked. "What about communications, Jax? I looked at that too. There're loads of different opportunities there. Some within the BRDF, and others between the central controls of each globe. Think I could do it?"

"I'm sure you'd be capable of anything you put your mind to. If I hadn't been handed BRAF I'd definitely apply to work in the brewery. Can you imagine? Just spend your days making beer, inventing new flavours and stuff like that? I've always liked work that is creative as well as physical."

"You're going to stick to flying though, right? It was awesome watching you yesterday. You looked absolutely in control at all times, and you looked like you were enjoying it too."

"I'm not sure whether they'll let me. At the moment, basic pilot training is compulsory for all BRDF candidates. No idea why, so I'm just going through that phase of my training. They haven't yet asked me what I want to do when I graduate at the end of the process. I'll probably end up polishing the boots of the entire force."

Libby laughed. "You really don't know how good you are, do you? Your entire crew responds to you, you exude authority without coming across as a power grabber, and you're the only rookie pilot in history ever to have won that combat scenario. At least, that's what Harris was telling everyone last night. You need to believe in yourself, Jaxon."

My face was burning up under her gaze, and I could feel myself blushing. I was never very good at taking compliments, but then I never really got any, so it's not like I'd had any practice. I was about to say something back when Amanda walked in, looked at Libby and said, "Hennessey is waiting for you by SECO 2." Then, glancing down at Libby's impossibly pert breasts she added, "Probably ought to put some clothes on though." She walked through to the toilet block without a backward glance, and Libby looked at me and mimed cat claws before giggling and pulling her fatigues on.

"See you later, Jax. Cheers for the chat."

"Later, Lib. Good luck."

She waved over her shoulder and sauntered out.

"You work fast." Amanda had reappeared and was leaning on the walled entrance to the toilets.

"Not really. Opportunity was there, so I took it." I shrugged.

"Did you really nail me on as an imposter?"

"'Fraid so. The moment I saw you put Leon down, I knew you weren't just another Occo. We'd barely been here more than four or five days. Plus, when I balled him out in front of the crew, you were totally impassive. Everyone else was dialled in. I decided you needed watching."

"Well, keep working at it. I'll try to get close to Mark and see how that goes."

"No, don't. Laura's got Mark. I'd already paired them up in Stage 1, and the only reason they didn't end up doing more than a day is because, well, you know why. It made sense to pair them up again. Why don't you have a crack at Eloise?"

"I thought you were working Eloise?"

"I wasn't 'working' anybody." I was back to low-talking. We had the advantage of doors to the dorm here, but even so, I didn't want to be overheard. "All I knew until an hour ago was that something wasn't right with Mark, and either Eloise or Libby, or both of them, are AoG spies. I don't know how to investigate. I'm literally just observing and reporting back what I see. Eloise approached me for help, so I took that opportunity, and Libby's just done the same. But I don't know what questions to ask. How to probe, or analyse what they're saying. They both seem really nice." I shrugged again. I was doing a lot of that lately.

Amanda looked thoughtful for a minute. "What if it's neither of them?"

"What if it's both of them?"

"I'm being serious, Jax. Who else has the opportunity to move around freely and unmonitored, and has access to both land and air-sides?"

"Only Harris and Hennessey."

"And you and Laura."

"We don't walk around unmonitored, and in case you hadn't noticed, we're escorted everywhere."

"Not today you weren't. You left Cooper's office together, and alone."

"Sure, but we walked directly to DECON 4, and straight through to here. We also left through the front doors, so were out of sight of the front desk for maybe twenty metres before we hit a wall of security. And, if you take a look outside, there are cameras everywhere externally, so it would be ridiculously easy to prove that. It's not me or Laura. Laura shouldn't even be here. They brought her back over from Command in Whitehall and then put her straight in—no warning, nothing. She was expecting to go back to Whitehall."

"Fair enough, so what about Harris and Hennessey?"

"Why would they wait until now? Why would they show their hand to me, Laura, and you and involve us in investigative discussions about an internal risk? It doesn't make sense."

"So we're back to Libby and Eloise."

"I didn't say that. I just said it's not Harris or Hennessey. There's at least twenty marines in Opps, plus another half a dozen in SECO 2, plus all the guys outside of DECON 4, where they spend the entire day face to face with..." I stopped. A penny had dropped.

"With? Come on, Jax. What have you just thought?"

"Where's the only place in the entire facility where BRMC and ICP spend twenty-four hours a day, three metres from each other?"

"DECON 4. You don't think...?"

"I do. Makes perfect sense. How difficult would it be for two officers to lean a hand through the fence and shake by way of a greeting? I bet they do it every day."

"I bet they do too. Bloody hell, Jax. It's got to be worth checking."

"We need to tell Harris or Hennessey."

"No, we don't. You do."

"Amanda..."

She held her hand up and stopped me. "Jax, you speak to them every day. I can't start getting all buddy-buddy with them, or it'll look wrong. Sorry, this one has to come from you. At least they can start looking into it."

"Fair one. Well, no time like the present."

I wandered about for a bit, but no sign of Harris or Hennessey. I grabbed a coffee and sat down on the sofas, flicking through the work manifesto hollotab that Libby had mentioned. She was right—there were literally hundreds of available occupations, and some which I just couldn't imagine existing in space. There was a complete section on agriculture, and an explanation that they entirely filled one globe with crops—wheat, corn, vegetables, rapeseed and tons of others, and an entry that talked about the allotments within every globe. I guessed there were a lot of mouths to feed, and as the sun was the same from up there—if not brighter being that it wasn't being filtered by a layer of smog, cloud, and whatever else provided a barrier to Earth—it must be just as easy to grow crops in a temperature- and humidity-controlled environment as it was on Earth. If not easier.

I thumbed through the volume for a while, stopping now and then to read a bit more, and as I was slurping the dregs of my coffee Aoife walked in, hair still damp and reeking of oil. Amanda was right.

"How'd it go?" I asked.

"Urgh. It was okay. I just met with that woman who first brought us in to Echo."

"Cooper?"

"Yes, her. How do you remember her name?"

Shit. Me and my mouth. "She challenged me before we went through DECON 1, remember? And she's not exactly hard on the eye."

"For fuck's sake, Jaxon. Don't you have enough women throwing themselves at you?"

"I..."

"Don't bother. Anyway, she was talking about opportunities and security and all that. It was all I could do to keep from nodding off. And there's more of that shit to come, apparently." She rolled her eyes at me.

"What are you leaning towards so far? Anything particular?"

"I don't know, Jax. I think they need to give us more time to look at things. It's a massive decision and there are so many options open. I was thinking about teaching. I always wanted to be a teacher when I was a kid."

"They have schools up there?"

"There's at least two schools in every populated globe. Nine million people—gotta be a lot of kids, eh?"

It hadn't even occurred to me that there'd be children up there, but now I thought about it I felt stupid for not realising there would be. Originally, I had thought that they'd sent more women up than men, because of some sort of primeval instinct to procreate, but I'd been conflicted about that sort of cave-dweller mentality ever since I saw the make-up of this crew. I'd made some assumptions that were foolish, really.

"I can see you as a teacher," I said, not really meaning a word of it.

"Can you really? Thanks, Jax. What about you? Carrying on with that pilot stuff?"

"If they'll let me. Finally found something I'm half-decent at."

"Yeah, you've gotta play to your strengths. Imagine what you'll see as well, flying around in space looking for little green men." She giggled.

At that moment, Hennessey walked in. "Ah, Aoife. Come and join me in Training 1."

"Actually, Sara, can I have five minutes with you first? I've been waiting for either you or Tyrone to show up. Sorry Aoife, I won't be long."

"No worries. I'm going to shower this shit out of my hair, anyway."

I walked over to Hennessey, who gave me a searching look. "What is it?"

"I have an idea how communications may be getting out." I explained my theory about the border post by DECON 4, and the connectivity between BRMC and ICP. She listened and looked thoughtful.

"How easy would it be to pass a note over, or whisper a few words as they said hello or goodbye to each other?"

"There's about fifty of them out there. This facility is totally locked down."

"Yes, I agree, but there's only a small number working the gates. Do they do the same job every day or rotate?"

"Well, they tend to do it in stints. So maybe a week on the gate, a week on the scanners, and a week walking the square. They aren't the same guys that are in Opps—that comprises BRAF and BRMC. Outside, it's all BRMC. I don't know about the ICP routine, though. I'll ask Amy when I see her next."

"Don't leave it too long. If what Harris said is correct, we've only got a week before that window closes."

"Are you giving out orders to commissioned officers now, Jax?"

"I—"

"I like a man who takes control." She winked at me and walked away. Fuck's sake.

CHAPTER NINETEEN

THE ASSESSMENT PHASE continued over the next couple of days. It made little difference to my day-to-day activities as I'd already been given my designation, but the crew were nervous about where they'd eventually be placed. The purpose of the assessments was to understand both the desires of the occupants and their capabilities, and reading between the lines in the evening conversations I'd say these sessions were quite intense. There were definitely some cracks forming, and stress levels were elevated throughout the crew. Only Laura seemed to be unaffected, but then, like me, she already knew what her designation would be, so I suppose there was little for her to stress about.

I'd been continuing my sessions with Eloise, and we were now up to eighty minutes in the hydrotherapy pool. Our next conditioning assessment was in a few days' time, and for the first time since we'd started the training, I was feeling good about it. I didn't expect to go the distance, but I knew I was improving dramatically.

I headed over to Opps—Addison had hinted that there was a new challenge coming for me today. I wondered if it was another combat mission in the Sim, or perhaps another shuttle escort mission—I'd done two of those since.

I walked into the Flight Readiness room and took a seat on one of the Armadillo-installation chairs, when Addison walked in.

"You won't be needing that today. Here, I've got something for you." He handed me a box that felt quite heavy for its size.

"If this is a severed head, I'm going to be very upset."

He laughed. "Open it."

I ripped open the top, and folded back the flaps, and there inside was a black flight suit with 'Jaxon' on the front pocket, and the BRAF insignia on the arm.

"My own flight suit? Wow!"

"Well, get it on then. We've got a mission to get to."

I looked up at Addison, searching for the answer, but he just laughed again and said, "You'll see."

I suited up and put my flight boots on, and then headed through the armoury to a door at the far end that Addison had disappeared through. I entered a small room, with an airlock entrance. I pushed through the airlock and as I opened the second door I was hit by a gust of cold air. I was stood on a gantry, overlooking the launch pad. Addison was waiting for me at the far end, so I walked over.

"Today's the day, Jaxon."

"The day for what?"

"The day you get your cherry popped in an actual cockpit. You're taking Sigma 2 up. I'll be in Sigma 1. We're escorting the Nova Pilgrim to Berty this morning."

I couldn't believe it. I was so desperate to get into an actual Sigma, but now it was happening I was really nervous.

Addison led me down the stairs and across the Launch Bay, under the huge fuselage of the Nova Pilgrim—it was so much bigger out here than it looked from Launch View or the Stage 2 rec room. We crossed to the building opposite Launch View, past an array of military vehicles and through a door at the far end into what was unmistakably a briefing room. Addison shook hands with a couple of guys as we walked in—the shuttle pilots, as it turned out—who had light blue flight suits with the BR Navy emblem on them. He then continued, walking over to a table in the corner and gesturing for me to sit down.

"You've done your training for this. This is no different, except now you've got SQIID drives, so you'll hardly feel any inertia. This is your first solo flight, Jaxon, so do everything by the book, exactly as you've been taught. Do a good job and I might have a surprise for you when we get up there."

I nodded, and Addison took me through the briefing, flight path, trajectory and docking procedures. He took my hollotab from me, loaded it into a dock and added some additional software, and when he handed it back the screen had "Jaxon 'Red October' Leith" across it.

"That's your call sign from now on. You are no longer 'Flight' and I am no longer 'Wing'. I will refer to you as 'Red' and you will call me 'Ocelot'—long story, not for today. You'll be taking the lead all the way up to Berty. Once we're on our final approach, you'll roll out starboard and let the Nova Pilgrim pass you and land. Once she's down, you're to set down on her starboard flank. Okay?"

I nodded. I could feel my heart pounding in my chest. Addison could clearly sense how nervous I was and put his hand on my shoulder. "It's just like training. You won't even realise you're not in a Sim. You're going to be fine. Just remember what you've been taught."

He got up and nodded towards the doors. I grabbed my hollotab and followed him outside.

"Look up." Addison was pointing at the far corner. The mullioned windows from Stage 2 were there, and Aoife, Libby and Jennifer were all standing in the window waving. I waved back and then walked out to my Sigma.

Because this was the first time I'd actually been inside the craft, I was a bit worried about looking stupid trying to get in it, but I needn't have been. One of the ground crew was already there with some moveable steps, and the hatch was already open for me. I thanked him as I climbed inside, and he nodded back and said "Godspeed", before closing the hatch behind me.

I loaded my hollotab into the dock and took the pilot's seat on the left. My screens lit up, and all systems came online. I looked through the window and saw Addison climbing into his Sigma, and the pilots of the Nova Pilgrim walking up the rear-loading ramp. I ran through my system checks, slowly and deliberately, and then ran a visual check to make sure there were no ground crew in the vicinity. Once I was sure it was clear, I flicked on the two gyro-spheres and powered up the reactor. I could feel the entire craft come to life, and a powerful pulse signature was piercing through me.

For the first time, it dawned on me that I was about to pilot an actual craft. I'd never crashed the Sim, and I wasn't sure that was even possible, but regardless, this was the real thing. Any mistakes could cost me my life, or the lives of those around me. At this thought my nerves kicked in in a big way, and every sinew in my body tightened.

I looked over at Addison, and he gave me the thumbs up from his cockpit. I switched to comms and heard his unmistakable voice come through.

"Tower, this is Ocelot. Request permission to launch."

"Ocelot, skies are clear and you are all set."

"Tower, this is Red October. Request permission to launch."

"Red October, you are clear for launch."

I throttled forward slowly and lifted her five metres off the deck.

"Red October, this is Ocelot. When you're ready, take us out."

"Copy that, Ocelot. Engage VTOL in three, two, one... mark."

We both shot up into the air at breakneck speed, but Addison was right. It actually felt odd without the inertia suit pressing me down into my seat. It was a bit like standing on an escalator—you know you're moving, but there's no sense other than your vision.

We hit the three-hundred-metre ceiling and stopped, before going through a clockwise three-hundred-and-sixty-degree sweep of the skies.

"Red October to Nova Pilgrim. You are clear to ascend."

"Roger that, Red."

I watched as the shuttle moved slowly up, and the stanchions dropped to the sides before she shot up and stopped between us.

"Lead the way, Red."

I acknowledged the transmission, rotated outwards, pointed her up and throttled forward. The screen above my head showed the rear camera, and I could see the Pilgrim filling the frame behind me. We passed through 1,500 knots, maintained that speed, and rolled slightly to adjust our trajectory through the atmosphere.

There was a very slight shudder as we broke through into space, and as always, I could barely contain my wonder at the view. Except, this was my first time actually seeing it for real. I can't say that it looked any different, but somehow it felt different.

I rolled left and guided the Pilgrim into our orbital pathway, gathering speed until we hit 25,000 kph. Once we reached our orbital speed, the spheres were idled and we let our momentum bring us up behind the Bertram. I could see the station just ahead of us, maybe fifteen minutes away, its spheres rotating gracefully on an angled arc. I couldn't imagine ever tiring of this view.

My comms lit up. "Bertram Tower, this is Nova Pilgrim requesting permission to dock."

"Nova Pilgrim, glad to have you home. Globe XI, Dock 3, please. Proceed at your leisure. Tower out."

"Red October, take us home. Pilgrim out."

"Aye aye, Sir. Follow my lead." *Aye, aye?* Jesus fucking Christ.

The station rotated clockwise on its axis, and the Globe XI docking bay was under the huge steel tunnel that connected them together, so we had to fly into the gap between Globes XI and XII, and gradually orbit with them around the central sphere, before lining up and gliding in. The station itself was travelling at 7.69 km/s, or 24,940 kph, so our relative speed was important until we closed in upon our destination bay. The Bertram Ramsay was constantly spinning to maintain its internal gravity, so there was a tricky moment when we'd have to speed up to the relative velocity of the globe in which we were docking, and time it so that in a single movement we passed into the gaps between the globes and parked it straight in the bay, or the protocol was to abort and hold for the next rotation. Once we were on the final approach, I rolled out right and held my velocity to let the Pilgrim pass.

"All yours, Nova Pilgrim."

"Thank you kindly, Red October. Thanks for the ride."

I watched as the huge shuttle slowed until it matched the pace of the station rotation and then eased forward, the landing gear lowering, and the stanchions lifting slowly as it entered the cavernous interior of Dock 3. I pulled in behind, and to starboard, and watched Addison take his Sigma to the port side to land. As I brought it alongside Nova Pilgrim, I rotated ninety degrees left so I was looking directly at the shuttle, and then set her down.

It was an exhilarating feeling, watching the huge dock doors close up and waiting for the green pressure light on my hollotab to illuminate, which it did after a few minutes. I popped the hatch and unclipped my harness. One of the ground crew was walking over with my stairs, so I waited and then clambered down. My first steps in actual space. Mind blown.

Addison sauntered over along with the two Nova Pilgrim pilots, and everyone shook my hand and congratulated me on a job well done. I was chuffed to bits, although I really hadn't done very much except point and throttle. The guidance computers kept me in the lane for the duration of the ride in, and I only went manual on final approach. I'd said it before—a ten-year-old could have done it.

Addison motioned for me to follow him, and we wandered over to the far corner where a glass elevator was waiting for us.

"Marvellous job, Jaxon. We'll be heading back shortly. The Pilgrim is just dropping off supplies, but we have a couple of crews coming up tomorrow so need to be back there. As promised, I thought you'd enjoy this."

We stood in the mag-lift as it rose at express speeds, higher and higher until it passed through the ceiling of the dock, and went dark for about ten seconds, before re-emerging inside what looked like a giant snow globe. It was unbelievable to behold. Of course, I'd seen the buildings from outside when I was in the Sim, but nothing could prepare me for what I was seeing here. There were two principal buildings in the centre, both over a hundred storeys high. They were surrounded by landscaped gardens and pools with fountains. There were lights on in the buildings and the left side was totally in shadow. The shadows were winding round in graceful arcs as the station rotated. The glass dome was so clear it was almost invisible, save for the huge metal construction that was holding it all together. In the distance I could see Earth, half in darkness, but so beautiful. The moon was passing the horizon, and I caught the merest glimpse of it before it disappeared behind the planet.

The mag-lift came to a halt, and Addison stepped off onto a tiled walkway with a ramp leading down to the gardens. He ignored the ramp and turned left, keeping the steel wall on our left side. I followed him along the walkway and only noticed after a minute that it felt like we were walking uphill. Then I remembered the first briefing that Harris gave us, talking about the gravity being one hundred and four per cent, and I could almost feel myself getting heavier. It was only as we were a hundred metres up the path that I realised I could only see part of the globe because of the partition wall on the left. It became glass further up, but way, way further up. Maybe three or four hundred metres.

"This is the BRAF command centre. This is where we live and work when we're on station," explained Addison.

"Where's the accommodation?" I asked.

"You're looking at it. Those two central buildings are all apartments for BRAF personnel. Beyond the buildings, towards the outer hull, there are two mess halls, a couple of bars, and more gardens. It's incredibly tranquil."

"Amazing. So what's behind the wall here?"

"That's the Flight Control Centre and Admiralty. Obviously the main hangar is below us now—you've already seen that, but the rest of the dock level is our fleet of Sigmas."

"And shuttles?"

"There are only two shuttles. One of them is in Hangar Four at the moment, being serviced. It'll be out of commission for another five months before it comes back into service. The Nova Pilgrim runs virtually twenty-four hours a day, to the various Compression sites around the world. It's an immense operation."

"Wait, there's only one shuttle working right now?"

"Yes, why?"

"Fuck. That's it!"

"What's it? Jaxon?"

"Sir, sorry, I can't tell you. But I need to get back to Echo immediately. They've got an immense problem on their hands, and the shuttle needs to stay here. It can't come back to Echo. At least not immediately."

Addison looked at me for a minute, as if weighing up his options. "Come with me."

I followed Addison back into the mag-lift, and this time it rotated as it dropped. I was gutted not to have been able to see more of the station, but this was too important to ignore. As we cleared the dark patch between floors, the mag-lift descended into an enormous hangar.

"Jesus Christ. There must be two hundred Sigmas down there."

"Not even close. Nearly four hundred in all. And there's the other shuttle, on the right side under the huge number four—see it?"

I could just about make it out from here. The size of these globes was just utterly beyond comprehension, and I got the distinct impression that the partition wall split the globe 70/30 in favour of this side. It was endless. I could just about make out another hangar door at the far end.

"Is that the way we go out?" I pointed at it.

"That's a door to another docking bay. That wall there is exactly opposite this one; on the far side of that is another accommodation area, for BRMC. And see that tunnel running across the ceiling? That's the Loop." Then, seeing the blank expression on my face, "It's a magnetic train. It circulates all day every day, between every globe, transporting people and freight. It stops by each globe once every two hours, twenty-four hours a day. Four trains, two going clockwise and two counter-clockwise."

"How do you sleep at night with all the daylight coming in?"

"Well, it's set to daytime now. We work on Zulu time up here." Another blank look from me. "Greenwich Mean Time. All clocks here are sync'd with London. Anyway, once it gets to 8 pm the glass darkens to block out the light, and the internal illuminations come on—just bright enough so you can see where you're walking, but otherwise pretty dim."

The mag-lift came to a halt, and Addison exited and turned right, stopping in an office about fifty metres up, where he asked to have our launch data uploaded to our hollotabs, before putting a call through on the comms system to Fleet Command. He spoke to them for a couple of minutes and then hung up and waved me over. I followed him through the corridor at the back, and out through a door into the hangar we'd arrived in. He handed me my hollotab and nodded at my Sigma.

"We'll take yours."

Thirty minutes later we were on the ground at Echo. Addison had insisted that I take the controls all the way home—no complaints from me at all, but time was of the essence, so I binned-off any thought of taking the scenic route and actually stalled my take-off until we were in the optimal position for re-entry over the United Coalition of Britain.

The moment the hatch was popped, I was out and charging for the stairs in the corner. Addison didn't follow me. He'd pressed me for more information during the flight home, but I just repeated that I couldn't tell him anything.

"I'm sorry, Addison, I just can't say. I know it's a lot to ask, but I need you to trust me."

He seemed to accept that, albeit begrudgingly, and nodded to me as I left. "Good job today, Jax."

I waved a thanks and headed up the stairs and along the walkway to the airlock door behind Opps. After closing the inner door, I weaved my way through the building and was just going through the screens when the far one opened and Harris was standing there. I'd never been more pleased to see him in my life. I grabbed him and pulled him back through into Opps, then round to Launch View.

"Tyrone, it's the shuttle."

"What's the shuttle?"

"The AoG target. There's only one in commission right now—the Nova Pilgrim. The other one is out of action being serviced, and will be for five months. If something happens to the Pilgrim, that's the evacuation halted. And that's what we're looking for, right?"

"Christ. How did you figure that out?"

I told him about my flight up and my conversation with Addison. "I think you're right, Jaxon. Where's the Pilgrim now?"

"I told Addison it couldn't return until I'd spoken to you guys, so it's still on the Bertram."

"And they just accepted that and grounded it?"

I shrugged. "Apparently."

"Unreal. I can't get Aoife to keep her bunk tidy without getting both barrels, but you can ground a space shuttle just by asking nicely. I'll be having to salute you soon."

"You'll find that difficult while you're carrying my bags."

Harris laughed and then stepped out, motioning for me to follow. We stopped in SECO 2, but no sign of Hennessey, Laura or Amanda, so we walked through to the Stage 2 rec room, where Amanda and Laura were chilling together on the sofas.

"Tyrone—why don't you find Sara, and brief Grealish and Cooper. We can't all go back through. I'll take Laura and Amanda through to the demo room in Stage 1 and tell them what's going on."

Harris nodded and went in search of Hennessey.

As I approached the sofas, Amanda looked up. "Nice scrubs, Jaxon. How was the flight?"

"No time for that now. Come with me, both of you. Assessment time," I added, as Eloise walked in. I gave her a quick wave and walked out into the SECO 2 corridor. Amanda and Laura were both behind me as I buzzed us through into Stage 1. We were just walking through to the demo room, when the klaxons sounded and lights started flashing all over the place.

The three of us pulled on our rebreathers, and watched as the two new crews flapped about, trying desperately to figure out what they were supposed to do. I wondered if we'd looked that ridiculous.

We walked into the demo room, bubbles on heads, and took a seat at the table by the stage area. The klaxons gave up after a minute, and I could hear the BRMC trainer chewing out the crew for being dead already. We'd only been here five weeks, and already I felt like a veteran.

I checked the room to make sure we were alone, and then I explained to Laura and Amanda what I'd discovered on my flight up to the Bertram. They both agreed that this was the likely target.

Laura looked at us both in turn. "Mark and I were in engineering today, going through the shuttle diagrams, in a classroom environment. He was much more animated than he has been recently."

"We cannot let him get anywhere near that shuttle when it comes back," said Amanda.

"We still don't know it's him," I reminded them. "At best, the evidence is circumstantial."

"Jaxon, he has the motive. We killed his parents. How difficult do you think it would be to convince him we're the enemy? And we're giving him the opportunity on a plate. Is that a risk you're willing to take?"

"What could he actually do though?" asked Laura. "I mean, realistically, if you wanted to ground the shuttle, what would you do to make it happen?"

I had no idea. "Could he make a bomb with the chemicals in the kitchen? We've already had one person killed by them."

"Wait... What?! Who?" Amanda sat bolt upright, looking between the two of us.

"You don't know?"

“Know what, Jaxon?” Her eyes flashed dangerously.

“Leon was killed by injection. Needle full of chlorhexidine under the arm. Huge anaphylactic shock and then suffocated because his throat was swollen. Needle traced back to the kitchen med kit. Whoever did it stored the contents of the EpiPen, then refilled it after they’d killed Leon. That’s why our focus has been on Eloise and Libby. Neither of them was wearing a bio-band at the time, and the trace program showed neither left the kitchen that day until the end of their shift.”

“For fuck’s sake!” Amanda jumped to her feet and raced out of the room. I looked at Laura and we both legged it after her.

CHAPTER TWENTY

HARRIS AND HENNESSEY entered Cooper's office, where they found her sitting in her chair looking out of the window.

"Tyrone? Sara? I wasn't expecting you." Then, seeing the look on their faces, "What's wrong? What's happened?"

"Where's the colonel? He needs to hear this," replied Harris.

Cooper tapped her comms device and waited. "Andrew, I've got Tyrone and Sara here. Can you come down? Okay, thanks. He's on his way," she said, switching off her comms. "What's this about?"

"We know how they're going to stop the evacuation. Jaxon figured it out. That bloke might just be one of the best recruits we've ever gained in this program, if not the best. He is so switched on."

There was a sharp knock, and Grealish entered. "What's going on?"

"Sir, the AoG are targeting the shuttle. That's how they're planning to sabotage the evac," replied Harris.

"That won't stop the evacuation. There are two shuttles for redundancy, precisely in case something happens to the first one. There are also two more being built as we speak, although they won't be completed for a few months. How can you know this, anyway?"

"Jaxon just took his maiden flight to the Bertram. Escorted the Nova Pilgrim from Echo and took her all the way in. While he was there, he discovered that the second shuttle is out of action for five months, whilst they perform essential maintenance on it. If we lose the Pilgrim, that's the entire transport network down."

"It still doesn't make sense. All the intel over the last couple of years has been about them destroying the Bertram. How can they do that if they can't get up there?"

There was a full minute's silence while each of them digested this, and gradually, one by one, they all looked up with horror on their faces.

"They're already on the Bertram. They've already got agents up there."

"Jaxon told them to ground the shuttle and leave it up there in case someone attacked it down here. Shit!"

"Okay, okay. Let's not panic. If we assume the shuttle is the likely target, then we can also assume that they've already infiltrated the Bertram. So what can we do about it? Sara, Tyrone, I don't have comms with the Bertram. Do you have someone you trust up there?"

"Yes, Sir," they both replied, simultaneously.

"Okay, get in touch with them and talk them through it. Increase security around the shuttle, and for god's sake get it launched and back here."

"But Sir, what if the threat is earthbound? We'd be handing them a target."

"Better an earthbound attack than one that happens on the Bertram. There's an awful lot we can do to restrict access here. Get Jaxon on comms, now."

Harris tapped his comms and called through to Jaxon.

"Hello? Hello?"

"Jaxon, it's Harris."

"Tyrone, you scared the crap out of me. I didn't know we had comms on the bio-monitors."

"You don't. They're on your bio-band. Anyway, not the point. Colonel Grealish wants a word. Hold. Sir?"

"Jaxon, it's Grealish. Are you away from listening ears?"

"I can be. Give me a minute." They could hear a door open, and then Jaxon's voice rang through again, with a slight echo. "Okay, I'm out in the SECO 2 corridor. Fire away."

"Tyrone tells me you've just been up to the Bertram?"

"Yes, Sir."

"And you came up with this idea that the AoG is going to disable the shuttle somehow."

"That's correct."

"Well, we've been going through it here and it might well be that they already compromised the Bertram and they'll disable the shuttle on site, which would completely detach the Bertram from Earth. If you had to stop that happening and you were up there, what would you do? None of us here have ever been in the hangar long enough to look at it properly."

"Well, that's actually an easy one, Sir. I'd evacuate the hangar, depressurise it, and open the bay doors. Nobody could enter it after depressurisation, and even if they could, they'd be sucked into space. The Pilgrim and the Sigmas all have magnetic docking gear, so they won't move."

"Okay, so how do we make that happen?"

"I'm not sure it's one for open comms, Sir. I could grab Addison and fly up, but I'd have to brief him. He's already acted only on my word once. I'm not sure he would twice without wanting an explanation."

"Okay, tell him the bare minimum. We've received a threat to the shuttle. It needs protecting. This is the plan. Got it?"

"Sir."

I clicked off my comms and walked back into SECO 2, where Laura and Amanda were checking through the feeds on the day of Leon's death. Amanda was scrolling through hours of footage, looking for what, I had no clue.

"Guys, I have to go. I need to get to the Bertram, but I'll be back in a couple of hours. Let me know if you find anything."

They both completely ignored me, totally engrossed in the bio-feeds and security camera footage. I ran through the tunnel to Opps, and into the main control centre. I asked them to put a call out for Addison to meet me at the Launch Bay, and then proceeded through the armoury and the airlock, onto the gantry. It was getting dark, and whilst I'd flown in space, I hadn't yet flown at night on Earth. My brain was trying to rationalise what the difference would be, but in the end I stopped thinking about it before my head exploded.

As I walked across to the Sigma, Addison opened the doors to the briefing room. I waved him over and shouted for him to grab someone from the ground crew. He disappeared back inside while I stood under the port stanchion of the Sigma and then reappeared a moment later with the same guy that helped me up earlier. He grabbed the steps and wheeled them over.

We got strapped in and I handed over control to Addison. "You fly, I'll talk. It's important, and it's also to stay between us. We're not on vox, are we?"

"No, but the flight recorder is always running."

"How often do they get listened to?"

"Only when there's an incident."

"Fine, try not to have one of those."

We took off and Addison wasted no time throttling to max and shooting us through the stratosphere into space. I told him about the intel to take out the shuttle, and the plan to keep it under guard until we could secure Echo completely and bring it down here. He listened attentively and didn't interrupt. When I'd finished, he looked over at me.

"Christ, Jaxon. How long have you known about the threat?"

"Remember a couple of hours ago when I made them leave the shuttle there while we came home? That long. I figured it out when you said about the other shuttle being out of service."

He said nothing after that. I could almost hear the cogs turning in his head, but unless he had some sort of prophetic insight, he was about to come to the same conclusion as me.

"If they have infiltrated Berty, and that's a big 'if', how the bloody hell are we supposed to flush them out before we hit deep space?"

"I honestly have no clue. I've been involved in this for just over five weeks, and it still makes my head spin."

"Do you know how many souls we have on board already? Six point two million. Already up there. That's the population of Birmingham, already on Berty."

"It's an impossible task. I get it, and people much cleverer than you or I will figure it out, but we can do something now, to mitigate the threat that we know about. We need to do that and then head back. They're going to secure Echo in the interim—total lockdown until they can put a plan into place to securely bring the shuttle back."

"What about all the other launch sites?"

"Not our problem. And well beyond our means to protect. The intel specifically identified Echo."

We were on our final approach to Globe XI. I could see the giant bay doors opening for us, and the shuttle still sitting on its pad where we left it. Addison went through the motions and parked it at the far end of the hangar, away from the shuttle. "Time is of the essence, so no sense making us walk half a mile to the control centre."

"Let's visit the Admiralty."

We took the stairs on our right to the mag-lift and then ascended to the command centre. Addison led me through a small vestibule into a bustling office, full of holloscreens and BRDF personnel, to an office in the back corner. Behind a desk was a BRMC captain, working on his holloscreen. He looked up as we entered, and then, seeing Addison, stood up and saluted.

"Sir. How can I help you, Sir?" I hadn't realised that Addison was so high ranking until this moment.

"We need to see the admiral. It's urgent."

"Yes, Sir." He tapped his comms and announced us, then gesticulated to the door on his left. "Go right in, Sir."

We knocked and entered an ornately-furnished office. It was an odd combination of hi-tech equipment and antique furniture. There were holloscreens covering two of the walls, with various data scrolling through them, plus what looked like a news channel and a radar array. The wall at the far end was floor-to-ceiling glass, with a spectacular view of the BRAF accommodation and the other globes beyond. Sitting behind a mahogany desk was a hulk of a man. He must have been three hundred and fifty pounds, and looked to be about sixty years old, with a bushy grey moustache and close-cropped hair. There was a small placard on the desk with the moniker Admiral H. Leigh Willard. He didn't look up from his screen as we entered.

Addison stopped in front of the desk and brought himself to attention, before saluting the admiral. I followed suit, feeling completely ridiculous, having never even attempted a salute before. I must have got away with it though, as neither of them said anything.

A full twenty seconds passed before the admiral looked up. "Addison, my boy. How the devil are you!" he exclaimed, leaning his ample frame back into the protesting chair.

"I'm very well thank you, Sir. Apologies for disturbing you like this."

"Not at all, not at all. Is this the chappy?" He nodded towards me, without breaking eye contact with Addison.

"Sir?"

"Addison, is this the little scrotum that grounded my shuttle?" I was taken aback by how quickly his tone had gone from jovial to contemptuous.

"This is Jaxon Leith, Sir. He's a BRAF trainee. And yes, it was his call to ground the shuttle."

He turned to look at me for the first time. "And who the fuck does he think he is, ordering my shuttle to be grounded? Has his training been fast-tracked so that he already outranks me here?" His voice was a balanced mix of nonchalant and dangerous.

"No, Sir. We have received intelligence of a credible threat to the Bertram. Jaxon here is working counter-intel during his training. He has a higher clearance than me, Sir. Perhaps I should let him explain?"

He stared at us both, cold fury rippling the deep lines all over his face. "I couldn't give a rat's arse how high his clearance is. Nobody, especially not a fucking trainee, waltzes into my space station and orders the grounding of the one operational shuttle that we currently have. Nobody."

Fuck this. I was trying to save them. I couldn't have cared less about rank or protocol. "Admiral, we have credible intel that..."

"Don't you fucking talk to me. You will stand there, with your mouth shut, and if I want your fucking opinion, I'll give it to you." Flecks of spit flew from his mouth as he screamed at me.

I wasn't going to stand for this. Clearly this was a pointless exercise already, so I just turned and left Addison there. I could hear the admiral bellowing through the closing door, but honestly, I couldn't have cared less at that moment. I walked through to the mag-lift and descended to the Launch Bay, where I had intended to wait for Addison. As I went to enter the walkway, the airlock door was closed, and a flashing red beacon above it warned me that the shuttle bay was depressurised. I turned left onto the raised gantry and ran along until I got to the viewing platform. I arrived just in time to see the back end of the shuttle leaving the Bertram.

Addison turned up five minutes later, looking distinctly pissed off. He joined me at the viewing platform and looked out over the empty bay.

"So much for trying to help."

"Jaxon, you shouldn't have walked out. He's all piss and wind."

"Oh, I see. So you explained the problem, which he listened to objectively, and then made a risk assessment before ordering a total lockdown then?"

"No, he bawled me out for listening to a word you said, then made several threats about revoking your access to the station permanently, reassigning you as a toilet cleaner in Swindon, and then he told me to fuck off."

"Sounds reasonable. So what are we going to do, Addison? The shuttle has gone. They aren't listening, and I'm out of ideas."

"Let's get back to Echo. You'll need to speak to whoever it is you report to. This is out of our hands. But hear this, Jaxon." He turned to face me, finger jabbing into my chest. "If you want to continue flying, you'll have to keep your head down for a bit. Walking out on the admiral was foolish. You're military now, and if you want to get on in life, you sometimes have to play the game." He shook his head at me and walked away.

We arrived back at Echo an hour later, having barely spoken on the flight home. I thanked Addison for taking me up and then walked back through Opps to SECO 2. I found Amanda and Laura still wading through hours of footage on different cameras.

"How's it going?" I could see from their faces that the answer was probably "not well".

Amanda completely ignored me, but Laura turned and spoke. "Nothing so far, but Amanda is convinced that the footage will show someone else entering or leaving the dorm when Leon was murdered."

"Haven't they already been through all of this? Surely that would have been the first priority?"

"Apparently. But it can't be possible for someone to enter or leave without being seen on at least one of the camera feeds, unless they were in there all day, and we've already been through the footage from the night before. Nobody enters or leaves during the night, and then everyone leaves in the morning, so we're now going through the daytime feeds."

"Christ. Okay, I'll let you get back to it. I need to find Harris or Hennessey."

"Harris was in Stage 2 last I saw, but that was half an hour ago."

I left SECO 2 and walked up the corridor to Stage 2. When I entered the rec room, it was like a ghost town. Mark was sitting in the corner, reading something, but it was otherwise completely empty. I looked around in all the rooms and found Aoife and Libby in Conditioning—they just waved at me from the treadmill and hydrotherapy pool—and Jennifer in with Hennessey in the training room. Hennessey looked up as I entered, and shook her head at me as if to say "not now", so I headed back out of Stage 2 and did a quick recce of Stage 1. I wove my way back through to Opps, but there was no sign of Harris here either. I had to assume he was somewhere talking to Eloise.

Back at Stage 2, I grabbed a coffee and walked over to the windows overlooking the Launch Bay. I felt completely helpless and frustrated by the admiral's reaction. I didn't ask for this. And I didn't fancy being stuck on a giant glass space station with an unknown terrorist on board. I couldn't fathom who of our crew could be such a person. Even Mark, despite all the motivation he might have to avenge his parents, didn't seem the sort to want to callously destroy lives. But then I remembered the beating he gave Leon, and it made me realise that there was definitely some pent-up rage in there. His story about his sister rang true at the time, but with all I'd discovered since, I was doubting everything.

I meandered about for another fifteen minutes until finally Harris walked in with Eloise. They were chatting away about what I did not know, when suddenly Amanda came bursting into the room behind them.

Everyone turned at the sound of the door crashing open. I could just see Laura in the background through the doorway. I swear everything went into slow motion. Amanda's face was contorted with concentration and anger, and she ran at Harris and Eloise.

Harris's reactions were lightning-fast. His training was instantly visible. He stepped back and planted his rear foot, bringing his hands up to a defensive position. Eloise reacted simultaneously and stepped back and around behind Harris, using him as a human shield, fear and shock plastered all over her face. I watched as Amanda launched herself at Harris, grabbing the front of his fatigues, and spinning him round and over her trailing leg. It was an awesome sight to behold, seeing this small woman drop a guy like Harris. Everyone was just frozen, watching this mini-battle play out.

Before Harris had even hit the deck, Eloise had vaulted over his legs and was running at Laura in the doorway. That's when my brain kicked in, and I could see what was happening. Amanda let go of Harris as he tumbled to the ground and turned on the spot, sprinting after Eloise. Laura reacted too late to the oncoming charge, and Eloise knocked her with brutal force against the corridor wall. I saw Laura collide with the brickwork and then drop to the floor. I pushed off on my back foot and raced after

Amanda, as Eloise turned the corner and headed for the airlock. As she reached it, her footsteps faltered momentarily; the red lights were on. Someone was already inside. She regained her stride and continued to pound her way down to Stage 1. Amanda was gaining; the brief pause whilst Eloise checked the airlock had given Amanda an extra step, and she was travelling faster now.

Eloise got to the partition doors between SECO 2 and Stage 1, and with a glance behind her she knew she'd never get them open in time. I was ten or fifteen metres back from them both when Amanda barrelled into Eloise at full speed, the pair of them knocking the door clean off its hinges. They went sprawling into Stage 1, still clinging to one another. Their combined momentum had carried Eloise on top of Amanda, and she was swinging her fists like a cornered lioness, mercilessly striking Amanda around the face. Amanda tried to get closer so Eloise was unable to get a full swing in. I arrived just as her fist was coming back for another strike and threw myself at Eloise, grabbing her round the neck and chest and using my mass to carry us both away from Amanda.

I gripped her as tightly as I could in a bear hug and squeezed so she couldn't get away. Her arms and legs were flailing madly, her head bucking backwards at my face, smashing into my nose and mouth, and she was making noises like a wildcat, hissing and spitting. I rolled onto my back, just in time to see Amanda launch a vicious blow at Eloise's head, and then she went still.

I released her, letting her body fall to the side, as Amanda jumped over my legs, and brought one of Eloise's arms up behind her back, but there was little point. Eloise was out cold. I could feel myself panting from the twenty seconds of intense exertion. Amanda let go of Eloise and fell back to the carpet, sweat pouring from her brow.

Harris chose this moment to come running in, and stopped, hands on knees, looking at the three of us on the floor.

"What the fuck is going on here?"

"I'm guessing Eloise was the infil. Amanda and Laura have been going through the security feed all day." Then I remembered. "Oh, shit, Laura!"

I jumped up and ran down the SECO 2 corridor, to where Laura was slumped in a heap against the wall. She was murmuring slightly. I laid her down gently on her side and put her in the recovery position. As I was adjusting her, Hennessey walked through.

"What the fuck is going on, Jaxon?" I could see Aoife, Jennifer, Libby and Mark all peering round the rec room, fifteen yards behind her.

I lowered my voice. "We found our infiltrator. She's out for the count in Stage 1. Laura needs a medic—can you send for one?"

Hennessey walked round me and off up the corridor on our left, presumably to the infirmary. I looked up at the crew. "Can one of you grab me a couple of small towels and soak one in cold water, please?"

Aoife turned immediately and headed off to the dorm. I called Jennifer and Libby over. "Look after her. When Aoife gets back with the towels, just press gently against the back of her head. She took a hell of a bang."

I got up and left Laura in their hands, then walked back through to Stage 1. Eloise was still unconscious, her bloodied, mangled face pressed against the carpet.

Amanda sat up, wincing as her raw knuckles pushed against the rough fibres. "I saw her on the feed. Just after Aoife and Mark left the dorm. She must have come inside while I was still in there and hidden under a bed or something."

"How did she get out of the kitchen without her bio-band?" Harris asked,

"That's what I saw on the feed. One of the guys from Crew 40 opened the door for her."

"So he's in on it too? Jesus, they're about to go into Stage 3."

"No, no, I don't think so. I think he was just being gentlemanly. Anyway, her sleeves are rolled down to cover her wrists, but the bio-feed shows she's definitely not wearing a band. I paused the feed on the holloscreen in the middle of SECO 2 if you want to check it out. What are we going to do with her?"

Harris leaned over Eloise's inert body and looked back at us. "We need to cuff her and extricate her from this facility. They have cells land-side. Let me get on comms and sort it."

I was aching all over from the sudden change in pace and the impact of taking Eloise off Amanda, and I could feel blood dripping from my nose where her head had struck back at me. Despite this, I couldn't help thinking 'one down…'

CHAPTER TWENTY-ONE

THE NEXT FEW days were a blur. The ICP took custody of Eloise within an hour of the incident, once she'd come round, but by all accounts, she was refusing to speak. Grealish was undoubtedly happier that we were finally making some progress, but the whole crew seemed a bit more strained.

Hennessey had called us all into the rec room the following morning and explained that Eloise had been an infiltrator, had murdered Leon, and was planning an attack on the space station, costing millions of lives, including our own. The rest of the crew looked stunned at this revelation, and I couldn't blame them. If I hadn't been party to the investigation, I would have reacted in the exact same way.

Amanda could no longer maintain her cover. Too many people had seen her tackling Eloise and putting Harris on the deck, and despite many hours of discussion, no credible cover story could be invented that would stand up under scrutiny, so Hennessey introduced her to the crew as an undercover operative for the ICP, and told us that Amanda would stay with us for the duration of our time in Echo before joining the BRDF ranks on the Bertram. The weight of her double life lifted, Amanda visibly relaxed, and seemed much more bubbly after this. I was reminded of the old adage *'the truth will set you free'*.

Laura spent the night in the infirmary with a mild concussion, but came back to the dorm the following morning with a lump the size of a golf ball on her head, and a badly bruised shoulder. I'd been in with her for an hour while they checked me out, but aside from a bloody nose, I was none the worse for wear. Amanda had broken a couple of fingers. She claimed it was as a result of colliding with the door, but I thought it more likely a result of her fist colliding with Eloise's head. She had a beautiful shiner on her left eye, and bruising around her neck and abdomen, but they released her with little delay.

I was hauled into a BRDF Command Centre in Stage 3 by the air-side CO of Echo, Brigadier General Martinson, and bawled out for my behaviour on the Bertram. Both Harris and Hennessey, upon hearing that I was being disciplined, came bowling into the brigadier's office and launched into an explanation of my 'mission' and the intel. He then hauled them over the coals for withholding this information from the command structure, until they explained that we had an infiltrator within the BRMC, and that the only way to maintain our cover was to keep all intel to a closed group.

A five-minute call to Colonel Grealish put the whole thing to bed, and the brigadier's demeanour became considerably warmer after that. He promised to put a call in to the Admiralty to explain, which I thanked him for, before being dismissed.

The ICP brought me in for a full debrief and interrogation, on all events leading up to Eloise's exposure as an AoG spy. The consensus was that the scene in the showers was manufactured to deflect any suspicion away from her, and to cosy up to me. If that were true, then I really was out of my depth here. I had been completely taken in, hook, line and sinker.

Laura and Amanda had to undergo a similar process, and both looked absolutely knackered when it was all over. Amanda was the flavour of the month in the crew, and the next few nights she was the centre of attention, answering questions about her work and the events leading up to Eloise's exposure as an infiltrator. Laura, conversely, looked distinctly unhappy about this, and I suspected there was a little jealousy there, what with Laura also being an ICP undercover officer, albeit undiscovered.

On the third evening after Eloise's arrest, the entire crew was sitting round the sofas, and the subject came back to Amanda and her undercover work. Laura sat there for about a minute, before getting up and leaving for the dorm. I followed her inside, where I found her lying on her bed, hands behind her head, staring up at the ceiling.

"Come on you. Arse out of bed. We're going for a steam." I reached my hand down and gently hauled her upright in a single movement. The pair of us grabbed our gear and wandered round to Opps, where we found the conditioning room empty. I stripped off, grabbed a towel and entered the steam room, and was joined a minute later by Laura.

She'd wrapped a towel around her middle, covering her chest and falling mid-thigh. I could see the livid bruises on her shoulder, which were turning a rather dark purple colour with yellow around the edges. She was moving a little gingerly, but given the impact, I wasn't at all surprised.

"What's going on? You seem really stressed at the moment."

"It's nothing, Jax. Don't worry about it."

"I will worry about it. We've had a monstrous few weeks in here, and, like you, I'm getting a bit stir crazy and ready to move on."

"Look, it'll just seem really childish, and honestly, I'll be fine tomorrow."

"Listen, Laura, I get it. Amanda is getting all this praise, and none of them have a clue about your contribution and your job as an undercover ICP operative. But you're looking at this all the wrong way."

"How am I looking at this the wrong way? Everything you've just said is fact."

"Because Amanda's cover is blown. She is no longer an effective asset until she gets on board the Bertram. She is no longer of any use to our ongoing investigation, because she's been outed by her action, which renders her useless."

She looked slightly mollified, so I decided to push the point home a bit harder. "You, on the other hand, are completely under the radar. If, and it's a big 'if', Mark turns out to be the other infil, then he's going to stay right away from Amanda, and he'll not suspect anyone else. Who could believe that there would be more than one undercover ICP officer in one tiny crew? There's only seven of us left, and the good news is, we now know it's not Libby, we already knew it wasn't Jennifer or Aoife, and so there's only one target remaining, and as the only undercover ICP officer left you get to take him down all by yourself."

"I won't, though. Even Amanda told me to avoid another public showdown, because it limits my options on the Bertram. Right now, nobody knows who I am, so I can still work counter-intel. If I blow my cover, I'm just another grunt."

"Maybe, but Amanda is out-out. She's done, you're not. You did a better job of remaining undercover, don't forget that."

"You're a decent man, Jaxon."

"Yes, well, don't tell anyone else. I'm currently trading off the reputation of publicly tackling a woman half my size." She laughed and certainly relaxed a bit more after that.

We stayed in the steam room until we were both relatively pickled and then headed back to the dorm to chill out. Just as we entered there was a blue glow from outside, and the familiar pulsing sensation enveloped us. We walked to the window where the crew were all gathered watching, and there, twenty metres off the ground, was the Nova Pilgrim, slowly setting down on the pad, with two Sigmas circling overhead. We watched as the shuttle powered down, and the ramp at the back lowered.

Six people descended, one of whom was an enormous man with a bushy moustache...

The man sat quietly in the corner of the room, thinking about the next stage of the plan. The others were in the meeting room, discussing the next moves. The door was open just a fraction, so he could hear them. He liked sitting in the shadows in the corner and listening. It enabled him to think without the clutter of close voices distracting him. He could hear the man speaking.

"We have him under control now. He will do as he is asked. They cannot be allowed to continue. If he fails, kill them."

He sat there for a while, listening and waiting. A moment later, a woman entered from the far door, and stopped as she neared the open door to the meeting.

He watched as she crept slowly, ear turned towards the doorway, completely unaware of his presence. These were not the actions of a dedicated Acolyte, and there had been many conversations about suspected leaks of their plans and information. Right here, and right now, he could see how they had been compromised. She would have to be dealt with.

He stood up and walked slowly and quietly until he was behind her. Then he leaned around her with one hand and pulled the door open, whilst the other hand pushed into the small of her back as he shoved her into the room.

The other men looked up quizzically. "She was outside, listening to every word. What would you like me to do with her?"

An hour later, Hennessey appeared in the rec room, and looked around for a moment before catching my eye. She wandered over to the sofas and pulled a note out of her pocket, read something on it, and then put it back.

"Jaxon, Amanda and Laura, sorry it's so late, but we have some bigwigs on site from the Bertram and your presence is required. They want your account of the events three days ago."

I looked at Amanda and Laura and then back at Hennessey. "What, now? It's nearly midnight."

"Yes, now. They're heading back to the station shortly." She turned and walked out, and the three of us followed. Hennessey turned left out of the rec room, and up a long corridor, past the infirmary, to a mag-lift on the right. Hennessey presented her bio-band, and the lift opened for us all to enter. She said nothing and did nothing, so I assumed there was only one destination for this lift, and it felt like we were going down.

"What was with the note?" asked Laura.

Sara smiled. "Trying to make it look like some official order from higher up is all."

The mag-lift doors opened onto a narrow passageway which Hennessey turned left into. The walls were plainly decorated in off-white, with a faded green linoleum floor, and flat lights fitted into the walls at regular intervals. We followed the passageway for a short distance, and then through a door to the right into another passageway much longer than the first. There was a door at the far end, with windows, but no light from the other side, which gave me the impression that this was an external door.

A moment later, Hennessey opened the door onto a small, covered courtyard, with several military vehicles parked in it. The left side was completely open, and the Nova Pilgrim sat inert on the launch pad, flanked by the two Sigmas. I wondered for a moment if we were heading to the Bertram, but Hennessey continued to walk to a door in the far right corner, which opened onto a stairwell. We climbed up two floors until we reached a small vestibule with a door on the left. Hennessey knocked and entered, with the three of us in tow.

We were in a large meeting room, with glass all down the right side, overlooking the Launch Bay. The hexagonal exoskeleton criss-crossed over the windows, lit up by the lights inside the room. A conference table with maybe twenty seats was sat neatly in the centre of the room and was currently half-occupied. The admiral's vast frame filled the head of the table, and he looked imperiously at the three of us. They ushered us to seats in the middle, nearer the group. Grealish and Cooper were both there, as were Harris and Addison, along with the five others that (presumably) arrived with Admiral Willard.

I sat between Laura and Cooper, with Amanda opposite, next to Addison and Hennessey. The admiral looked up at us and spoke.

"I have just been briefed on the emerging threat of the AoG. I understand that one infiltrator has been flushed out and is in custody, and that there is another in Crew 41 that has yet to be identified. That about the long and short of it, Andrew?"

Grealish looked up. "Yes, Sir, that's pretty much it. Although there is only one potential candidate now in Crew 41 who we suspect."

"So why aren't we arresting them and removing the threat if we know who it is?" This from an older man in BRMC fatigues opposite Grealish, with the name 'Lavigne' on his chest patch.

"General, the evidence is still very circumstantial, and until we have definitive proof, we need to treat him as any other Occo."

"Andrew, the general is right. If there's only one candidate, and you have the intel that says we have a second infiltrator, it would be prudent to act upon it now. Prevention versus cure and all that jazz."

"Admiral, Barclay, Watkins and Leith here are our operatives inside Echo. They've been on this from the beginning, and it's thanks to them we've found one infiltrator already, but this operation remains unfinished." Grealish looked over at me. "Jaxon, why don't you bring us up to speed?"

Talk about being put on the spot. "Yes, Sir. Admiral, the intelligence so far is that the AoG are planning two different attacks. One, to halt the evacuation, and the other, to destroy the Bertram Ramsay. This intel came directly from Colonel Grealish's source inside the AoG. The only way to halt the evacuation, given the number of facilities worldwide like this one, is to disable the transport network. When I was up on the Bertram last week, I saw that the second shuttle is currently not flight-worthy, and apparently not likely to be for several months, which led me to the conclusion that the Nova Pilgrim was the only sensible target. I admit, at the time I felt it was better kept secure on Globe XI."

"And now you think the threat is on the Bertram?"

Harris stepped in at this point. "I think it's the only conclusion that makes sense, Admiral. If the AoG destroy the shuttle here, they halt transportation long enough that no further evacuation can ever occur without putting the Bertram at the same risk as the planet. So in order for them to achieve their main objective, they must have people already on board to do the damage."

"And you concur with this assessment, Colonel?"

"I do. The last six weeks have been an intense investigation to discover the identities of the AoG infiltrators at Echo. So far we have one AoG defector dead, and his killer in custody. We have separate intel that suggests that killing Prouse was her primary objective, so the larger play here—to destroy the Bertram—falls to another unidentified individual."

"Who you believe you have identified. Which brings me back to my original point—why isn't he being removed from the facility right now?"

Amanda bristled, but managed to keep her cool. "Because, Sir, if we are correct, and this individual is part of a plot to destroy the Bertram Ramsay, then it stands to reason that he's not the only one. When we create a plan, we build in redundancies—alternative options should the first option fail. If we accept that as fact, then we must also accept that there are more of these people on the Bertram Ramsay already. And if we remove our suspect from this facility, we lose our only lead to discover their whereabouts and identity."

"So this is a catch and release scenario?" said the general. "You want to let this person loose on the Bertram, so they can lead you to the other operatives?"

"That's pretty much the complete picture, General, yes." Grealish sighed and leaned back in his chair. "Admiral, may I speak freely here?"

"Of course, Andrew. Tell us what's on your mind."

"Thank you, Sir. Look, Amanda has been undercover on this operation for a year, but she's now burned. Tyrone and Sara are BRMC, and so their activities are already suspicious to anyone who is an enemy of Earth, which leaves us with two operatives that nobody suspects—Laura and Jaxon.

"They've worked hard on this. It's thanks to Jaxon that we understand the scope of the plot, and it's thanks to Amanda and Laura that we discovered one of the infiltrators in Echo. Nobody suspects either Laura or Jaxon of being counter-intelligence operatives, because both are immersed in the Compression process.

"By far the bigger issue here is that we also know we have traitors in the BRMC and ICP on site. Some of the intelligence that's been fed back to us directly concerns events that have occurred inside Echo, and since BRMC can't leave, and ICP can't enter, our only conclusion is that one person inside is colluding with another outside. Our full focus now is to discover these individuals before the tour rotation in four days, otherwise we'll be facing at least another two AoG operatives on the Bertram."

"There's also something else we might consider." I figured now was the best time to mention it, as the admiral was at least minimally acquiescent. "If I were AoG, and I wanted to destroy the Bertram Ramsay, by far the easiest way to achieve that would be to prevent it from leaving Earth's orbit. Strand it here, and everyone on board may as well be on Earth."

There was a moment of silence as the people around me digested this. It had only just occurred to me, so I couldn't pretend I had some amazing foresight here.

"I just asked myself what I would do if it were my mission. And that's what I'd do. No need to destroy the Bertram if there's an effective weapon already en route."

Grealish looked at me, then back at the admiral. "Sir, Jaxon's right. If they could keep the Bertram in orbit, they wouldn't have to do anything else. It would succumb to the same fate as Earth. So, given that as a scenario, what could they do to prevent the Bertram leaving orbit? What would be the ideal target?"

"Nigel?" The admiral addressed one of the other men in the room who had, thus far, remained silent.

"Well, there are many critical systems, but all of them have local redundancies—oxygen generators, water reclaimers and the like are all systems installed in every globe. Each globe also has its own power and propulsion, should they need to separate from the main body. In essence, they are all individual ecospheres connected together. The central command globe houses the primary propulsion system and the Quirillium Nucleus. So, if it were me, that would be my target. The entire station would be stranded if that was taken out, and none of the other propulsion systems can operate while connected to the hub."

He continued. "I would also consider breaching the reactor. Any meaningful damage could render it unstable, and it wouldn't take long before the entire station is a nuclear wasteland. The globes could detach and seal, but their individual propulsion systems are inadequate to eject them from Earth's gravitational pull. They'd be dead in the water."

The admiral looked thoughtful. "Okay, let's assume this is their plan. General, I need a plan of action for the defence of these critical systems implemented ASAP. In the meantime, continue your investigations. We'll send the Nova Pilgrim with four Sigmas from now on, and we'll decompress the bay whenever it's docked."

"And Jaxon..." I looked up. "If you ever walk out on me when I'm bollocking you again, I'll lock you in the dock when we decompress."

CHAPTER TWENTY-TWO

I COULDN'T SLEEP THAT night. Too many things running around in my head. Mark was still on the outskirts of the group, but with Amanda as the centre of attention it was no wonder he was cagey. The thing worrying me was the flow of intelligence out of Echo. There'd been no news since I mentioned the possibility of the DECON 4 gate being compromised as the only viable option, unless it was Addison or one of the other pilots and they were lobbing messages out of the Sigma windows. I shook that ridiculous notion from my head and got myself out of bed.

The clock on my bio-band read 04:55. Barely four hours since I went to bed in the first place. Today was going to be a long day, but not much I could do about it. We had another conditioning assessment today, and I hoped that the extra hours spent with Eloise were going to pay off.

I still felt slightly humiliated by that whole situation. It had occurred to me that she was faking, but my ego prevented me from seeing it. In my defence, she had embraced me naked, which, at the time, seemed entirely unnecessary. I'd assumed she was trying to get more of a reaction from me, but not to manipulate me. In fact, the only woman I hadn't seen naked so far was Jennifer. To be fair to Amanda, everyone had seen her in the buff when she tackled Leon. I definitely needed to kick my ego to the curb.

Eloise was an absolute master, as it turns out, and I wondered why I hadn't received more grief for not being cynical enough. Especially from Laura—I was expecting all sorts of sly comments, but since the events of four nights ago, she'd been rather subdued. Part of me was also hoping that she'd join me in the showers again, but she'd shown almost no interest since that night, and I wondered if there was a little regret there.

I had a quick shower and then went for a walk. I had no real purpose, but I needed coffee and the Stage 2 kitchen wasn't yet open, so I walked around to Stage 1, which had coffee on the go twenty-four-seven. The whole of Echo was a ghost town, but it had barely ticked past 05:00, so I wasn't surprised. There wouldn't be any meaningful activity until closer to 06:30, which gave me plenty of time to ponder the current situation.

I filled a mug with coffee, and walked through to the demo room, with all the pictures of the Bertram Ramsay in. It was a remarkable piece of engineering, and these images really didn't do it justice. It was incredible to think that each of these globes was self-sufficient and could separate from the hub and navigate under their own power. Each globe must have a dock of some sort as well, or they'd be trapped inside forever. I made a mental note to ask Addison about it next time I saw him.

I was about to head back when a BRMC officer walked into the room and leaned over a desk in the corner, writing something on a piece of paper. I was surprised by his presence at this hour. I checked my bio-band—05:13—and then looked back at my new companion. His body language seemed all wrong—I can't explain why—and he just seemed, I don't know, fidgety and tense. I took a slow step back into the shadows to watch. I was in my black flight fatigues, so I was hoping he wouldn't see me. Conversely, he was in his whites and seemed to glow in the morning light. I could see sweat forming on his forehead—this was a man under pressure.

The fog suddenly lifted from my head as the adrenaline kicked in. Every sense was alert, and I could feel my muscles tightening. I remained still and silent and just watched as he folded the note, looked around to see if he was alone, and then tucked it behind a painting of the Nova Pilgrim by the staging area, before turning about and walking back through to the Stage 1 rec room. He was nervous and jumpy; no question about it.

My brain was racing. There were several choices available to me here. I could extract the note and read it, but if someone walked in while I did that it would either implicate me or blow the dead drop. Perhaps I could sit and wait and see who arrived, but that could be tomorrow for all I knew. I could run and get Harris, but then I might miss the person collecting. Or I could follow the BRMC officer and see where he went. That would be difficult, with such narrow corridors and no place to hide. I could always just stroll along with my coffee, as nonchalant as you like, and just be myself, but I didn't trust myself to keep a game face.

The best option, I concluded, would be to sit in the Stage 1 rec room, in sight of the drop, and all exits, and just drink my coffee and trust that someone would come looking for me at some point. I figured our BRMC guy would be on the camera feeds, so he'd be easy to identify, and probably follow his path to his destination through all the cameras. I had an exact timeframe, so it wouldn't be nearly as painful as it had been to catch Eloise on the feed.

I grabbed a refill from the pot, careful to keep my eyes on the prize, and bedded myself in for the long haul. They didn't expect me anywhere before 14:00 today, and I think my crew would assume I was off flying if not in the rec room, so I wasn't hopeful of company soon. I couldn't ask one of the other BRMC guys to fetch Harris either, as I couldn't be sure who I could trust, so it looked like I'd be camped out for a while.

It gave me some time to think it through. It seemed an odd place to have a dead drop. The only personnel with access to air-side were BRMC, so this surely couldn't be the direct leak? And if I was right, then why all the subterfuge? I could walk up to anyone in my crew, or BRMC personnel, and hand them a note, and nobody would give it a second thought. This guy looked under real strain too, and I considered the possibility that he was doing this under duress. Which meant that someone on the inside was piling on the pressure.

None of it was making sense. Even if it were true that he was being coerced into compliance, that didn't explain the need for a dead drop air-side. I'd seen plenty of occasions where BRMC officers were bawling out the grunts, both in SECO 2 and Opps, which made the drop even more irrelevant. If I were a grunt and an officer barked at me and told me to hand something over, it would attract zero attention. Literally zero. Even a member of the team of equivalent rank. I'd seen a few spats since I'd been here, and mostly people shrugged and ignored it.

The only rational explanation was that this note was not meant to be found or collected—at least not easily or immediately. It appeared that this was an insurance policy if something went wrong—maybe a last will and testament. The thought made me shudder, and I could feel goosebumps on my arms. Perhaps it was the smoking gun we needed, and it named the person who was pulling his strings. I took a deep breath and mentally stepped back. I was forming too many conclusions here, and that sort of thinking had already cost one life. Better I kept an open mind for now and discussed it with someone else before taking any action.

About an hour later, things were getting uncomfortable. I was on my fourth coffee, and my bladder was protesting. I dared not walk through to the dorms as they were both occupied, and the nearest WC outside of the dorms was back in the room with the note. It would just be my luck that the two minutes I took to relieve myself would be the two minutes in which the note vanished and I missed the recipient (if there was one) and any grounds for questioning the officer who left it. I crossed my legs and stopped drinking.

Grealish was pacing. It was 06:45, and he had barely slept. The current situation unnerved him. They had no actual idea what the AoG were planning, and despite their suspicions, he grudgingly conceded that Mark Hanson had done nothing so far that incriminated himself at all. The evidence about his parents and the Valiant was powerfully suggestive, but there simply wasn't any proof that he even knew that it wasn't an accident.

The leak of information outwards was also bothering him. The maintenance crew had made subtle shifts to the camera positions at the checkpoint to see if they could identify any sort of collaborative behaviour between ICP and BRMC, but so far nothing out of the ordinary had occurred.

He was just thinking about taking a walk down there to check it out in person, when a call came through on his comms.

"Grealish."

"Sir, it's Cooper. I've had a call from the front desk. They've got a badly injured woman down there, insisting on seeing you."

"Well, who is she?"

"She's refusing to talk, Sir. Not to anyone except you. What do you want me to do?"

Christ, he thought. Just what he needed right now—more drama. He sighed heavily. "Okay, bring her up to your office—tag her so she can't roam, and buzz me when she's in there."

"Sir." Cooper clicked off her comms and headed for the mag-lift. She walked down the long corridor to the vestibule at the front, where she found a woman clutching her side, blood pouring down her hands, and her face severely beaten. The woman looked up at her and said, "No. Only Colonel Grealish."

Cooper looked over at the guy behind the front desk. "I'm taking her up to the colonel's office. I need a bio-band now and send some medics up there immediately."

She took the band and gently clipped it to the woman's free wrist and then guided her through the doors. She was walking very gingerly, and her breath was becoming more and more laboured with each painful step. The walk back took nearly ten minutes at the only pace this woman could manage, and by the time they arrived at Cooper's office, her breath was rasping and she was making all sorts of noises.

Cooper sat the woman down in the nearest chair and then buzzed Grealish. The medics turned up before Grealish, but the woman just shook them off. "No time. Get them out. Nobody can know."

Cooper looked at the two medics, who seemed visibly distressed at being unable to help the woman, and asked them to wait down the hallway on the bench. She promised to call them in when they were done. Grealish turned up just as the medics were leaving.

He nodded to Cooper and then looked at the woman. His eyes widened in disbelief. "Andrea? What's happened?" He looked back at Cooper. "Get those medics back in here now."

"No. NO. There's no time, Andrew. We're already too late."

"Tell me what's happened to you." He said it with a fatherly voice, but with just enough of an edge to make it sound like an order.

"Communications still coming from Echo, but not directly. They're coming from the Bertram. They've got someone inside Echo ready to take out the entire facility. It's a suicide mission. I don't think he's AoG, but they're manipulating him somehow. They're everywhere. I thought there were only two, but I was wrong. So wrong. At least three more already on the Bertram."

"How do you know this? We need the source, Andrea."

She looked up at Grealish, eyes wide with fear. "They caught me listening in on a meeting. Stupid of me. I didn't check the room first. Someone already in there. Tried to run, but they stopped me and put me in a cyber-car. I didn't know where they were taking me. I managed to open the boot and jump out, but it was travelling too fast."

She was becoming progressively out of breath, and her words were beginning to slur. Her eyes were taking heavy, long blinks, and the blood was dripping from her hand and arm, pooling on the floor beneath her.

"They put me back in the boot and drove me here. Threw me out half a mile away."

"I'm getting you some medical help now. Cooper?"

"Sir." Cooper walked to the door and called the medics back in with some urgency.

"I'm sorry," Andrea said, tears glistening in her glassy eyes. She took a deep breath and went still.

It was another half an hour before I couldn't hold it any longer. I'd spent the last thirty minutes thinking through the best way to handle the situation, and the only conclusion I could come to was that I'd have to take the note on the way to the bathroom, and potentially put it back afterwards. I figured that anyone turning up for it would probably take a minute to have a look around when they didn't find the note, so worse-case scenario I'd bag whoever was collecting as I left the toilet. They'd better hope I'd washed my hands.

Mind made up, I left the table and strolled purposefully towards the painting. Echo was still a ghost town, so there was little possibility of anyone catching me removing the note, and I suspected it was unlikely anyone would turn up to retrieve it. I looked around as I approached the painting, and seeing the empty rec room I turned, lifted the corner of the picture, grabbed the note, pushing it into my top pocket as I headed for the loo.

A couple of minutes later I exited, and as expected, was greeted with complete silence and stillness. The problem now was that the note was burning a hole in my pocket. I couldn't decide whether to retake my seat and continue my self-sanctioned stake-out, find Harris or Hennessey and tell them about the note, or open it and read it myself and then decide.

I walked back towards Stage 2. I decided there was no point waiting any longer for someone to turn up. The cameras would catch anyone looking anyway, so that seemed like the least necessary option. I felt it would be intrusive of me to open the note myself, which was stupid, because it was clearly of some importance, and why should it matter who opened it, as long as they were on 'our' team. No, the sensible choice was to find an authority figure, tell them what I'd witnessed, hand over the note, and absolve myself of any further responsibility.

But that was an issue in itself. I couldn't detach myself, and I couldn't get out of my mind the way the man looked as he wrote and planted the note. He was petrified. That was genuine fear, I could see. I should have recognised it sooner and not spent the last hour and a half waiting for someone to turn up. I quickened my pace and went straight to SECO 2, to see if I could find Harris or Hennessey. A couple of guys were still in from the night shift, and I asked if they'd laid eyes on any of our superiors, but they just shook their heads.

I turned and pushed through the double doors to Opps, where I found Harris coming out of the conditioning room. I grabbed him and pulled him through to Launch View.

"What's got your knickers in a knot?"

I explained about my early start, and the BRMC guy, and the note. Harris hung on every word without interrupting.

I'd barely finished when he responded. "Well, let's go and get it then."

I pulled it out of my pocket before he could stand and laid it on the table between us. We both stared at it for a minute, and then Harris tentatively picked it up and opened it. He read it out.

"Please find my girls. I won't be around much longer. They've said they'll kill them if I don't do it. When you find them, tell them I did everything I could to save them. Forgive me."

Jesus fucking Christ. Harris just looked at me.

"We need to find him. Now!"

He got up and started sprinting for the doors. I followed him out through Opps and straight into SECO 2. He pulled up the camera feeds on the same holloscreen that Amanda and Laura used to find Eloise, and looked up at me. "What time?"

"It was 05:13 on my bio-band when he entered the demo room."

"Jesus fucking Christ, Jaxon. That's almost two hours ago."

"I thought it was a dead drop, Tyrone. Not a suicide note."

He just pulled a face and went back to the screen.

Harris pulled up the feed and skipped back to 05:10. There were six camera views on the screen; I walked into view in the rec room, and grabbed a coffee, then I jumped to another camera and entered the demo room, where there were two cameras trained—one above the passageway looking directly towards the airlock, and one at the far right side facing the stage area, with the exit airlock in the top corner.

"What were you doing, wandering around Stage 1? You understand the powers that be are on the lookout for strange activity?"

"It's not 'strange activity'. I couldn't sleep and the kitchen in Stage 2 doesn't open until 6 am, so I went to Stage 1 for a coffee, and then decided to have a nose about. And in case you've forgotten, it's a bloody good job I did."

"Here he is. Right on cue." The camera showed the back of the man's head as he walked in. He looked right and then headed across and left to the table by the stage.

"How the hell has he not seen you?" Harris turned to look at me. I shrugged. Looking at the second feed now, I could see both of us in frame. Me, on the left side with my back against the wall, and the man, who must have been no more than ten or fifteen metres away, at the table.

Harris watched it play out, but from this angle it was impossible to see his face. He turned to the right and Harris paused the feed.

"Do you recognise him?" I asked.

Harris stared hard at the screen and squinted. "It's difficult to tell. It's still quite dark in there, but light enough that the cameras have switched off the infrared." We watched as the man walked out of the demo room, straight underneath the camera above the passageway, but he was looking down and it was hard to discern his features.

"We need to follow his path through the cameras. Jaxon, you take over. I need to call this in."

I sat at the desk and switched between the cameras until I had the feed from above the SECO 2 corridor entrance in the Stage 1 rec room. I ran it back twenty seconds and then watched as the man walked into the rec room and directly across to the double doors. Then I switched to the next set—there was one on the other side of the doors, facing down the corridor with SECO 2 on the right, Opps on the left, and Stage 2 at the end on the left, although the Stage 2 door was out of shot. The other cameras were above the SECO 2 door, in the Opps corridor facing the double doors, above the Stage 2 entrance, and above the mag-lift.

I tried to catch him so that I could read his name patch, but it was almost as if he was evading the cameras. He walked past SECO 2, Opps and Stage 2 into the corridor that Hennessey had taken us down the night before. I watched him stop at the mag-lift and then get in it. I didn't have any further feed access.

"Tyrone. Tyrone!" He held up one finger while he finished his conversation.

"What is it?"

"He's gone in the mag-lift down the corridor from Stage 2. I can't see anything beyond that. And no clear shot of his face on any camera. If I had to guess, I'd say he was deliberately avoiding them."

"Shit. This is a real problem. I've just woken Hennessey and told her to get an armed patrol down here now. She's working on it, but we have to find this guy. Come on."

Harris ran out of SECO 2 with me on his heels, and headed down to the mag-lift. We stepped in and waited for what seemed like an eternity for it to move, then back out of the mag-lift into the green-lino passageway.

"Why don't we have to go through an airlock to get outside here?" It hadn't even occurred to me last night, but now I thought about it, it was odd.

"The mag-lifts are airlocks. It depressurises on the way down. Anyway, not the time for that conversation. We're going to have to sweep the grounds."

"Tyrone, wait." I stopped in the second passage and waited for him to turn around. "We're going about this all wrong. If you were a terrorist organisation, and you were manipulating someone to set off a bomb, where would you put it? Somewhere to cause maximum casualties, or somewhere to cause maximum damage. The Pilgrim isn't here, so they aren't targeting that."

"Difficult one. The Pilgrim is due shortly, so we can't write it off just yet. The BRMC barracks are home to about two hundred of us. There are connected dorms with about thirty people in each.

It would have to be a massive bomb to take out more than one or two."

"Unless they bring the building down?"

"Unlikely. You'd need to blow all the support struts of every building as they're all connected. No, this is a localised attack on this facility, so if I wanted to cause the most damage..." He broke off and looked up, panic etched all over his face.

"Opps! If I wanted to cause the most damage, I'd target Opps. All the communications arrays are there, along with the flight tower and our direct comms to the Bertram, not to mention more high-ranking BRDF than anywhere else in this facility."

He paused for a brief moment and then took off on a run through the passage to the courtyard at the end, before hurling himself left to the far corner of the launch pad, where the stairs go up to the Opps gantry and the airlock. I ran as fast as I could after him, but he was faster. He piled up the stairs, two at a time, and raced down the gantry to the Opps airlock. I caught up just as he was opening it.

We waited for it to pressurise and then ran through the armoury into Flight Readiness. Tyrone suddenly stopped, and it was all I could do to avoid crashing into him at full pelt. He walked back to the armoury, punched a code into the cabinet and pulled out two Proxys, one of which he handed to me.

"Hold it horizontal and squeeze the stippled end three times." I did as he asked, and my bio-band sounded a small tone and flashed red.

"That's now coded to you and can't be used by anyone else until you unpair it from your bio-band. You know how to use it?" I did, but I'd never actually tried. In the interests of expediency, I just nodded once.

We walked quickly through Opps, checking each room but finding nobody that looked out of place. Hennessey walked in with a dozen armed BRMC grunts just as we were coming back through the sim room.

"Sergeant, what's happening?"

Harris quickly explained and passed over the note, which Hennessey read with wide eyes and a frown. "Where did he go?"

"We don't know. Jaxon followed him on the cameras to the mag-lift in the Stage 2 corridor, and then we lost him. But that was over two hours—"

A commotion interrupted the conversation over at the airlock. Raised voices could be heard, and Harris sprinted back through with myself, Hennessey and her small platoon close behind.

"Back off. BACK OFF!"

It was the guy from the demo room. He had tears pouring down his face, and he looked absolutely terrified. His entire body was shaking. There were two BRDF officers squaring off with him. In his right hand was a bag, with a coiled cable coming out of it to a device in his left hand. Harris walked between them.

"Brian, what are you doing? What's going on?"

"Tyrone, I can't tell you. I've left a note behind the painting of the Pilgrim in the demo room. It'll make sense once I've gone. I have to do this."

"Brian, we've already got the note. Tell us where they've taken your girls. We can send a cyber-car and a squad to get them. I'll send our best marines."

"They're on the Bertram, Tyrone." His words were coming through dry sobs, and the shaking was getting worse. "They took them from our apartment. My Emily, and our twin daughters. They're only six."

He dissolved into tears and Tyrone motioned for us all to back away a few steps. This was a man on the edge, and under impossible duress.

"Who are they, Brian? How can we find them?"

"I don't know who they are. I DON'T KNOW." He screamed, spit flying from his mouth. He had snot and tears streaming down his face and chin, and he'd flushed so dark he was almost purple.

Harris held out his Proxy. "Brian, I don't want to have to do this, but we can't let that bomb go off. You understand, don't you? There are innocent people here that will get badly hurt if that detonates. Is that what you want, Brian? To watch your friends die with you?"

I could have told him that was completely the wrong thing to say. This guy was prepared to kill himself to save his wife and kids. In his situation, I wouldn't have cared less about collateral damage to humans or structures.

Harris sensed he was losing him and held out his Proxy in warning.

"Don't you do it, Tyrone," he sobbed. "It's a dead-man's switch. I drop, it goes off."

I stepped forward with my palms outstretched. "Brian, why hasn't it gone off then? It's because you don't want to do it."

He dropped to his knees and wailed. "I don't want to die. I don't want to die. They'll kill them, though. They said I had to die when I set the bomb off or they'll kill my girls. What can I do, Tyrone? Help me." He pleaded on his knees, face contorted in pain and fear.

Suddenly there was a familiar pulsing sensation, and I could see blue light emanating through the airlock windows. I looked around at Hennessey, and she had fear in her eyes too. She turned and ran for the comms panel. I turned back to see Brian looking out of the window, and then he slowly turned back to Harris.

An eerie calm had come over his face.

Everything went into slow motion again, for the second time in a week. I grabbed Harris by the lapels and dragged him backwards from the room, onto the floor, held my Proxy upright and squeezed the bottom end. Then the world ended.

CHAPTER TWENTY-THREE

WHEN I CAME to, the building was in tatters. There was a hole the size of a bus through the airlock and armoury walls. Air was rushing out thanks to the pressure, which also took the smoke with it, but it was fanning the flames which were roaring over the gantry. Harris was out cold on the floor next to me, and as I looked around, the two marines that were closest were in a shit state, crumpled on the floor by the entrance to Flight Readiness.

The small group of marines that Hennessey had brought in with her seemed to be okay, although they were all on their arses and wriggling fingers in their ears. The walls between the armoury and Flight Readiness had protected them somewhat.

My Proxy was still on, but glitching badly. I could feel the shield edge against my legs, flickering on and off. As the seconds ticked by, I felt distinct elements of pain in my legs. I looked down and my flight suit was shredded. There were sharp metal bits sticking out of my shins and calves, and I could see blood trickling down.

I could feel the pulsating gyro-spheres from the Pilgrim and guessed it was still hovering above the launch pad. The light was a mixture of blue and dancing orange from the flames.

A klaxon sounded above us, and suddenly the gusting breeze stopped. I guessed they'd switch off the pressure, so we were now operating at normal atmosphere. I wondered, stupidly, if that meant we'd all have to go through DECON again.

Smoke was filling the room, and other noises were filtering in. I could hear a lot of groaning, and some screams that sounded like they were outside. The ground crew would have been out for the Pilgrim to land, but they were far enough away to be shielded from most of the blast by the gantry, I hoped.

I pushed myself up very slowly and assessed my condition. There was a ringing in my ears, but it was faint and fading. My right forearm felt like someone had hit it with a sledgehammer. I was still gripping my Proxy like my life depended on it, and a small voice in my brain told me to let it go, which I did.

My back and arse felt bruised too, but that was hardly surprising; I must have hit the deck quite hard. Everything was a blur and I could hear voices now, coming from behind us in the Opps centre. There were people moving through, and medics attending to the bodies on the floor.

I checked Harris was breathing and shouted for a medic, before shuffling over to the marine that was on my left when the bomb detonated. He had blood cascading out of his nose and ears, and the left side of his face was blackened and dead-looking. I checked his pulse and couldn't find one, but then I could barely feel my fingers. I shifted him around so that he was lying with his back to the wall and legs outstretched along the skirting. His hands had debris imbedded all over them, and I guessed he'd tried to shield himself from the blast and they'd taken the brunt of the impact.

The pulsing got louder and stronger, and I could feel it throbbing through my shoulders and neck. I heard the familiar winding sound of the Pilgrim's landing gear coming down. I guessed it must be relatively safe out there if they were still going to land.

One of the medics got to me and started fussing about my face, but I brushed him off and told him to look after the two marines at the front first. My injuries weren't life-threatening. Theirs might be.

Harris stirred; I pulled myself over to him and gently rolled him onto his side so he was facing me. His cheeks and hair were singed, and his legs looked to be in a similar state to mine.

"What the fuck happened?" he shouted hoarsely over the wailing of the klaxons.

"Don't try to move, mate. Medics will get to you in a second. You took a big hit there."

"Why aren't we both dead? We were yards away."

"Who the fuck knows? Managed to deploy my Proxy while I was saving your arse. You can thank me later. I've still got bags that need carrying."

He laughed, but it quickly turned to a coughing fit and a grimace, and he clutched his chest. He'd hit the deck face first, so I expect he'd broken a few ribs in the maelstrom. Another medic got to us now, and I pointed them to Harris.

I looked back and saw Hennessey standing there, hands on head, in total bewilderment. She looked completely unscathed, probably because she'd put some distance between herself and Brian when the bomb went off. The marines were picking themselves up now, and a couple of them were helping the medics and clearing debris away. The Flight Readiness room had vents and ducts swinging from the ceiling, and it looked like the lockers had fallen over in a twisted mess of metal.

The medics were getting Harris strapped on to a stretcher on my right, and the other two were doing the same with the marine on my left. He must be still alive, which was good news. The other marine they'd left where he was, and there were some already cordoning off the area. Not so good news for him.

The whole back side of the armoury was missing, and the areas around the hole were scorched and twisted. There was a fire crew outside putting the flames out from the gantry. Time seemed to be fluid at the moment, and I wondered how much had elapsed since the blast. My brain was numb. I kept having random, inconsequential thoughts. My vision was fading in and out too, and I could feel a pounding sensation developing in the back of my head.

The medics hoisted Harris away, and another pair came over to me. I could hear them making an assessment, but I was dizzy and struggling to make sense of the words. Many hands lifted me and I was comforted by how gentle they seemed to be. I opened my eyes again to see what was going on, but everything was spinning, and my entire body felt like it was vibrating. One of the medics put his hand to my head and pushed it back down, and everything went black.

The following twenty-four hours felt like a year. Command put Compression Echo and the fifteen adjacent sites on total lockdown. The shuttle had been forced to land as it was struck by debris which compromised the hull, so they sealed the whole Launch Bay off to everyone while the ground crew and engineers did their bit.

For the first time in Compression history, the site was swarming with ICP investigators. Crews were isolated to their Stages, and they herded BRMC personnel back to the barracks, with the exception of those on roster at Opps and SECO 2.

When I woke up I could hear voices around me, but they were foggy and muffled like I had cotton wool in my ears or something. My legs were stinging and my back was aching, but I didn't feel quite as broken as I suspected I should.

I opened my eyes and looked around. I was in an infirmary, but I couldn't say with any conviction that it was the one in Stage 2. It looked bigger, although I'd only previously seen it from the doorway. There were probably twelve beds in here, all occupied by people in various states of injury. I tried to sit up and felt a sharp pain in my hand. When I looked down, I discovered a needle inserted into the back of my hand and taped down. I followed the tube up to an IV, which was dripping slowly.

To my right was a woman—I couldn't make out her face, but she had short, dark hair that seemed to be matted with blood. On my left was the marine who had taken the brunt of the blast, or at least I assumed that's who it was. He had bandages all over his face, wrapped tightly around, and his arm was in a cast along with both of his legs. They'd hooked him up to a machine that bleeped softly every few seconds.

I shuffled myself backwards until I was a little more upright, which attracted the attention of the medical team. A woman approached me wearing camo fatigues with a red cross on her shoulder, and introduced herself as Medical Officer Jane Pullman.

"You took quite a hit there, Jaxon. I'm amazed you're still alive. Do you remember what happened?"

"Vividly," I replied, and she laughed.

"Yes, I'm sure that's not something you'll forget for a while. Anyway, how are you feeling?"

We chatted back and forth for a bit. She told me that the damage to my legs was superficial and everything had been glued up in the HolloDoc and was starting to heal. My arm was a livid purple colour from my wrist all the way up to my shoulder, and incredibly tender to touch. I'd bruised my backside and my back in the fall, and taken a hell of a bang on my head, which explained the vision problems and the headache, but I'd be fine in a couple of days and able to resume light duties.

"And I mean light. You are lucky to be alive after that ordeal, so you just remember that, when you're deciding whether to do some combat training."

I smiled, and she walked away. She'd disconnected my IV, which was basically a painkiller, so I swung my legs over the side of the bed and gingerly stood up. My shins were stinging and felt really tight, but with so much glue on my wounds it wasn't surprising.

There was a fresh flight suit in my locker, so I ditched the robe and put it on, then had a quick look around the ward for Harris, but there was no sign of him. I wandered out of the door and looked left. It turned out I was in the Stage 2 infirmary, so I took the short walk over to the Stage 2 entrance and headed into the rec room. The crew were all at the windows overlooking the Launch Bay. They turned as I walked in.

"Jaxon!!" Laura screamed and ran at me. I frantically waved her off before she launched herself on me and did any more damage. She pulled up and then put her arms gently around me.

"I thought you were dead. We all did," she said through tears.

"They didn't tell you I was okay?"

"Nobody told us anything. We've been locked in for the last twenty-four hours."

"I'm not surprised. They locked the whole site down, I think. There are police everywhere though. I saw some in the SECO 2 corridor as I came over."

"Yes, everyone has been interviewed. They're taking statements from everybody on site."

The rest of the crew crowded around me and started asking questions. I motioned them to the dorm, and they all followed. I needed to lie down. My back was aching, and honestly, I could probably have slept for another half a day. My system was full of drugs, and clearly they weren't ready to disperse the fog that clouded my ability to think.

I told them everything that had happened, omitting the part about the note and the dead drop. I didn't need them asking questions about that around Mark. Amanda and Laura could read between the lines—I could see it in their eyes, but the entire story would have to wait until I could isolate us from the rest of the crew.

We sat around chatting for an hour, and then were interrupted by a marine I'd never seen before. He was holding a hollotab, which he looked at as he walked in.

"I'm looking for Jaxon Leith, Amanda Barclay, and Laura Watkins."

"What the fuck is it with you three being called off for secret meetings, eh? That's twice this week." Aoife looked properly pissed off.

I feigned an 'injury voice' for her benefit. "Don't worry about it, Aoife. It'll just be the Eloise shit all over again. I expect it's the same people that did this." I pointed towards the windows, even though there were at least two walls in the way. She just raised her eyebrows at me.

We followed the marine through the rec room to the corridor and walked down to the airlock at the skybridge. He escorted us through and then pointed us to where Cooper was standing. She just nodded, and we followed her back to her office where Grealish and Hennessey were patiently waiting.

"Where's Tyrone?" I asked as soon as we walked in.

"He's been airlifted to Chelsea Barracks University Hospital. We don't have the necessary medical gear here to put him back together properly, but don't worry. He'll be back in a few days," replied Hennessey.

Grealish stood up and walked to the window, then turned and sat against the window ledge.

"Well, we are in the shit. Remember our inside source in the AoG? They kicked her half to death and then threw her out of a moving car just up the road. She managed to warn us and died on this floor ten seconds before the bomb went off in Echo. How are you doing, Jaxon? Sara told me you'd taken the brunt of it?"

"Lucky to be alive, Sir. And very grateful to be honest."

"As are we. Sara also told me about the note and what happened subsequently. I shudder to think how many bodies we'd be clearing up if he'd gone unchallenged."

"Note? What note?" asked Amanda.

Sara explained the day's events, and I chimed in occasionally to fill in the gaps. Neither of them knew I had been talking to the guy when he detonated the bomb. Laura looked at me anxiously, motherly concern all over her face.

Grealish took control again. "Okay, so here's what we know. Someone on the Bertram kidnapped Brian Latimer's wife and twin daughters, and was holding them hostage in order to manipulate Brian. He hasn't seen his family for six months since his rotation down here, which was due to end yesterday, so he was under incredible stress.

"Obviously they targeted Opps, though it's unclear why, as yet. It wasn't a target for body count purposes, or they'd have bombed the barracks."

"Could it just be the AoG sending us a message, Sir?" asked Laura.

"I don't think that's their style. I think this was a specific target. All the intel so far has been about Echo, and we're no closer to understanding why."

"Hang on a minute." My mind was suddenly racing. I could feel pain all over my body as my brain shook off the fog that had been clogging up my senses. "You said he'd been stationed down here for six months? Six?"

"That's correct. Why?"

"What do you mean 'why'? How the fuck did he get his hands on a bomb? This wasn't some kitchen-chemical-chuck-in-a-bit-of-fertiliser-and-a-bag-of-sugar explosion. This was a device with a trigger and a dead-man's switch. So how did he get his hands on it?" I could see the dawning comprehension on the faces around me.

Cooper recovered first. "Well, it can't have come in from land-side. You've seen and been through the scanners at DECON 4. In DECON 1 you walk in as naked as the day you were born and are given new kit on the other side. Everything that goes into DECON 1 we incinerate, ergo no bomb."

"And that's exactly my point. This can only have come from the Bertram. And what's worse is that for that to be true, it must have been built there. I assume all Compression sites have similar security and procedures for entry?"

Hennessey spoke. "Almost carbon copies. Same layout, same process, everything. Nothing gets in from land-side. That's how we can easily rotate crews between each site, because everything is the same."

"Well, then you've not only got a terrorist on the Bertram, but they're building bombs there. And flying them down here. Any number of people could have done it. Could be a pilot. Could be one of the ground crew in Globe XI in cahoots with a member of ground crew down here. How difficult would it be for them to send notes to each other inside cargo, or in a hidden dead drop on the Pilgrim?"

Hennessey seemed most troubled by this. "Jaxon's right. This can't be an ICP issue. It has to be BRDF or ground crew."

"There's still information getting out, Sara," I reminded her. "It can't all be an internal issue. Someone land-side is receiving messages and relaying them, and we're no closer to figuring out how, let alone who."

"Well, we need to start making progress immediately. They're evacuating all Compression personnel in the next week and closing the process off to any further Occos. Crews 42 and 43 will be the last to ever pass through this facility."

"What?" said Laura. "They're ditching the site?"

"The brass thinks it's better to stem the flow of incoming now and prevent any further breaches. It makes sense for a change. Now they only have to deal with existing problems, and not new ones."

"So, basically we've got a week left to figure out who's leaking information from this site, before we join a space station that we know to be compromised." Hennessey was totally matter-of-fact about it.

"What about Mark?" He hadn't been mentioned so far, and I wondered if he was no longer in the picture.

"Mark Hanson is what we call a 'person of interest'. I still need you guys to keep a close eye on him, but he's a lower priority than finding the ICP leak land-side. Or figuring out how intel is getting out, with or without ICP collusion."

"We know there's ICP collusion. Otherwise how did Mark, Leon and Eloise get into this facility?" It seemed so long ago that this intel was our priority concern.

"It doesn't matter now. Everyone has been ordered off site on rotation, so a new crew is already in. Whoever it was got away with it. And since there're no further crews incoming, it's no longer a problem.

"That said, the brass have given me carte blanche to set up a counter-intel team on the Bertram, specifically to deal with the on-site threat. And that's you six, including Tyrone. Amanda, strangely, being compromised as you have been may actually be an advantage because nobody will expect your involvement any more. I'm pulling some strings to get you all stationed where you'll be most effective, and I'm still working on identifying locations to meet safely when we're on board."

"Any questions?"

There was a general shaking of heads.

"Find them, or we all die."

CHAPTER TWENTY-FOUR

I WAS INTERVIEWED A couple of days later by two ICP inspectors. Grealish had warned me not to disclose my involvement in the counter-intel, but it was difficult to explain my decisions without hinting at it.

They made me re-tell my account over and over again; I assumed because they were looking for some deviation in my story. They pulled up the feed from the cameras that Harris and I had been scrolling through, and asked me a lot of questions about why I'd chosen to sit there and watch the painting, or why I'd chosen to keep myself hidden from Brian Latimer when he was writing the note. Always I gave the same answer—something didn't feel right. He seemed 'off'. I couldn't explain why I felt that way, or what had triggered that thought process. And ultimately, I'd gone to a superior and reported it, so they were going to have a hard time implicating me in any Machiavellian plot.

They also asked me a lot of questions about my involvement with Eloise, but that was much more straightforward. I had literally reacted when I saw her run. Why would she have run if she'd done nothing wrong? So my brain had kicked in and told me she needed to be brought down.

"A number of your crew have said you were getting quite close to her? Private sessions in Conditioning and the such like?"

I told them about the first encounter in the shower, and how I'd been totally taken in by her vulnerability and had promised to help get her up to speed. I felt stupid talking about it and perhaps they sensed this, because they wrapped it up quickly after that and the lead questioner held out his hand to me.

"From what I've heard so far, you did an incredibly brave thing a few nights ago. You undoubtedly saved lives with your actions. Your crew is lucky to have you."

I was immensely grateful to hear those words, and I relaxed considerably as they escorted me back to the dorm.

Laura had warmed up significantly too, and had decided it was her personal responsibility to attend to my wounds and dressings and to keep me fed and watered while I recovered. She even offered to help me get clean in the showers that morning.

"Oh, for fuck's sake get a cubicle, you two!" Aoife was her usual delicate self and rolled her eyes as she said it, but without any malice and with a hint of a smile on her face. Everyone laughed.

Harris turned up a few hours later with a walking stick and a lot of dressings on the side of his head. He had one arm in a sling, and looked decidedly worse than I did, I surmised. The crew applauded good-naturedly when he walked in, and he smiled. What took me aback was that when he approached me by the sofas, he flung his good arm around me and brought me in to a hug.

"You saved my life, mate. Thank you."

"Nah, I just needed a soft landing spot." He laughed, and so did the crew.

The day carried on in a similar manner, and I was feeling happy for the first time in a while, despite the aches and pains which seemed to have expanded to other areas of my body. There were still major concerns facing us, but for today they seemed a little less pressing.

Later that evening, everyone in Echo was summoned to a general assembly out in the Launch Bay. They'd set a make-shift stage at one end by the stairs to the gantry, and over two hundred of us were escorted from our dorms and barracks to the Launch Bay, which was surrounded by a heavy presence of well-armed marines. The rest of the site was on total lockdown, and the only inhabited places were Opps and SECO 2, which remained online and functional.

Grealish, Addison and General Lavigne were all on the stage, sitting behind a podium which was being secured by two BRMC officers. I could see Cooper at the front by the stage, and a smattering of ICP that I'd passed in the corridors of Echo Command. Above and to the left, the gantry was still cordoned off. The outside of the building was still blackened and burned, but the debris had been cleared away and a temporary wall had been erected where the airlock once stood.

General Lavigne stepped up to the podium when everyone was gathered, and a hush fell over the assembled crowd as he spoke.

"Three nights ago, an attack was launched on this facility by the Acolytes of Gaia. You will all be aware by now that there is an intense ICP investigation underway as to how this attack came about, and who was behind it. Everything is being done to ensure the safety of our crews and serving officers in this facility and aboard the Bertram Ramsay. I would like to ask that each of you remain vigilant, and alert, and report anything out of the ordinary, however trivial it may seem. Together we will overcome this terrorist scourge and continue on our mission to save humanity from extinction."

There was a smattering of applause, but after only one or two claps it stopped. The general seemed oblivious.

"Because of this attack, we have moved forward the timetable for evacuation. In the next seven days, every person in this facility will be transported to the Bertram Ramsay, where you will begin the next chapters of your lives as astronauts."

Conversations broke out almost everywhere. I hadn't realised that the general population wasn't aware of the evacuation order.

The general called the gathering to order. "Before we end this assembly, there are a couple of things I'd like to bring to your attention. In the events of three days ago, we lost a well-respected colleague. Sergeant Paul Chamberlain lost his life in the service of protecting his friends and colleagues in the Corps. The flags above Compression sites around the world fly at half-mast today, in memory of a courageous man, taken from us too soon."

A bugler began playing 'Taps', and the entire crowd fell silent and bowed their heads. The general, and the marines around the outskirts of the Launch Bay, saluted and held it for the duration of the tune. It was an emotional moment, with the silence being so stark and real, only broken by the soulful, distressing notes of the bugle. I could see tears cascading down many faces of the surrounding marines, and of the Opps crew. As the last notes were played, the assembled mass broke into applause for a full minute before the general stepped back to the podium.

"There is someone else amongst us who deserves a special mention. He was the closest to the threat, and yet threw himself in front of a colleague and dragged them out of harm's way, before immediately attending to the marine who had the worst injuries, despite being badly injured himself. There are at least two men here that owe their lives to this man, and had he not intervened when he did, there would undoubtedly have been many, many more casualties. And so, it is with great pride that I offer his first rank as a serving BRAF officer. Please welcome to the stage, Lieutenant Jaxon Leith."

The universe stood still for a moment. I couldn't believe I'd just heard my name. I was still emotional from the moving tribute to Sergeant Chamberlain. There was a push in the small of my back, and Laura was grinning at me, eyes glistening with tears, and her face red from crying. Many hands began shunting me forward. "Jaxon, move! He's calling you!"

I stepped out of the crowd to the side and walked what seemed like a mile to the stage. The noise around me was deafening. The crowd was clapping, cheering and whistling as I walked to the front. Harris greeted me at the bottom of the steps and ushered me up with a massive grin on his face, arm still in a sling. I helped him up the steps with his walking stick in hand and then stepped towards the podium.

"Sergeant Harris will bestow this great honour upon you, Lieutenant Leith. Your presence of mind and courage are commensurate with the best traditions of outstanding military contribution. Many of us stand here in your presence today, because of your actions and unquestionable valour, and your determination to preserve the life of others, at great risk to your own. Congratulations on earning your first military rank, Lieutenant, and on behalf of everyone at Echo, both military and civilian, we thank you and honour you, for your bravery, and for your selflessness under enormous pressure. Sergeant Harris?"

Tyrone turned to the general and took from him a set of gold wings, which he pinned above my name patch on my flight suit. He stepped back and saluted me. "Congratulations, Lieutenant Leith."

I returned his salute. I could feel tears burning the backs of my eyes, and I had to grit my teeth to stop my lips from wobbling.

The general spoke again as I stood alone on the stage, aware that all eyes were on me. "Not only has Lieutenant Leith earned his first commission, but in recognition of the exceptional bravery and courage he displayed in the face of overwhelming odds he is hereby awarded the Victoria Cross."

Fat tears were rolling down my face, and I was struggling to remain in control. Six weeks ago, I was wandering The Bleeds, aimlessly frittering my life away. And now, I stood on a stage being rewarded for doing what any other person would have done in my shoes.

Tyrone retrieved the medal from the general and asked me to lower my head as he placed it over and around my neck.

"History dictates that we award the Victoria Cross for 'most conspicuous bravery, or some daring or pre-eminent act of valour or self-sacrifice, or extreme devotion to duty in the presence of the enemy'. I think you, Lieutenant Leith, exemplify this statement more than any other in recent memory, and it is with great pride that we bestow this honour upon you."

The crowd erupted again, with applause and whistling.

"Salute the general, and then turn about and fuck off… Sir," whispered Harris with a smile on his face, as my head was bowed in front of him.

I brought my legs together sharply and saluted the general who saluted me back, and then I left the stage, to my immense relief, albeit in a shit state.

That night was a muted celebration in the dorm. We were still in lockdown, and not able to leave unless called out by ICP investigators. My crew gave me a warm reception though, and in all honesty, I felt like they were talking about someone else. I didn't believe I had done anything that others wouldn't have in those circumstances. I certainly didn't think it merited such lavish praise, rank, and medals.

It was nice to not have to think about anything, and just let the conversation wash over me for once. I'd been in the thick of it pretty much since I got here, so a night off wasn't such a big ask. Laura delivered on her promise of helping me wash myself in the showers. She was gentle and sexy and just a little dangerous, which definitely increased the pleasure.

Harris brought me my new flight suit the following morning, with the wings stitched above the name patch in place of the bronze wings that now sat on my locker, and a purple ribbon below with a small, bronze Maltese Cross in the centre, upon which was etched a lion guarding a crown—my Victoria Cross Medal Ribbon.

"You should be very proud of that, mate. I heard the general talking to the brigadier this morning. You are definitely the flavour of the month, and I expect you'll get a few more pats on the back before the week is out."

"Yes, well, at least I've got a medal and some wings to put in the bags you're going to be carrying for me now."

Harris laughed and slapped my shoulder, and then hastily apologised as I winced. I was still badly bruised on my arm and my back, and I was struggling to sleep properly as a result. It was nothing compared to Tyrone's injuries though—he really had taken the brunt of the impact, despite my attempted intervention. He was in good spirits, and his mood was infectious. Everyone in Crew 41 was smiling, irrespective of the current situation. Even Mark seemed lifted and was more engaging.

The repairs to the Pilgrim had been prioritised, and it was flight-worthy less than a day after the explosion. It was arriving on site twice a day now, and we watched as hundreds of crew members and marines were evacuated to the Bertram daily. There was a definite decrease in noise in the hallways and communal areas, as fewer and fewer personnel roamed the premises.

With five weeks still to go in our Compression regime, Harris and Hennessey laid out the plans for our course completion once on board the Bertram. The consensus was that the fitness was a priority, and whilst we'd made solid gains in our assessments, there was still some work to be done. I was told it would not be necessary to complete the course, as I would immediately join the BRAF once I got to the Bertram, and that, given my injuries, it was unlikely I'd be fit by the time the course ended anyway. Harris promised to join me in Conditioning once he was fit again, so that we could both get back to optimal fitness as we began our duties aboard the space station.

The next few days were subdued. It had been an intense internment, and I reflected on just how much had happened in the last seven weeks. I was still curious about the identity of the man at the bus depot, and wondered how much influence, if any, he'd had on the circumstances around Leon, Eloise and Brian Latimer. His face still haunted my dreams, and I was determined that he would see justice for his involvement in events at Echo.

I couldn't help feeling we still faced an uphill struggle aboard the Bertram Ramsay, with so many loose ends. Eloise continued to be interrogated, although she was still refusing to talk. She'd been moved to a cell at ICP Command in Whitehall and denied any access to the outside world. Given her beliefs and the impending apocalypse, I suspected that her incarceration meant very little to her, or the ICP.

There were still no leads on the leak of information from Echo site to the AoG, and with no operatives in the upper echelons of the enemy organisation, the flow of intelligence had all but stopped completely. Brian Latimer's wife and children were still missing, and I was out of the loop on what was occurring in that investigation, and as far as I could tell from my interviews with ICP investigators, they were still none-the-wiser as to how a bomb could have been manufactured on the Bertram and smuggled to Earth.

There seemed so many unanswered questions that it made my head spin just to think about it. Grealish's side project to have us as a specialist unit on the Bertram had not been mentioned since that initial meeting, and in the very little time I could get with Amanda and Laura alone, we speculated on how that would manifest itself once we got up there.

Now that I had my wings I would still need to complete my flight training, and fly sorties with the BRAF, but we would leave Earth's orbit before very long and I found myself overcome with emotion at the thought of never seeing my home again.

I wasn't the only one. As our departure grew nearer, I found the entire crew had become a little withdrawn. Even Libby's serene smile had somehow become forced and didn't extend to her eyes. Some of us were leaving people behind and some, like me, were all alone in the world, but this primeval instinct to return to our home was taking a toll on the mood in the camp.

There was some excitement, too, but everyone was careful about being overtly upbeat about the prospect of living on a space station. A few of the crew had never flown before, with the exceptions of Laura and Amanda, who had frequently been transported in ICP Grasshoppers, and Mark, who as a previously serving member of the Air Force had had many opportunities to see the world from above the clouds. Libby and Jennifer had moments of anxiety at the thought of boarding the Pilgrim, balanced with excitement over such a historically significant adventure.

As the days passed, they asked more and more questions about the Bertram, and I tried my best to give some sense of the immense size and the incredible feat of engineering it was. My experience aboard was limited to my two short stints on Globe XI, but even these relatively insignificant moments seemed to thrill and amaze the crew. I told them about the buildings and the paths and fountains, and about how 'normal' the residential areas seemed to be, with the gardens and streets. Of course, I had barely seen even a third of Globe 11. Addison had told me about the other residential areas, and how whole globes were filled with homes, with farms on the levels below them, plus all the engineering works within each globe that allowed it to be self-sufficient, and detachable from the core.

The conversations never ceased, and I was grateful for it. We'd been cooped up in Stage 2 with very limited access to anything for nearly a week, but the crew was fast becoming my family and we spent most of the days either gathered around the sofas, or chatting in the dorm where we could lie down. Laura spent most evenings leaning against me with her feet curled up on the sofa, holding my hand or squeezing my thighs when she got animated about something. There were lulls in the mood for sure, and there were tears fairly regularly, but I think this was just fear and trepidation.

Nobody talked about the explosion or Eloise any more, I thought, because those subjects were the primary catalyst for the mood in the camp deteriorating. I knew I wasn't the only one worrying about the potential consequences of a saboteur on board a huge vessel in the vast vacuum of space. I wondered how we'd feel, watching the Earth grow smaller in the distance, and whether anyone at the higher levels had anticipated the reaction of the masses now on board.

The very last day was the quietest. We'd become used to this home, and it was all about to change in a big way. The crew had packed their meagre belongings the day before, which only took about ten minutes. I'd asked Harris if we could have permission to take the crew to Opps Conditioning and use the steam room and sauna for our last day here. He managed to get us a couple of hours in the late afternoon. It was an enjoyable time, and the conversation flowed freely and more excitedly. We all sat around in towels, letting the heat soak into us, and just talked about our lives and families before, and our hopes and dreams of the future.

Upon our return to Stage 2, refreshed and both eager for the night to pass, and nervous about our future, we had one last drink on the sofas before going to bed early. Tomorrow was going to be some day.

CHAPTER TWENTY-FIVE

THE FOLLOWING MORNING was the first time in seven weeks that I was not the first to wake. I doubt anyone had slept particularly well, and I'd certainly heard a few get up in the night which was unusual.

There was a palpable excitement in the air. Today was always going to come, with or without the drama of the last seven weeks, and whilst our internment had been five weeks shorter than planned, it still felt like we'd been together for months on end.

I could hear laughter coming from the shower block, and needing to get cleaned up before the journey, I extricated myself from my bunk and wandered around to the showers. Laura, Libby and Jennifer were all in there, standing around in just their knickers, and laughing about something. It was only as I walked in that they all stopped, looked at each other and giggled. I mentally ticked Jennifer off the list of women whose bodies remained a mystery to me and shook my head. Fuck's sake.

I didn't ask what the conversation was about. The sudden stop when I entered gave me a pretty good idea. I grabbed a towel and headed into a cubicle between Libby and Jennifer and proceeded to soak myself in the hot jets of water. My mind started to meander, and I wondered whether the water pressure would be this good on the Bertram Ramsay.

When I'd finished I dried off, pulled my flight suit on, marvelling at the new inclusions on the left breast, and walked through to the rec room to grab a coffee. It was only just gone 06:00, so the coffee was scalding hot and fresh. The entire crew joined me in the next fifteen minutes. Everyone had come out of the dorm, bags in hand, along with their kit bags and belts, ready to head off.

Harris and Hennessey joined us around 07:00, and sat with us for a coffee while we waited for our call to the transport. Addison turned up about half an hour later, and wasted no time enamouring himself to all five of the ladies with his well-spoken Surrey accent and his chiselled looks. He smiled easily, and they fawned over him for ten minutes before he actually got around to the reason he was there.

"Lieutenant." It took me a minute before I realised he meant me.

"Sir?" Since when did I call him 'Sir'?

"As this is your crew's maiden voyage to the Bertram Ramsay, I wondered if you wanted to escort them from one of the Sigmas?"

"Actually, Addison, I think I'd like to sit this one out and just travel up with my crew, if that's okay?" To be completely honest, I was still bruised and battered, and wasn't at all sure I should be in charge of anything.

He smiled. "I expected nothing else. I'll be in Sigma 1 and I'll put three of my best in the other Sigmas. Not the best, of course. The best wants to travel up with his crew…" He winked at me and said, "I'll see you up there shortly."

He bade the rest of the crew farewell with his warmest smile and jovial tone, which the ladies lapped up, and then departed for the Opps centre.

I spent the next ten minutes being referred to as 'Lieutenant' and fending off requests for more personal introductions. I laughed at their feigned offended looks when I told them they weren't good enough. The crew was smiling, and I expect it was a relief for them all to get to this moment. We looked out of the windows as the familiar pulsing sensation filled the room at 08:00, and the Nova Pilgrim descended onto the launch pad with the four Sigmas settling on either quarter.

They called us for boarding shortly after 08:15, and I could feel the tension escalate among the crew. They escorted us to the mag-lift, and down through the tunnel to the courtyard where we joined a line of marines who were walking up the rear ramp of the Pilgrim. I'd always been impressed by its structure, but had never seen the inside, so I was intrigued as we walked up the ramp, and into what was clearly a cargo bay, to some steps in the far corner. We followed the rest of the passengers up the steps, along a short gantry, and then through a door into a lavishly furnished passenger cabin.

There were seats for at least four hundred people up here, with six columns of four. Laura grabbed my hand and led me to one of the window seats on the port side. I was stopped in my tracks a couple of times, as marines wanted to shake my hand and thank me for my efforts last week. It was odd for me, having such high praise from strangers, and I tried to be cool about it, but undoubtedly failed.

Laura sat by the window, in a big, cream faux-leather chair. There were no frills about the seats but they looked, and were, comfortable, with plenty of room to stretch out our legs in front of us. We had five-point mag-harnesses installed into each seat, the same as on the Sigmas, so the pair of us got ourselves strapped in and ready. The interior of the cabin was bright and airy, with holloscreens at the front showing forward cameras and GPS tracking data, along with several other metrics including altitude, airspeed, distance from destination, distance from departure and time elapsed.

I could see the rest of the crew getting excited as they took their seats. Mark sat next to Amanda, which surprised me slightly, but they seemed to be chatting and getting along. Libby and Jennifer were behind them, eyeing up a number of the marines to their right, who were just as interested.

I left my eyes on Jennifer, just for a moment longer. Of all the crew, she was the one I'd had least interaction with. I saw her talking to the others, so she wasn't shy, and of course we'd spoken, but nothing beyond the daily platitudes and work assignments. She seemed happy enough, particularly at the moment, as the pair of them were giggling like schoolgirls at the marines surrounding them.

I drew my eyes away and looked through the cabin. The ground crew had checked everything and everyone and made sure we were okay and comfortable for the journey, which they expected would take just under one hour. They waved us off and left through the loading ramp before clearing the pad. It wasn't long before we could feel the pulsing sensation of the gyro-spheres, and the captain announced over the comms system:

"Welcome to the Nova Pilgrim. For those of you who haven't been on board before, there are bags in the seat backs in front of you should you feel unwell during the trip. Flight time today is fifty-five minutes. Your new home awaits, and I hope you enjoy the ride."

There was a small jolt as the landing gear disengaged, and then we could feel ourselves rising as the stanchions remained static until we were hovering ten metres above the launch pad. I watched the Sigma on our left take off, and shoot up to three hundred metres, where I knew the four of them would do a three-hundred-and-sixty-degree reconnaissance before signalling to the Pilgrim to ascend.

The vibrating stopped as the SQIID drives kicked in, and then we were airborne. Laura almost screamed at the speed we rose at, and she wasn't the only one. There was a considerable amount of laughter throughout the cabin as the crew reached three hundred metres and stalled next to the Sigmas. I got a slap on the leg for laughing, and a coy look, which meant I'd be paying for that later.

Not for the first time this week, I pondered on the future with Laura. Neither of us had expressly said anything about it, but we were both very comfortable in each other's company, and there was no lack of attraction. I was more concerned about the long-term implications, should things not work out between us, but Tyrone had already broached this with me last night.

"There's nearly seven million people up there, mate. And twelve separate globes to live in. I reckon you could spend the rest of your life on the Bertram and never come across eighty per cent of the occupants."

He was probably right, and really, I had bigger things to worry myself with than a new romance. It was a brave new world up there, with a million things to think about. The challenge we faced together was bigger than those that immediately burdened us. There were questions unanswered, and an invisible yet deadly foe in our midst, and I reminded myself that our destiny had not yet been decided.

Our only mission was to ensure the continuity of our species, and hope above hope that Earth would be safe in our absence, so that one day we may appreciate its beauty once more.

EPILOGUE

"Everything will be okay in the end. If it's not okay, then it's not the end."

- John Lennon

I CAN FEEL THE walls around me closing in. Despite the enormity of the Bertram Ramsay, I have a palpable sense of trepidation and claustrophobia. Our planet may be small, in the context of the huge gas-giants and the vast nebula across the universe, but it is huge for one man. And I am only one man.

My movements will forever be constricted to the metal walkways of these artificial cities. I will never again feel a summer breeze on my face, or listen to the rain as it patters over my balcony in The Bleeds.

The crew had been buoyant and excited as we approached the bay doors of Globe XI. The smiles and wide eyes and fascinated looks adorned their faces until the doors of the bay closed, and a sense of profound melancholy swept through the cabin.

Even those among us who have lived sporadically between the Bertram and the barracks in Compression are deeply subdued.

This is our last journey.

In three months we will leave Earth's orbit and begin the perilous voyage into deep space. Our destination is anywhere and nowhere. With almost seven million souls aboard, the Bertram Ramsay has become a modern Arc, saving us from the fate that awaits Earth.

The majority will go about their daily tasks, thankful for their lives and the liberty afforded to them in these cities of wonder. It will take years, in all likelihood, to relinquish ourselves of the guilt, of the feelings of deep shame and heartache at the loss of our civilisation. The air is thick with hope and fear, tinged with a crushing sorrow.

For some of us, a small minority, our survival depends on the success of our mission. Among us is a ruthless, invisible killer, biding their time, slowly penetrating the depths of our vessel-of-hope, poised, ready to strike when the time comes.

My crew are my family now. Libby, Jennifer and Aoife are oblivious to our worries and the covert mission that consumes Laura, Amanda and myself. Mark is on the peripheries of everything, and still someone that needs investigating for his role in past or future events. He's been so quiet since the incident with Leon that it has been hard to develop any sort of relationship with him. Laura is probably closest, although seeing him sitting with Amanda on the shuttle made me wonder if he could truly be a threat. He knows who she really is, after all.

There are those among us who would do us harm, and it is our duty to flush them out and make them pay for their cowardice and hate.

"Hey, handsome."

Laura's voice draws me out from my dark reverie. "Hey."

"You've been lost in your thoughts all morning. Everything okay?"

"I'm okay. Just thinking about what happens next. Do you remember that man in the crowd when I arrived at the bus station?"

"Of course. He's been flagged for years, but nobody knows who he is. Why?"

"I think of him all the time. I'd bet my life he's on this station."

"Are you worried about what might happen?"

"Not worried, no. Apprehensive, I suppose. Somewhere in this space station someone is holding a woman and her daughters hostage. Elsewhere there are others, plotting and devising ways to disrupt our lives and destroy our home. Where do we even begin?" I stare at the ceiling, unable to comprehend our path.

"It seems a mammoth task, I know it does. But I've spent the last two years chasing these people, and it's a lot harder to do when they have an entire planet to hide on. This vessel is a blip compared, and they'll show themselves, eventually."

"You think so?"

"I do. They can't hide in the shadows forever."

"So where do we start?" I look into those beautiful blue-green eyes. She is stronger than me, and filled with purpose and confidence, and I need both right now. I am struggling to come to terms with the enormity of this mission.

Laura pulls back the covers, her elegant curves naked and splendid in the dappled sunlight, her breasts barely touching my chest, as she winks at me and kisses her way down to my naval.

Fuck's sake.

TO BE CONTINUED...

ABOUT THE AUTHOR

AWARD-WINNING PRODUCT DESIGNER and entrepreneur Danny Lenihan was born in West London, raised in Chessington and now lives in the Shires with his two children, Evie and George, a smattering of Hobbits and the occasional wallaby. A former press photographer and stand-up comedian, Danny spends his days designing for his two global brands, 3 Legged Thing and Morally Toxic.

A passionate writer, Danny has contributed to several books (actually one, but he bought two copies) prior to penning his own, and has had articles published worldwide. He has written for TV, film and radio, and hosts his own, utterly childish, comedy podcast.

Previously a finalist in the Great British Entrepreneur Awards, Danny shot to notoriety in the photographic industry when he launched his own tripod brand, 3 Legged Thing in 2010. Defying convention and focusing on innovation and engineering, Danny's designs are widely considered to be the industry benchmark in camera support technology, winning the prestigious Lucie Technical Award in 2017.

For more than a decade, Danny ruined the world as a stand-up comedian, during which time he featured and starred in three British horror movies (in which he died four times, a record only recently beaten by Tom Cruise in 'Edge of Tomorrow': Tom cheated though.) and was a frequent panellist and contributor to BBC Radio. Danny composed the musical score to Pat Higgins' debut horror movie, *Trashhouse.*

He can also speak to cats.

@DannyLenihan
@DannyLenihan
@DanLenihan
in/dannylenihan
dannylenihan.com

ACKNOWLEDGEMENTS

THIS BOOK WOULD not have been possible without the love and support of my beautiful children, Evie and George. Through some of the hardest times in recent memory, they have been the oxygen in my lungs, and the blood running through my heart.

My original story was inspired by an interview on BBC Radio 2, with Professor Brian Cox, who talked about wandering planets, and speculated on their paths and histories, and Andy Weir who somehow made sci-fi more earthly and relatable.

To my beta readers, who helped me shape my world, and gave their time so a stranger could blossom—Teresa, Alex, Nina, Lisa, Diana, Alison, Nicola, Clinton, Drew, Peter, David, Craig, Chip and many others I have probably missed—forgive me.

To Liz Ward, my editor, and probably my saviour, who has been instrumental in keeping me in my lane, and focussed.

I should also thank my team at 3 Legged Thing, for working so hard and so diligently, that I could spend my time concentrating on my kids, and writing this book. Their combined excellence and support these last few months has been a huge weight off my shoulders, impossible to quantify with my limited vocabulary.

Most of all I want to thank my mum, for encouraging me to read as a child, and for always being there for me, no matter what.

Rogue was written to champion the little guy. The one who nobody expects anything of, that meanders through life aimlessly, drifting into the abyss of lost souls.

It is about taking that one chance, that single opportunity to change the path he's walking, to make himself heard within the cacophony of disconsolate voices that pervade his mind.

There's a Jaxon Leith inside us all, just waiting to be untethered from convention, and leap free from our social bondage, taking control of our destiny. Seizing opportunity is as much about creating something as it is about taking chances.

Rogue is about breaking through the clouds that dampen our aspirations. It's about quietening the voices that tell us "*you can't do it*" or "*you're not good enough*". It is about taking the first steps towards bettering ourselves, fighting for what is right, seeking improvement and creating a legacy for our children that enables them to stand tall and be counted.

We should all aspire to work hard, show compassion, be kind and loyal, stand up to social inequality, racial injustice, and prejudice in all forms.

I wrote this novel because, one day, I want to be able to look my kids in the eye and tell them "*I did the best I could*", even though I fell a thousand times, made bad decisions, treated people poorly, and let myself down over and over again, I did it all with a flawed nature, an inescapable humanity, and a good heart.

Danny

Lightning Source UK Ltd.
Milton Keynes UK
UKHW021019220322
400428UK00005B/226

9 781838 476403